I0593477

Mission
Budapest

Mission Budapest

SUSAN C. TURNER

Copyrighted Material

Mission Budapest
by Susan C. Turner

2023 Harry Douglas Press Paperback Edition
Copyright © 2023 by Susan C. Turner
All rights reserved

This book is a work of fiction. All incidents, all dialogue, and all characters—with the exception of well-known historical and public figures—are products of the author's imagination and are not to be construed as real. Where real-life figures appear, the situations, incidents, and dialogues concerning those persons are fictional. In all other respects, resemblance to persons living or dead is entirely coincidental.

No part of this publication may be reproduced, stored in a retrieval system or transmitted, in any form or by any means—electronic, mechanical, photo-copying, recording or otherwise—without prior written permission from the publisher, except for the inclusion of brief quotations in a review.

Published in the United States of America by Harry Douglas Press

Harry Douglas Press
704 West Swann Avenue
Tampa, FL 33606
USA
www.harrydouglaspress.com

ISBNs:
978-0-9847232-7-0 (softcover)
978-0-9847232-8-7 (eBook)

Printed in the United States of America

Cover and Interior design: 1106 Design

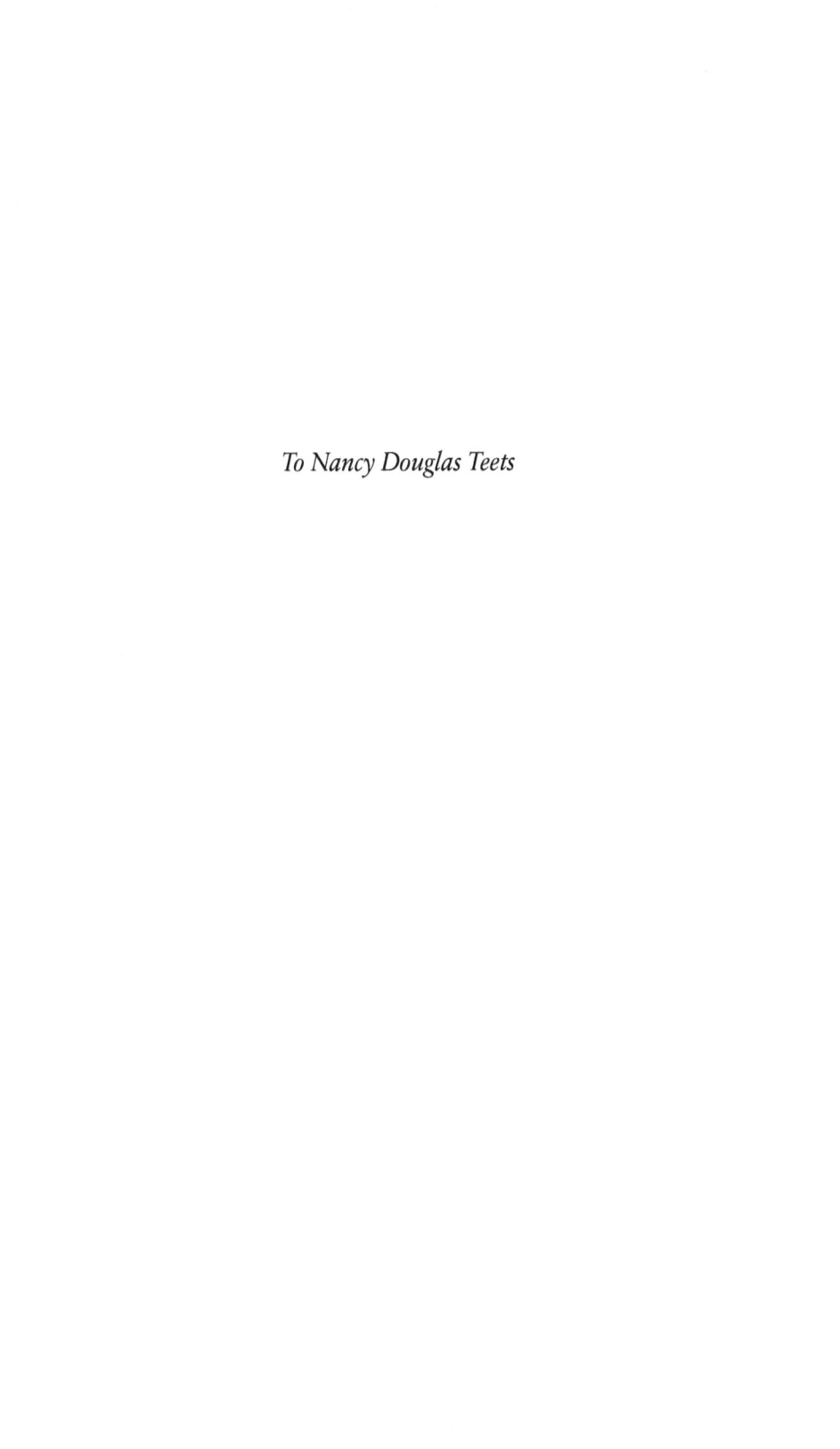

To Nancy Douglas Teets

Count me not with the wicked
and with the workers of iniquity,
who speak peace with their neighbours,
but mischief is in their hearts.
—Psalms 28:3

Chapter One

31 May 1938, **Budapest**. Unhurried, Tennyson Neale strolls south along the boulevard, lost among the crowd, nodding the obligatory greeting to strangers who meet his eye. The street is filled with evening walkers—regulars and a smattering of tourists—taking in the shop window displays. Arm-in-arm, they pause to admire a ruffled yellow parasol and a silver-handled cane. They point out a colorful stack of tea tins and rack of neckties. Black taxis creep past, windows down, their occupants searching for an outdoor café to pass the idle hours. On the corner, a newspaper kiosk is closing, the busy part of the day gone. The owner winds up the last bit of worn canvas awning. Behind him, two boys pass the end of a cigarette back and forth, each drawing a long drag before the taller boy flicks the butt into the gutter. The kiosk owner speaks softly to them, and they carry away what remains of the day's unsold items.

When the clock tower strikes nine, Neale looks once over each shoulder, cuts left and moves quickly to the rear entry of 60 Andrássy Avenue. In the alleyway, he flattens his body against a shadowed wall and stands dead still, listening to a metallic sound in the distance, straining to hear a scuff of footsteps or an involuntary cough. No time for lapses, he tells himself, the assignment nearly done. In three days, with the right amount of luck, he'll be lifting a pint at the Elephant and Castle, a good-looking brunette on his arm, an ample measure of quid in his pocket.

Broad stone steps littered with the day's debris lead up to a heavy wooden door, its extended hinges visible. Concealed by the half wall of the handrail, Neale hunches low and takes the stairs in two strides. He jams the pick into the lock, opens the door, and steps soundlessly across the threshold. Inside, he crouches, letting his eyes adjust to the deeper darkness in the room. The door secured, he switches on the hand torch. Earlier that evening, he had blackened the edges of its chamber to create a highly focused beam. Unlikely to be detected, it is the perfect light source for the photographs he requires. If memory serves, the office he seeks is last on the right. He takes a moment to study the long passage, then stands and makes his way down the marbled hall. He passes each doorway, registering a series of tiny sounds—a lamp's electric buzz, a night bird's wings flapping against a window. The rhythmic ticking of a clock reminds him of the need for haste.

The office door stands ajar. Curtains drawn, he locates the file drawers and thumbs the tabs. Aligned in rows, arranged by date, the files consist of correspondence among government representatives, official agencies, and newspaper articles of recent events. Nothing of importance. He wonders why he's been directed here, of all places. Of all nights.

He abandons the cabinet search and shines the torch on four file folders stacked neatly on top. Too convenient. In the first folder, he finds three photographs, each enlarged to fit precisely to folder size. Regent Miklós Horthy walking with his son. A familiar-looking British diplomat in discussion with Hitler's newly appointed Foreign Minister Ribbentrop. The American ambassador, Hugh Wilson, entering a meeting in Berlin's Adlon Hotel.

The second folder contains two typewritten memoranda. These are in German, which Neale understands. One, dated 21 May, regards two Germans killed in Sudetenland, purportedly by Czech police, noting that German Nazis in the region were told to provoke trouble. The other, dated three days ago, 28 May, reports that Hitler called together his senior staff at the Reich Chancellery and instructed Wilhelm Keitel, Commander-in-Chief of the High Command of the Armed Forces of the Third Reich, to draw up plans to erase Czechoslovakia from the European map.

From the third folder, Neale extracts a report and skims its contents.

Dated 30 May
Case Green TOP SECRET MILITARY

Cover directive by Keitel for Führer Adolf Hitler in response to his recent declaration: *"It is my unalterable decision to smash Czechoslovakia by military action in the near future. It is the business of the political leadership to await or bring about the suitable moment from a political and military point of view. Czechoslovakia stands in the way of certain German victory and the extension of German coastlines into Belgium and the Netherlands."*

The remaining pages set forth details of an imminent military operation against the Czechs. The last page shows areas abutting Germany, including maps of Sudetenland, Bohemia, and Moravia. A proposal for Hungary's redrawn boundaries accompanies the invasion plan.

Neale stifles a whistle. Holy Christ.

He does not know what he was expecting, but this isn't close. He wonders again who directed him here. The date on the last report explains the timing. Door unlocked, alarms unset, files in open view. All too easy. He imagines all manner of motives. What he holds in his hand explains the reports of German maneuvers in Bavaria and activity along the Czech border.

Setting the torch steady, he snaps pictures, counts an extra second to capture the clearest image, hopes the film he selected proves sufficiently sensitive. He works rapidly, stopping only to wipe sweat from his eyes or adjust the light. Within minutes, he runs off forty stills—two of each page of Keitel's report and accompanying maps, the pictures and memoranda in the other folders. Satisfied, he arranges the contents to their original condition and stacks them back atop the cabinet. Extinguishing the torch, he feels his way along the corridor, a cold sweat inside his shirt. He wonders how much of this is coincidence, how much a clever plant. He is not eager to do favors for nameless political power figures purely to further their own ends.

He hears the rain outside—a downpour has begun. He slips the camera, the torch, and two film cases under his jacket. As he approaches the back door, he silently counts off the seconds. Ten beats at a time until he reaches a total of two minutes. By then, anyone who might have observed the dim light or noted his footsteps will have burst in. Once out the door, he jumps down the steps, strides quickly—best not to run—to the alley entrance, and checks his watch.

He will call her, arrange a late meeting. A quick wash and a shave. Enough time to drop the film cases and safely stow his work. The dispatch is due out at dawn.

𝄞𝄞

Her instructions specify the northeast corner of Klauzál Square on Dob Street. Neale bolts the tram at an earlier stop, an automatic habit of late, and cuts a long diagonal across the square, observing the sounds of the night, the leather bag tight against his ribs. Earlier at the apartment, he shaved, showered, and changed from the high-necked black turtleneck and dark trousers to more suitable summer clothing—a light blue long-sleeved shirt, gray flannels, and navy sports jacket—the casual attire of a proper English tourist out to meet his lady friend. Luckily, the rain has ceased.

The Kádár café is situated down a quiet back street between a milliner's shop and a bakery. Out front, tables with faded blue umbrellas stand amid puddles of water. Surveying the lively street scene—women in colorful dresses, couples arm-in-arm, cars trolling the curb, loud radio music—he guesses that the bar and café owners in this district pay a generous price for the relaxed curfew laws. Still, he notes a scattering of official uniforms. On his first pass, he ambles past the café, hands in pockets, whistling a nameless tune, the muted light of the street lanterns casting elongated shadows on the roadway. Scanning left and right, he crosses the street and approaches from the opposite side. A worn speaker's stand—in another life, a professor's lectern—signals the entrance.

When he inquires about an outside table, the host gives him a hard look. "Umbrella tables are used only in daylight hours."

Just as well. Neale inhales a last breath of fresh air. The café will reek of cheap cigars and plum brandy. He walks into the semidarkness and takes a table in the corner, facing the entry.

"*Jó estét uram.* Good evening sir. What will you order?" The waiter holds up a freshly washed glass and wipes it with a towel.

"*Gulyás à la Székely.* Goulash with sauerkraut and sour cream. *Szalon Sör.* Beer, pale ale." He decides he is hungry, even at this late hour.

He judges the goulash neither good nor bad—lukewarm veal stew has never appealed to him—but it satisfies his hunger and gives him something to do while he listens to the patrons' conversations, voices rising and falling, hoarse shouting, arguments in progress. Hungarians and their endless political debates. Fanatical patriots with loud opinions and inflated gestures. Neale is not indifferent to their conspiratorial causes. He simply does not understand their disparate passions. He likens it to trying to tie crooked sticks into a tidy bundle. In any case, he chooses not to agonize over their furtive conversations. In the beginning of his service, he cared enough to discover the rightness and wrongness of a thing. Played it straight. Acted faithfully. Now, he refuses to engage in such moral deliberations. He sees no advantage in the effort.

It was she who first suggested the exchange of money for secrets. A bit of business on the side, she said. It crossed his mind that she worked for the secret police. Or worse. He surprised himself how swiftly those reservations passed. No use in soul searching, he reasoned. Money meant freedom. Gather enough of it, and he will leave the service behind. These last few months, his missions have gone stale—gathering, transmitting, destroying items of incrimination. He has grown tired of obeying orders. Like other citizens of the empire, he envisions a future of self-rule.

Restless, he mops the last bit of goulash from the bottom of the bowl, orders another beer and waits. He notes the distant click of heels on the pavement, checks the street and makes out her delicate frame as she approaches the entry. He gulps a swallow of beer, wipes his mouth, and stands to greet her. The other voices grow silent as she passes each table and makes a point of smiling at each occupant. Hers is one of those sculpted faces. High cheekbones. Exquisite symmetry. She wears a fitted green skirt and matching ruffled blouse, her dark hair loose on her shoulders, a deep shade of plum fresh on her mouth.

The waiter brings them two small cups of Turkish kávé. They sip in silence. He lights a cigarette, passes it to her.

"So, it's of use to us?" She narrows her eyes as the smoke ring escapes her lips. One hand rests on his sleeve.

"You mean, is it any good?" He stretches his arms above his head and yawns—loudly so the other patrons will notice him—using the opportunity to scan the room once more. He pretends to laugh at something she said, then speaks softly. "The group in the corner, in the shadows, three of them, a nasty bunch."

Pretending not to hear, she stares at him, then at the burning ash of the cigarette. "I asked you a question."

"It's exactly what you need." He leans toward her, nuzzles her neck.

She stiffens, pushes his face away. "Where is it?"

"I'll have it for you tomorrow." He brings the cup to his lips, frowns at the acrid sweetness.

"How recent?" She takes one last puff and stubs out the cigarette, not looking at him.

"Very recent. Very significant," he says. "Precisely why the price has gone up by half."

"A new level of greed, even for you. You will have your money tonight. That was our agreement." She says it hastily, covering her lips with the napkin.

A moment passes before he responds. He will have to do some fast work. "US dollars or pounds sterling. I've no interest in forints." He takes her hand, presses it to his lips.

"When has it been different?" Her voice is strained. She gives him a murderous look. "Two o'clock, Chain Bridge, Pest side, the path along the river edge. There's an alcove under the stairs. He'll be prompt." She pushes back from the table. Her eyes direct his attention to the napkin under her cup.

Neale leans forward—his right hand on her neck, his thumb pressing the small indentation at the base of her throat—and draws her to him. He kisses her hard on the mouth.

"They need to think we're having a lovers' spat," he whispers. "That way they won't follow you."

She nods, an imperceptible inclination, then reaches out and slaps him hard. He grabs her hand, but she wrenches it free and rises from the chair, spilling remnants of the kávé, a fine spray finding the front of his shirt. He grabs the napkin and wipes at it. She turns and flees for the exit.

In mock surrender, Neale throws up his hands, shrugs, and smiles broadly at the men staring at him, taking a moment of pleasure as he walks past them. "Women," he mouths.

On his way out, he presses a wad of forints into the waiter's hand.

IIIII

It is well after two when Neale arrives at the river's edge, a deliberate ploy on his part. A way of ensuring he will escape detection by one authority or another, aware that police chiefs and their lieutenants do not relish waiting around in the small hours of the morning. Out on the river a foghorn sounds, water laps against a passing barge, a broad shimmer of moonlight floats on the surface. Staring at the current, strong and swift, he imagines the dark Danube flowing south, then east to the Black Sea on its slow, steady course.

He moves away from the edge and settles down to wait. Within five minutes, from a dark recess, the contact reveals himself, valise in hand. Has he been hiding there all this time? Neale had hoped—foolishly it seems to him now—she would be the one to accept the delivery. Without a word, the contact walks past him and descends a steep stairway to a narrow dock just above the water line. Neale sees little choice but to follow. From the darkness, in a single smooth glide, a skiff moves toward them, one man poised in the center, oars in hand. The man, wearing a broad-brimmed hat that obscures his face, reaches out and pulls the boat in until it rests, broadside, against the edge of the dock. In the darkness, Neale cannot be certain, but he has a vague notion, an uneasy notion, that he recognizes the man.

"Your payment is in the case." The contact's words, glacial and remote, break the stillness. "I will hand you the case. You will place the packet in the skiff. Then, you will return up the slope to the bridge."

Neale takes the valise, judges its weight, holds it on one knee and flips open the locks to assure himself of its contents. Even in the dim light, he makes out the stacks of pound notes. Satisfied, he leans forward and places the packet he has brought on the floor of the boat. Silently, he shifts the money case to his right hand

and retreats up the stone stairway, eager to slip free of Budapest and its treacherous intrigues.

"We haven't quite finished," says the man in the boat.

It takes Tennyson Neale less than an instant to place that voice. Another to realize his fate.

Chapter Two

1 **June 1938, Baden-Baden.** "Seven-card stud, first two and last card down," the dealer announces in German, each word precisely articulated and held a beat longer than usual.

At the quarter hour past ten o'clock, dressed in a finely cut white dinner jacket and black tie, Harry Douglas takes his spot in Salon Number 4 of the swank Baden-Baden casino. The plush red carpet, finely painted murals, gleaming gold chandeliers, and gilt-framed ceilings conjure up the infamous extravagance of Bavarian royalty. It is, for certain, one of the more opulent places Harry has set foot. He is aware that he draws attention from other gaming patrons. Harry Douglas is lean and fit with dark close-cropped hair, pale gray eyes, an easy gait and a ready smile.

In swift order—the calculation practiced, almost automatic—he takes measure of the five men seated around the table. From past encounters, he knows the pinch-faced boastful Frenchman. Jacques Lanier, he of the manicured sideburns that neatly brush the edges of his jaw, is prone to childish tantrums, tosses cards that fail him, terrorizes the dealer who delivers them. Serious about his cards.

The elegant tuxedoed Hungarian Count, Vilmos Adami, an elite of the old school, sleek and smooth, fond of calling up his Magyar roots, is quick to raise, quicker to fold when the cards do not fall his way. Serious about his money. The Austrian executive Albert Renner—competitive to a fault, driven by numbers, theories, and an intense need to impress—reveals his winners and losers more surely than any player Harry has encountered. Busy hands, smug expressions, dancing feet. Serious about winning. Finally, the two starched and uniformed German officers—one husky and blond with pale eyebrows, one slight and darker—presumably on a short duty leave, can barely contain their brashness. There is nothing subtle about them. Moments ago, they arrived together, acknowledged the others with formal nods and audible clicking of heels and took possession of two chairs across from Harry, neglecting to introduce themselves.

Harry is determined not to show his loathing. He signals the waiter to replenish everyone's glass. These officers are, after all, the reason he has spent the whole of last week settled in this chair, biding time and resources at the high-stakes tables. In the lobby this evening, on his way to the salon, Harry noted groups of German officers in their splendid uniforms. Tall and well built, they smoke heavily, greet each other with stiff-armed salutes and take photographs with glittered women, careful not to include themselves among the tourists and gamblers. Given the other tables available, Harry wonders why these two summoned the nerve to break ranks and find their way here.

To warrant his place at the table, Harry possesses nothing more than a large measure of confidence, an observant eye, and a keen memory for cards. His fluency in French, Italian, and German serve him well, both in his work and at European gambling tables. That fluency, in fact, proved the deciding factor in his recruitment for this assignment. He had hoped the mission's timing might coincide with the start of horse racing season—at the Iffezheim racetrack, by far the leading track in Germany—but such temporal good luck was not to be. Field agents do not dictate the details of their MI6 duties.

His cover for the job is simple enough. He introduces himself as an agricultural specialist for a Canadian wheat production company, commissioned to collect data on the effects of warm springs on soil conditions. When questions arise, he was born to Scottish parents in Ontario, studied agriculture and animal husbandry at McGill, played poker to meet his expenses at university, and landed his specialist job a month after graduation. The warm springs of Baden-Baden, he tells his tablemates in exaggerated, halting German, are an obvious stop on his information-gathering tour. After a full day of tromping through soft black muck, he explains, he rewards himself with an evening at the gaming tables.

In reality, the British Foreign Service has received intelligence reports regarding German troop movements in and around Bavaria. At first, the Service passed off the information as speculation, but further details raised suspicions, and Harry was dispatched to observe conditions in the area. Tonight, the German officers in the casino arouse his interest. The right question at the right time may provoke a significant slip of information. Particularly if the two across from him believe his German to be less than fluent and his judgment reckless. As the dealer distributes the first cards, Harry raises his glass in salute to his competitors, feels the first warm burn of the whiskey, and vows to make the drink last through the night. Last night, he made a decision to limit his impulsive drinking. His career cannot afford another drunken bender.

Two hours later, Harry shifts in his chair. The game has progressed without incident, all six players winning a hand or two, Renner's chip count lowest. The Austrian started out lucky, but capricious Lady Luck deserted him. The more hands he loses, the more whiskey he consumes, the poorer his bets. Harry knows the cycle.

"Call and raise," says Count Adami. Deliberate, he places a handful of chips into the pot, taps his fingers on the table edge, and waits.

Renner scowls at his dwindling pile, shakes his head. He squints at his cards, sets down his whiskey glass with a rough thump. Composed, the Germans exchange looks. When Harry's eyes meet the one, he winks. Meaning what? A silent understanding? Amusement at the inebriated Austrian?

The hour grows late. Harry worries the Germans will take their leave. He has a transmittal report due at dawn with little to show for an evening's work.

"Another whiskey, sir?" asks the waiter.

Harry nods—another vow broken—glances at his watch. Renner still has not placed his bet.

"Your bet, Herr Renner," the dealer encourages.

Renner decides, throws in all his chips, sits silent as the Count matches his bet and turns over his hole card. The ace of diamonds completes the Count's full house.

Renner struggles to rise from his chair. He stands, leaning on the table for support. His head gives a series of jerky little movements before he bows to the group, an odd smile on his face. He turns and speaks directly to the Count, "You have beaten me tonight. Enjoy these silly games while you can. Your country will be the next trophy on the Führer's mantel."

His pronouncement hangs in the air, the others shifting their gaze from Renner to the Count to the German officers. Lanier, the Frenchman, suddenly serious, pokes a stub of cigarette into a brimming ashtray and says, "It is a delicate situation, monsieur. We must be deliberate. There are many possibilities. Patience."

"Too late for patience," slurs Renner. "The Nazis own Europe. It is a disgrace, the occupation in Austria. My country will never be the same. One is forbidden to wear a particular hat, to walk on a particular street, to frequent a particular business. Neighbors disappear. You are more than wrong, sir. There is no delicacy here."

Harry pretends to ignore the conversation, does nothing to convey his understanding of the exchange. He keeps his head down and reshuffles his cards.

The Count pushes back from the table and sips his cocktail contentedly. His gaze fixes on the Frenchman. "It will unfold. It is, as we speak, unfolding. Just as our game of skill and chance unfolds. If Chamberlain and Daladier keep their promises. If Britain stays. If France concedes. If the Russians raise. If Roosevelt plays. Does it matter? The answer is, of course, yes. It matters to all of us. This trading of power. Hitler wants war, not a brokered peace. For now, he contents himself with persecuting the Jews and the Romani. Soon, that will not be enough for him. The Austrian is right. We will live to regret our blind eye."

Harry sees the Germans' cold stare, their mouths grim.

Lanier responds, "We know what runs beneath your Hungarian concern. You will regain your lost ground. Your borders will expand once again. At what price?" Lanier pauses, the emphasis clear. "France and Britain will never allow this expansion."

The Count continues, "In the end, the English and French will be forced to abandon us. It is the Czechs who must fear. Germany will march into the Sudetenland. Benés will fight for his new country. He has no choice. I have watched the Czechs mobilize. Their tanks and fortresses are not a secret. It is their intent to defend themselves, but they are not strong enough to stand alone in Europe."

The husky German officer smiles, nudges the other. The slight one, who has had little to say—or drink—for the last two hours, speaks, a dismissive superiority in his tone. "It is easy to attack this new Czechoslovakia. It is surrounded on three sides. It will go soon enough."

So there it is. The plan is in place. How soon is "soon enough"?

"A curse on them all," Lanier almost spits his annoyance. He turns in his chair, refocuses his glare on the dealer. "Another hand, *s'il vous plaît.*"

War or no war, there is a game to finish. The men watch the first issue of cards. The room attendant approaches Harry and whispers in his ear, "A private call for you, sir, on the lobby telephone."

Harry rises casually. He leaves his chips on the table, though he suspects he will not return. "Gentlemen, my apologies. For this hand, you must excuse me." He makes his way out of the salon into the lobby. The attendant points to an elevated table where an ivory telephone receiver lay on its side. Buying time to assure himself no one is listening, he reaches into the inside pocket of his jacket, extracts a silver cigarette case, removes a thick Gauloise. The strong aroma of Turkish tobacco reminds him that he would dearly love to light up his beloved pipe. Instead, he squanders good money on this needless affectation. All the same, he places the cigarette between his lips, waits a moment before lighting up, eyes the receiver. He will make his remarks as cryptic as possible, and knows the other party will do the same.

"Douglas here."

For the moment it takes to draw the smoke deep into his lungs, he listens to his caller. He stares at the chandelier's shimmering reflection in the silver cigarette case. With a protracted sigh, he exhales a ring of smoke and follows its slow dissolution amidst the golden cherubs on the ceiling. "On my way."

The line goes dead.

ﬃﬃ

Though well past the hour for the last train to Munich, Harry makes his way to the Baden-Oos station, stands in a short ticket line, and arrives on Platform One in time to board the early express to Vienna. From there, he will make a connection and meet Mick in Budapest by ten in the morning. Later than they planned if he had gone via Munich, but quicker than waiting for the next express. He's never understood the term "express" as it applies to European trains.

He notices, on an adjacent platform, an exchange between an SS agent and a well-dressed young man carrying a briefcase, presumably a businessman on his way to an early morning meeting. After a brief conversation, the SS man raises his arm above his shoulder, the elbow straight. "Heil Hitler," his voice strident, the salute held an instant longer than necessary. In response, the second man makes a weak gesture—enough to satisfy an authority, enough half-heartedness to satisfy himself, perhaps. The faster Harry crosses over the German border, the better. He can barely tolerate the red flag hanging from the front of the station, the ugly black swastika two stories high.

In the midst of packing, Harry had the presence of mind to call the casino and instruct them to wire his winnings to his flat in Milan. A bit of blind luck and a three-night stream of good cards assured that he will leave Baden-Baden five thousand reichmarks richer than when he arrived. A tidy haul for a brief stint of international espionage. Subtracting currency fees and taxes is another matter. For the hundredth time, he marvels at the Third Reich's tax system and the reasons behind it.

Before 1933, the old German empire closed many of its casinos, citing gambling's immorality, reliance on superstitions, and negative family effects. A few short years later, the Nazi government, realizing easy money from wealthy foreign tourists, enacted strict new casino tax legislation and a residency ban. The lucrative Baden-Baden gaming salon, a mere fourteen kilometers from the French border, began collecting sizeable tax revenues from all manner of foreign players. He wonders how many marks Jacques Lanier has contributed to the Third Reich's coffers, and whether he appreciates the consequence of his contributions.

In the deep gray-blue light of morning, the quiet rumble of the train beneath him, Harry watches the affluent city fade into the darkness. The train gathers speed. Harry removes his fedora, sets it on the seat across from him, takes a small notebook from his pocket and begins jotting page after page of what he remembers. The last five years of Foreign Service have honed an already razor-sharp memory. He scribbles hurriedly, intent on capturing the exact words—the Count's declarations, Renner's discomfort, the Germans' reactions to Lanier and Renner—as well as the steady increase in the number of German military officers in the casino. At one point last night, when the number topped 150, he stopped counting. A definitive boost from his arrival a week ago. He jots a comment about a new airport in the area, too. There is something going on in Bavaria. That much is certain.

Alone in the coach, Harry withdraws the pipe from his pocket, tamps finely shredded tobacco into the bowl, sits for a moment savoring the sweet smell, lights a match and puffs, the aroma made sweeter by a calming warmth that settles in the palm of his hand. Beyond the window, the dawn emerges, and with it, a landscape of rich farmland. For the next hour, Harry resolves, he will do nothing but enjoy the view and the tobacco.

Within a few moments, however, a gentleman of not yet middle age—a light smattering of distinguished gray in hair and mustache, watch fob arced on a patterned waistcoat beneath a steel-gray linen jacket, a knotted silk tie, slightly askew, beneath a refined face—approaches from the rear of the coach and stops next to Harry's seat.

"Would you mind if I sit down?" he asks in German. A smile adds fullness to his face. Harry notes his tired eyes. Indeed, the man's entire demeanor strikes Harry as one of exhaustion.

"Suit yourself," he answers in English. He moves his hat, a gesture of acceptance if not hospitality, and continues puffing on his pipe.

The man lowers himself into the seat. "You're English," he says in a heavy accent.

"Canadian," says Harry. "You?"

"Hungarian. On my way home to Budapest."

"Do all Hungarians speak such polished German?" Harry wonders now which language he will be expected to speak with Budapest authorities. He does not care for translators who interfere with his real understanding of the situation.

"German has become the second language of Hungary. We conduct business with many German companies. Our children are educated to converse in both languages. At least those in certain homes," he says. "We must prepare our children for their future."

While the man is talking, Harry watches him. "What future is that?"

The man extends his hand, "My name is Jan Nagy."

"Harry Douglas." Harry sets the pipe on the window ledge and shakes Nagy's hand.

"I am a businessman, a manufacturer of colored glass. I own and operate several warehouses along the Danube. I have a wife and two sons. Young sons. The future for them will be of a different order." Nagy pauses, gazes out the window as if searching for a phantom on the horizon. "A different order than my wife and I have known in our beautiful Budapest."

A different order. That's one way to describe it. "How so?" Harry takes up his pipe again.

Passing a hand over his eyes, Nagy seems to gather himself. "Though Canadian, you are familiar, perhaps, with Europe's tense situation. In March, Hitler claimed he wanted to unite all Germans into one state, and his party seized power in Austria. Italy, France and Britain fear the power of a larger Germany, but they did nothing to stop this unification."

"Reluctant to engage, as they say," agrees Harry. "Not willing to use force over it. I follow the situation." Harry pauses, amused at his own understatement. "Hitler seemed convinced the Austrians wanted unification. Their vote was pretty decisive. Ninety-five percent in favor."

"How would you vote if Himmler and his SS agents stood next to the box to receive your ballot?"

"You're saying the vote wasn't secret. The voters coerced?" Harry knows full well the answer to his question.

"The voting was a public spectacle. The balloting a disgrace. One small farm village, in a secret ballot in March, voted almost 100 percent to maintain Austrian independence. Less than a month later, with uniforms hovering over them, they voted for annexation. Only a few were brave enough to stand fast. God knows what happened to them." Nagy moves his head from side to side, mumbles something in Hungarian Harry does not understand.

Harry raps out his pipe on a handkerchief, intent on examining the bowl's interior. The Nazis produce a flow of half-truths. He spent the better part of last year observing Austria's power elite move in Hitler's direction, but he keeps his voice neutral. "There are some Austrians who favor the union. They're not all victims. Many Austrians consider themselves German. Isn't Hitler himself native to Austria?"

Nagy folds his hands over his vest, nods. "You are right. Austrians have many contradictions. Some are indifferent. Some cheer Hitler when his armored car passes, and they welcome the German troops to their villages. They do not resist the authority. At the same time, thousands of leftist Democrats, Communists, and Jews are arrested and taken away. I know this."

"You're afraid this will happen to your sons." Harry speaks pointedly, focuses his attention on Nagy's face. Harry is well acquainted with rumors of mass disappearances of German intellectuals and wealthy Jewish merchants and financiers, their possessions now the property of the Third Reich.

"My sons, my wife, my wife's mother."

"Which are you, then?" Harry asks. "Communist? Jew? Liberal?"

Harry can almost see Nagy's mind doing somersaults. He is asking himself if he can trust this young Canadian. Nagy rises for a moment, cranes his neck, scans rows of seats.

Nagy's eyes droop. He speaks wearily. "My wife, Magda, is an actress, well-known in artistic and social circles. Beautiful. Talented. A tender mother to our sons. She was born a Jew in Budapest. Many times in the last year, since the Austrian annexation, I have urged her to take our sons to London or Paris. Until we see how the winds blow in Hungary."

Harry says nothing for a moment. Then, "How do the winds blow?"

"Our political state is fragile. Our leader, Regent Horthy, tries to protect us, but he is not strong. He is an aristocrat. He says he is done with war. He has seen too much of it. In the face of conflict, I think he will concede. Then, we will all drown in remorse. Magda refuses to flee. Just now, I have come from Paris where I found a small apartment. At least I will send my mother-in-law and my sons to safety. It will be difficult."

"You're sure Paris is safe for them?"

"No one believes France will go to war again. For now, I am confident they will not be harmed. Who knows what Hitler and his brutes will do? They are no more than thugs in uniform. I fear Austria is only the beginning." Nagy rubs his eyes, slumps back in his seat.

Harry cannot argue. At the same time, he chooses not to lend support to Nagy's fears. "You've had a long trip from Paris. You should sleep," he says, feeling inexplicably responsible for the man and his family.

"Only if you give your word you will wake me when we reach Vienna. I will buy you a coffee, and you will tell me about your journey."

Chapter Three

2 **June 1938, Budapest.** The train crawls into the station, stops with a hiss and a lurch. The sun burns through the open windows. Harry stands to stretch his back while the seats around him empty. Unlike the train from Baden-Baden to Vienna, this one is full of people travelling to Budapest and beyond. When he and Nagy boarded in Vienna, the scarcity of seats forced them into different coaches. Before their separation, Nagy presented his card and invited Harry to contact him. Harry likes the man, but doubts he will see him again. Not yet aware of the requirements for this new mission, he knows only that an agent is dead, and that he and Mick are to find out why.

Weary from sitting in the same position for hours, his arms and neck ache. He presses the scar on his cheekbone, feels the slight indentation where the bullet struck years ago. Ethiopia. Nothing simple there.

After a night of travelling, he is bone-tired, hungry. The prospect of a cold glass of lager cheers him. He tugs his tie into place, rolls down his shirtsleeves, buttons them at the cuff. Coat slung over one shoulder, hat perched on the back of his head, bag in hand, he steps down onto the platform. The crowd jostles around him. Swarms of railway police walk among the trains, some with heads down, others scanning the new arrivals.

On the rack of morning newspapers, the headline on the *Berliner Morgenpost* catches his eye, *Two Germans in Sudetenland Confirmed Killed by Czech Police.* A thought takes hold. The German officer's smug comment the night before, the certainty of it—*it will go soon enough.* A staged provocation. The murder of German nationals creates a motive for an offensive. Exactly what Hitler is after. Although Harry knows only bits of Hungarian—a difficult language, of little use other than in Hungary—he glances at the front page of the *Budapest Magyarság.* A photograph of Hitler, standing on a podium, gesturing to the map of Czechoslovakia in the background, solidifies Harry's suspicion. The tactics of deception are in place. Seized by an ominous gloom, he picks up a copy of the paper, folds it under his arm, and deposits the only forint he possesses into the payment bin.

The line at the passport checkpoint moves at a maddening crawl. Harry obtains the obligatory stamps and pushes his way through the horde of arriving visitors. Across the station, he catches sight of Jan Nagy and a fine-featured blonde woman Harry guesses to be Nagy's wife. Magda, the actress. Nagy lifts his hand to Harry in farewell. The woman turns toward Harry and says something to Nagy that makes him smile. She is every inch as beautiful as Nagy described.

Halfway to the taxi line, Harry feels a heavy hand on his shoulder.

"You're a grim-looking fellow."

"Impossible to sleep."

"Hear you walked away from a full house."

"It wasn't mine."

"Well then, no harm done." Mick grins.

Harry Douglas and Mick MacLeod met in the summer of 1933, raw recruits in the King's service. From their post in Milan they and a team of agents monitor activities of Mussolini's fascist government. For more than two years, they have observed and recorded Italy's military and political operations, the invasion and annexation of Ethiopia, and the dictator's growing alliance with Hitler. Among the best and brightest analysts on the team, Harry and Mick have earned a reputation for perseverance and thoroughness, not to mention the occasional lack of restraint. No strangers to Milan's night scene, they are frequently tested in some of the city's better and lesser social establishments, including the famed San Siro Racecourse.

Given their fluency in Western European languages, the two have become freewheelers, assigned sensitive investigative projects for Section Six. Though physically dissimilar—Mick a ginger-haired, red-cheeked Scot with muscular chest and shoulders, Harry dark-haired and slender of build—the two men make an imposing and memorable impression. In their time together, Harry has come to appreciate Mick as a good man in a fight. When things get rough, he remains. Put to the test, he turns into a Scottish street brawler with a hair trigger and a quick pair of fists. Harry, on the face of it the more urbane, is every inch as dangerous and reliable.

"Anything worth noting in Bavaria?"

"It's there, all right," says Harry. "Can't miss the buildup. Troops, airport. The German machine. Don't know why we've not been monitoring it more closely."

"Why do you suppose?"

"Not so much intelligence as communication failure, command not knowing the importance of the maneuvers. Worse yet, not connecting the evidence and events." Harry and Mick rarely speak of the failings of the British aristocracy and the unqualified people they manage to place in positions of authority. Sheer incompetence, some say. This Lord marries that Baron's cousin. That Baron a member of the second Earl's private club. Harry shifts his bag from one hand to the other and changes the subject. "What's the job here?"

"Tennyson Neale, one of our agents, stabbed, strung up on a lamppost at the east end of the Chain Bridge, found early yesterday morning. Might as well have had a sign around his neck."

Harry stops, surprised when tears form in his eyes. He is not a man who weeps.

"Neale? Tennyson Neale? You're sure?"

"You knew him?"

"He's a friend."

"Knew him well, then?"

"Another life. My first day at Six, I was a cocky little bastard, out to set the world afire. Tennyson Neale gave me a nod, bought me a drink. Said he could help, knew what I didn't. I paid him no mind. Let him collect the bill. Later when I asked around, I discovered I'd been drinking with a legend. The ace of Broadway."

"A healthy dose of humility."

"Later, we traded stories. His far better than mine. We worked a case together. Neale knew what he was doing. Had this instinctive sense for information, how to use it, how to protect a source. Didn't mind sharing the credits either. Obsessed with the service. King and Mother England."

"What earned him the big name?"

"Hard to say. He's daring, willing to do almost anything. Fearless, not reckless. A trace of coldness in the heart. All the same, I admire him."

The word "admire" did not come close to Harry's feelings for Tennyson Neale. Worship, he corrects silently. I worship his skill, his grace, his courage.

"When did you last see him?"

"I lost track. He's always on assignment. Never privy to where. A few months ago, I heard rumors he'd fallen from grace. Handed a dead-end assignment. I didn't believe it. Not true to form for Neale. I passed it off as idle gossip, tongues wagging. Neale never cares what people think of him."

Harry stops talking, his throat closing on the words. He's always thought of Neale as indestructible. His brain denies it, the fact now beginning to dawn. Tennyson Neale—collaborator, guide, idol—gone from this earth.

"We'll drop your bag, pay our respects." Mick takes Harry's bag, maneuvers him ahead to the taxi line. "You're to present yourself as solicitor representing the interests and properties of *Burlington Magazine* and of Neale, their employee. Esteemed editor's name is Herbert Read. Emphasize 'esteemed.'"

"Harry Douglas, Esquire." Harry considers the title, smiles a little, fights to calm the devastation in his heart. "*Burlington?* Art, isn't it? A bit stuffy."

"Frightfully. I'm staffer for Editor Read's assistant, Edith Hoffman. I've accompanied you to identify the body and collect Neale's effects."

"Do we know the first thing about art collectors?"

"As much as we know about English law. If anyone asks questions, I'll launch a rant about post-impressionist forgeries."

Mick waves a hand for the taxi driver. "Let's make what we can of the body, and find Neale's flat where we'll meet our contact, Cephus Brinkley. He'll fill us in, provide background."

"Cephus Brinkley. Never heard of him."

"Reuters' correspondent in Budapest. That's his cover. He's been at it so long, he considers himself a genuine member of the fourth estate, and an expert on the ups and downs of Hungarian politics."

"I had a short lesson on that myself last night," says Harry.

iiiii

It is another two hours before they finish examining Neale's body, collect his blood-encrusted shoes and clothing, and locate his apartment house. The concierge provides a key and leads them into the flat that was Neale's. A bright, high-ceilinged room simply furnished with double bed, night tables, bureau, and two cushioned chairs next to a pair of broad windows. The bed neatly made. A camera and three lenses of different lengths sit on the bureau top. Mick opens the closet door. A sorted collection of shirts, jackets and trousers smell faintly of cigarettes.

From a bedside table, the telephone bell rattles. Harry picks up the receiver and speaks a line of greeting. The line crackles with static and goes dead. He replaces the receiver and stands back. "Wrong number. Or I'm not the bloke the caller expected."

"Brinkley checking to see we've arrived," says Mick. "No surprise there. Any thoughts on the body?"

Harry remembers the hollow-eyed, gray figure on the morgue table, featureless, the color bled away. Nothing like the handsome Neale he knew. The coldness of the place—and an unlabeled emotion—had made him shiver. "I would have liked to see how he was strung up. How he was tied. Position of the head and arms. As a lanky fellow, Neale wouldn't be easy to hold in place on a lamppost. Bleeding like hell." Harry stares out the window, swallows hard. His voice nearly fades away. "Why the knife?" Neale deserved a better finish. "A pistol would have done the job. One clean shot." How much suffering did he endure?

While they wait for Brinkley, Harry walks a slow circuit around the perimeter of the room. He stands in its center, squints up at each ceiling crevice and through the large picture windows that face the river, the Royal Palace in the distance. Mick calls the reception desk, verifies dates of Neale's arrival and planned departure, and makes arrangements to meet the clerk on duty the night Neale was last seen. On hands and knees, Harry reaches under the bed to find a used coffee cup and a half-empty glass of what smells like Irish whiskey. He places them both on the nightstand. A collection of tripods is strewn along the bureau surface. A search of night table drawers reveals items of clothing, three cigarette packets—all open and nearly void of cigarettes— and an unopened bottle of Pálinka.

"What's this?" Mick holds the bottle aloft.

Cephus Brinkley saunters into the room, leaving the door ajar. "Pálinka. Hungarian fruit brandy. Potent bit of punch and flavor. An art form hereabouts." He stretches a hand toward Harry. "Cephus Brinkley. Met Mick last night." Brinkley relaxes into the overstuffed chair next to the window, elevates one foot on the marble sill. He wears an expensive suit of rich navy, a white silk shirt—monogrammed at the cuff—and brown leathers. He flips out a striped boarding school tie and smooths it over a slight paunch. Streaks of silver run through his thinning brown hair. A few lines around the eyes and mouth. Harry guesses his age at fifty plus, no more than sixty.

"You're familiar with the local custom." Harry closes the door. "When we finish here, you can point us in the direction of a cold pint of ale."

"A blue movie and a massage, if you've a mind. Budapest is famous for them." Brinkley winks in Harry's direction.

"Not one of my hobbies," says Harry.

"A matter of preference?" asks Brinkley. "There are many options in the city. We have our favorites."

A hint of animosity hangs in the air, Harry's judgment about Brinkley all too obvious.

Mick interrupts. "Fill us in on the case."

Brinkley stares down at his tie for a long moment, and then brings his gaze up to Mick. "Simple enough. Recover the body. Next of kin, all that."

"We've just come from the morgue. We've made arrangements to transfer Neale's body to London on the next available transport. May go out this afternoon. Tomorrow at the latest. A representative from *Burlington Magazine* contacted a sister in Folkestone."

"Efficient, you young chaps," says Brinkley. "I trust you'll handle the rest of the mission as easily." Brinkley rises from the chair, brushes an imaginary speck from his lapel, and straightens the knot on his tie. The genial manner is gone, replaced by a sudden abruptness. "You are to retrieve whatever information Neale gathered and get it to Broadway. He was scheduled to send out a dispatch yesterday morning, but it never appeared. Supposedly something big."

"Any idea what?" asks Mick.

"Not a clue." Brinkley checks his watch. "Whatever you get, bring it to me. I've cleared you with the Ambassador's staff, and I'll update them each day. They've nothing to add to what we already know." Again, he stares at his watch. "Let's get going with this background material. I have a deadline to meet."

"Tell us about Neale," says Harry. "What was he doing here?"

"I communicated with him several times, always about dispatch schedules and contacts. Not much to tell. He kept a low profile. Precisely what his mission was, I couldn't say." Brinkley rubs his hands together, changes the subject. "What do you know about Hungarian politics?" Brinkley paces a track between the bureau and the window. At the nightstand, he picks up the half-empty glass of whiskey, gives it a sniff, and tosses it down.

"We've had access to a considerable amount of research. But you're here on the ground," says Mick. "We need your impressions."

"I'll be brief. Miklós Horthy is the Regent of the Kingdom of Hungary." Brinkley emphasizes the word kingdom. "No need to go into the monarchy. Irrelevant to our issue. Suffice it to say Horthy holds a tight rein on power, has for eighteen years. Old nobility, war hero, polo player, married into society. You get the picture. Conservative, though not extreme right, he faces political upheaval. In the last year, he's deflected political factions that would depose him and transfer power to the more heavy-handed fascists. To save his position—some would argue his country—Horthy must publicly support Austrian annexation. If Horthy complies, Hitler guarantees Hungary's present borders. And adds to them when the Führer decides to take a bite out of Czechoslovakia."

"Horthy's major opponents?" asks Harry.

"National socialist party called Arrow Cross. Fascists. Right-wing racists. Similar to the Nazis. But, primarily, extreme nationalists. They believe in racial purity of the Hungarians, the original Magyars. Thus, they have not, to date, aligned themselves with the Germans. Nor would they choose to, unless it means more power for them."

"What are their issues?" asks Mick.

"Arrow Cross is militantly anti-Semitic, anti-capitalist, and anti-communist. An appalling bunch. Hopeless imbeciles. The whole lot of them. Horthy tries to keep them under control; but recently, with outside influence, they have gained ground, strength. They specialize in bribery, blackmail, violence."

"Are there others opposed to Horthy?" asks Mick.

"Yes. None as strong or determined as Arrow Cross." Brinkley stops, pivots on his heel as if searching the room, then adds vaguely, "A dip into Hungarian politics is akin to sticking your hand in a bear trap."

"Do you suppose Neale's dispatch had anything to do with this power struggle?" asks Harry.

"An almighty question mark. More likely with an event that is more immediate. Something soon to occur. Hitler is pressuring Horthy to appoint a friendlier cabinet."

"And then?" asks Mick.

"Horthy fears Hungary will become a puppet state of Germany. Ergo, the Hungarian parliament is expected to pass a second set of anti-Jewish laws that would lead to a stronger alliance, rather than an outright takeover, with both Germany and Austria. Horthy says he will protect the Jews. Many disagree. Anti-Semitism grows."

"Manifested by what?"

"The recent laws, passed in May, restrict Jews' participation in government, business ownership, professional licensure. The second set of laws on the docket defines Jews as a racial rather than religious group. That is, people with Jewish-born grandparents are declared Jewish."

Harry remembers Nagy's guarded remarks about his wife and children.

Brinkley continues. "Two hundred and fifty thousand Hungarian Jews have lost their income and right to vote. A proposed Third Jewish Law prohibits intermarriage and penalizes sexual relations between Jews and non-Jews."

The image of Nagy and his wife at the train station comes to mind.

When Brinkley finishes his briefing, Harry relates parts of his train conversation with Jan Nagy. Out of respect for Nagy and, truth be told, lack of confidence in Brinkley's discretion, Harry does not reveal Nagy's name or his wife's.

"Sounds as if your travelling companion had it right. Before it's over, this part of the world is going to get bloody," says Brinkley.

Harry walks to the window, turning Brinkley's remarks over in his mind. "To follow your logic, the night before his death, Neale might have learned something about Hitler's plans. He thought this information important enough to dispatch to headquarters. Information someone else thought important enough to stop him from sending."

Brinkley shrugs, glances from Mick to Harry and back again. "A good place to start." He takes a few seconds looking around the apartment, eyes alighting here and there, then settles his attention on Neale's cigarette packets, grabs one and shakes loose a cigarette. "You ought to be aware of two more players in Budapest. In Hungarian politics, anybody who is anybody knows everybody. Useful connections, if you will. No doubt, you will receive an invitation from one Laszlo Vací, head of the Hungarian Secret Police. Under the circumstances, I'd accept the request."

"Thus far, we've dealt with the Budapest Police Department," says Mick.

"How would Vací know we're here?" asks Harry.

"Vací knew the minute you stepped off the morning train." Brinkley clears his throat, a gesture of impatience. "Most likely, he knows we're meeting now."

"You said two players. Who's the other?" Harry watches Brinkley pocket the cigarette pack.

"Kristof Balas, self-proclaimed head of the Arrow Cross Party. Ferenc Szálasi is the formal leader, but he's in prison. Sentenced to three years. You'll see Balas soon enough. He makes his presence known. Doesn't waste time. I doubt you'll receive any invitations from him." Brinkley leaves as abruptly as he entered, pulling the door closed behind him.

"Likeable chap," remarks Mick.

"Eton stripes," says Harry. "There's a mean spirit beneath that stuffed shirt."

"You've never had a poet's grace," says Mick. "I suspect he's not all mouth and trousers."

"With any luck, we'll not run into him again," says Harry. "Now, let's search this room. Neale had to have a safe spot."

They start with the usual places. Harry slides under the bed, pulls himself along the floor, working his way along the bottom of the mattress. Mick removes the tank lid, pokes behind the water closet, checks under the hot- and cold-water taps, through and around the medicine cabinet and dustbins.

"Light fixtures?" asks Harry. "Wall prints?"

"I pulled a restaurant bill from the pocket of the dressing gown," says Mick. "A late supper at the Kádár café."

"After we finish here, we'll check on it," says Harry. "Could be they'll have something to drink. Besides Pálinka."

They roll up the carpet from one corner to the other. As they near the end, Mick notices a slight bulge between the finished edge and lining. Closer examination reveals a narrow flap, no more than ten centimeters in length, sewn into the lining. Reaching in, he extracts an envelope, the same dark shade as the carpet.

"Clever spot." He slits the edge of the envelope with his knife. Inside is a thin sheaf of papers, folded over once. "Lists of a sort, series of dates, three and four digits beside them, indecipherable without additional data. No photos or film. They are bound to be stashed somewhere. The camera gear has to turn up something useful."

"Check his clothing. The bag from the morgue." Harry removes the items and lays them out on the floor. He hands Mick the gray trousers, spotted in a range of browns.

"Stiff with blood."

"All the better," says Harry. "The police won't have touched them." He draws a small knife from his pocket, and uses it to pry the soles from the brown oxfords. "Bingo." Holding up a strip of celluloid toward the window, he remarks, "Looks to be a roll of negatives, more than twenty images. We'll need a magnifier. It's in my bag at the Gellért."

"Nothing in trousers, shirt collar or cuffs," says Mick. "What's left?"

"See if you can pull up that windowsill, the one where Brinkley planted his expensive leathers."

The sill lifts easily.

Mick crouches, runs his hand along the inside of the opening until he meets a small object. "A treasure trove." Mick pulls out a black-ringed notebook and leafs through it. "Our Neale displays an exceptionally neat hand. A conscientious public schooler." Tucked inside the last page is a business card, showing a camera tripod graphic above the name and address. "We may have found our photographs." He reads the card aloud. "Tamás Sándor Fényképészeti Film Fejlesztése. 16 Arany János utca. There's a note scribbled on the back. Same handwriting as the notebook."

"Before we down that pint, we need to get a good look at the Chain Bridge," says Harry.

⫼⫼

Neale's apartment building, the Corso, is located in the heart of the city and provides ready access to entertainment, shopping and eateries.

"We might find someone who remembers Neale. A bartender. A shopkeeper," says Mick.

Walking east, Harry and Mick find themselves on Vací ut amidst stalls of books, handmade linens, and a parade of tourists who stop to admire the intricate wrought iron grills that adorn the windows, or comment on a storefront window dressing. At the corner of Vací and Kossuth uts, the two men turn south toward the Danube.

The Széchenyi Chain Bridge, a vast iron and stone suspension bridge that spans the river, connects the two sides of the city. Buda on the western high ground, Pest on the flat eastern bank. A pair of carved stone lions looms over the entry. Harry is reminded of the posed bronze pair in Trafalgar Square. A string of elegant iron lampposts lines both sides of the structure, separating two lanes of traffic from a pedestrian walkway.

"Which post?" asks Harry.

"Shouldn't be hard to find," says Mick. "I doubt they've scrubbed it clean. We'll get particulars tomorrow morning at the station."

"You mentioned a sign around Neale's neck. What's that about?" asks Harry.

"Neale wore no sign. I was just remembering—relating—a history lesson from school. In the old days, London looters were hanged from the lamppost closest to their crime. They sometimes had signs around their necks listing what they had stolen." Mick shakes his head, walks a few steps ahead along the bridge. "Here on the continent, a lamppost exhibition means something different. Several years ago, the practice made its mark in Vienna. An Austrian newspaper contained a cartoon showing Jews dangling from the lampposts on a Vienna street, declaring this would happen when the unification took place. *Hang the Jews from the lampposts* is one of the Nazi slogans in Germany and Austria." Mick plunges his hands deep into his pockets.

"Neale wasn't a Jew." Harry eyes the base of each post. In truth, he knows nothing of Neale's religious nature. They never discussed faith. "I saw what you're describing just this morning. From the train window approaching the Vienna station, in the early light. Broken shop windows, painted signs. *Closed. No Jews Here.* I didn't know the anti-Semitic sentiment was so deliberate."

Harry stops abruptly, examines the dark traces on one particular post. "This is it." He takes out a small notepad and begins to write. After a moment, he looks up, pen poised above the page. "Why hang him up for public display? There has to be a reason. A signal to someone. Or a number of someones."

"Could be his cover was blown. A British spy in our midst."

Chapter Four

3 **June.** At two minutes before nine o'clock, beneath an overcast sky, Harry and Mick climb the marble steps to the elaborate front entrance of the Rendörség, Budapest Police Headquarters on Jozsef Attila ut, a block south of St. Stephen's Basilica.

"Before I offend these chaps," says Mick, "let me get my simple mind straight. In a few words, these Hungarians sport several political groups, each fighting to defeat the other. To a group, they want to keep out Germans and communists. Get power for themselves. Add to that, their knickers are in a twist about regaining territory they owned before the Czechs took it in 1918."

"Sounds right. Stick with questions about Neale, we'll be okay," says Harry. "I doubt the Budapest police have much time for political intrigue."

At the reception desk, they present their identification. A ruddy-faced security attendant—the smell of sweat heavy about him—records, in an official-looking ledger, their names and the purpose of their visit. For good measure, Harry insists the attendant add the word Esquire to his name.

They soon note the building's drab interior does not equal its ornate marble facade. A round unstylish woman with a flat voice and sturdy black shoes shows them to a second-floor office, bare except for a table and four chairs. A single opaque window, darkened by layers of dust, is shut tight. The unventilated air smells of mildew, partially masked by the odor of fresh varnish.

"Glad they didn't tidy up on our account," says Harry, seating himself on one of the hard chairs that sits around the metal table. "Where are the fellows with black mustaches, daggers in their belts?"

Mick removes a page from his folder, scans the questions they wrote last night. Harry detects a note of anxiety in his partner's typically unflappable manner.

In the time it takes to blink twice, the door opens. An enormous man—thick dark hair slicked back from a broad pale forehead—strides in. He is dressed in uniform, gold braiding, tasseled epaulets and ribbons on full display. Chief Marton Gaska grabs Mick's hand, then Harry's, within easy reach in the small space. He sinks into the chair at the head of the table. Both chair and table seem to quake, overwhelmed by the size of their visitor. Gaska mops sweat from the serious pouches beneath his eyes and wheezes into a soiled white handkerchief. Not waiting for introductions, in a voice louder than necessary, he launches into a monologue in Hungarian, punctuated by uncontrolled arm gestures and head shakes. At intervals, he looks toward the ceiling, pleading for divine intervention. It appears to Harry as if the occasional tear fills Gaska's eyes.

Harry and Mick dare not look at each other. They do take notice, however, of a young woman in a cherry-red sheath who entered the room after Gaska started to speak. At first, she stood alone in the arch of the doorway, observing the scene, eyes dwelling on each of them in turn. Mick against the opposite wall, Harry seated on one long side of the rectangular table, Gaska at its head facing the window. She moves behind a chair at right angle to Gaska and stands, studying the tabletop. When Gaska finishes speaking, he looks at her. She nods and repeats, in English, Gaska's remarks.

Harry, always appreciative of the female form, thinks this woman especially remarkable. The word alluring comes first to mind. Her striking face is far from beautiful, but the olive skin, unusual almond eyes and structured nose cause him to wonder about her lineage. Luxurious straight black hair, dark eyes. Almost Asian, with a bit of Romani. She bears a composed self-assurance. No hurry in her movements. Most disturbingly, she looks directly at him when she speaks, as if her message is meant for him alone. The slight rasp in her voice clinches it. Fascinated, he realizes he has little idea of the content of her remarks. Surely, Mick will be taking notes.

When she finishes speaking, she looks at Gaska, waiting for a sign. Finally, he smiles and motions for her to sit down. She pulls out the chair across from Harry and says, without extending a hand, "My name is Laura Savic. I am an interpreter with the police department and other state agencies in Budapest. Chief Gaska is ready to hear any questions you have. As you see, he is saddened by Mr. Neale's death. They were friends. He wishes to be of assistance." She glances at the folder in Mick's hand. "It appears you are prepared."

Mick steps forward, pulls out the last empty chair and sits down. "The Chief answered many of our questions. From the coroner yesterday, we learned that Tennyson Neale's body was found at four o'clock or thereabouts on the morning of 1 June, suspended by ropes from a lamppost on the east end of the Chain Bridge. He'd been stabbed many times, seven to be exact, in the front torso. He was not stabbed at the lamppost location, but had been moved to that position. It appears that he had been taken there quickly. Much of his blood pooled in his shoes and trouser cuffs, deposited beneath the post. Probable time of death was between three and four o'clock that same morning."

Mick pulls a second page from his notebook. "I am reading from the coroner's report, delivered to us by Chief Gaska's aide when we arrived. *Recovered from the body was a wallet containing Mr. Neale's identification, one hundred British pounds and fifty Hungarian forints. Jewelry included one 18K Cartier backwind tank wristwatch.*" Mick stops, clears his throat. "No mention of a key to his flat."

Laura Savic stares at Mick for a moment, the beginning of a question in her eyes. Then, she translates Mick's statements. Gaska says nothing. Face contorted, he breathes into his handkerchief and collapses in a fit of coughing that lasts a full minute. Laura calls into the corridor for a glass of water.

Harry picks up the conversation, careful to look at Gaska rather than the appealing interpreter. "Thank you for your cooperation. Our employer, *Burlington Magazine*, requests to know what clues the police have found in the area, where you speculate Mr. Neale was murdered, and if you know any reason why he was hung from the post. In addition, our employer inquires if your department is aware of similar murders in the area."

Laura Savic sits silent, staring at the back of her hand on the table. She speaks quietly to Gaska. Before she finishes her commentary, Gaska shakes his head and pushes himself up from the table. Without looking at them, he walks out the door, closing it behind him, leaving them to puzzle through his departure.

Thinking Gaska might return, they wait, staring at each other, then at Laura. She sighs, straightens her spine, sits forward in her chair. "Chief Gaska is unable to give further information regarding the circumstances of Mr. Neale's murder. He is unaware of any similar murders."

Mick waves the coroner's report in the air. "What the blazes? This is his idea of assistance? A long-winded speech. A coroner's report. That's the whole of it? We've no more information than we had yesterday." Mick drops the report on the table.

Laura Savic blinks twice. "Chief Gaska made certain the coroner's report was translated and provided to you in English." She pauses. "He was quite firm about this."

Harry tries to gauge the level of the game being played. Mick is right. They are no wiser than before they arrived. They have blown half the morning. Why had they expected the police to be helpful? Nothing so far suggests it. There are no photographs of the crime scene. No notes. Harry curses himself for not knowing more of the language, although Hungarian would hardly be useful on any other occasion. Gaska's behavior is more than odd. Is the man ill or playing the role to avoid their questions? He notes Laura Savic's reaction to Mick's outburst. She nods slightly, smooths an eyebrow, looks directly at Harry.

He decides to take a chance on her cooperation. She might know something. "We are required by my client, and by our own duty and decency, to find out as much as we can about Mr. Neale's death. What do you suggest?"

Without hesitation, she offers. "I suggest you take Mr. Neale's body and go back to England." She folds her hands into the lap of the red dress. This time, she does not look at him.

"That's not possible," Harry says. "My client requires the facts of Mr. Neale's last moments and his assailants."

"Chief Gaska was quite fond of Mr. Neale. If he could help, he would."

"Then we'll find someone who can," says Mick. "Who are the officers assigned to the case?"

"I will discuss your request with Chief Gaska." She rises from the chair and makes her way—she glides, Harry thinks—to the door.

Harry and Mick stand. Harry is reluctant to see Laura Savic leave. "When you have news for us, we're at the Gellért Hotel. I'm Harry Douglas. This is Mick MacLeod."

Over her shoulder, holding his eye, she says, "I know who you are." Then, she slips out the door.

"What the hell was that about?" asks Mick.

"She knows more than she's saying," says Harry. "She looks genuine enough. Outside the building, she's more likely to share something with us."

"Genuine enough. Is that what you call it?" asks Mick.

‖‖‖‖

Under a light drizzle, they walk north to St. Stephen's Square, frustrated by the fruitless morning. At a small café across from the basilica, a plate of stuffed cabbage and a loaf of brown bread between them, they examine the coroner's report.

"Reread that part," Harry points to a spot on the page, "about his personal effects."

"Recovered from the body was a wallet containing Mr. Neale's identification, one hundred British pounds and fifty Hungarian

forints. Jewelry included one 18K Cartier backwind tank wristwatch."
Mick pauses. "One 18K Cartier backwind tank wristwatch. Quite
a charm, that. What do you guess? A thousand pounds? More?"

Harry closes one eye, looks at his own worn wristwatch. Not
quite cheap as chips, but close. "It wasn't robbery." He finds it
impossible to picture the Cartier on Neale's wrist.

Mick raises an eyebrow. "How did Neale afford, or even think
about, a fine piece of trim like that watch?"

Chapter Five

3 June. Laura Savic checks her appearance in the mirror over the bar and applies a fresh coat of lipstick. Now that the sun is shining, she can dine outside along the river and think through the morning's events. She selects a table near the edge so she can watch the muddy water run its southerly course. Assured that the rain has not left a puddle on the chair seat, she sits down, lights a cigarette, inhales the sweet Turkish scent, holds the heat in her lungs an extra moment, closes her eyes. Harry Douglas took her by surprise, and she cannot let go of it.

Gaska, the deceitful old lecher, misled the British solicitor and his assistant this morning, feigned illness to avoid their questions and left her to fend them off. For what reason, she cannot fathom. She always assumed Gaska had a real affection for Neale. Surely, Gaska wants to find Neale's killer. She is unaware of Gaska's political leanings, but knows he is ambitious. Power hungry, like the rest of them. She hates working with him, but she needs the job, and she knows enough to keep silent. A new position requires papers, a work permit. None of which are readily available, and she dares not return to Prague to secure them. Budapest is tense, the pressure growing.

The others in the movement dropped the responsibility upon her, and she is determined to see it through. Stunned after Marek's death, she wanted to slide out of sight, become invisible. For a time, the sadness overwhelmed her. His memory, that peculiar emptiness he left behind, and the insistent urging from the others, did not allow her to abandon his cause. Now it has become her cause, her gift to him.

She fears she will fail him in some way. Moreover, that the sound of his voice, the blue of his eyes, the passion for his cause will slip away. If Marek were here, he would tell her what to do. "If you have the courage," he would say.

She tosses her cigarette into the river, watches it swirl into the bottomless eddy.

A river barge loaded with timber rides low in the water. Bound for Bucharest, she assumes, some eight hundred kilometers south and east. The flag suggests Komárno, the city of Marek's birth. She is back in that morning, answering the sharp knock at the door, reading the distraught faces—their defeat and grief—knowing without doubt that he is dead.

Harry Douglas presents a complication. A threat, perhaps? She knows nothing good will come of it. Of course, she can ignore his request, but she senses that he, like Marek, does not give up easily. There is a measure of intelligence, too. She cannot afford to have him make discoveries on his own. Not now when the path is almost clear. She relaxes into the chair, surveys the river traffic once more, and lights another cigarette.

Chapter Six

3 June. "Here it is. Number 16." Mick points to the faded wooden plaque above the door.

He and Harry step across the threshold. The door closes behind them, a bell jangles, a distant low buzzer sounds. The space is filled with an intense odor.

"Oranges?" Harry wrinkles his nose and brow. He leans over the low counter, surveys the shelves along the wall. While the shop seems a dingy place, the shelves are tidily arranged, envelopes of various size and color stacked in groups of two and three.

"Development chemicals," says Mick. "We're in the right place."

"Thought you didn't know the first thing about photography."

A quick little man of middle age emerges from a closed door at the rear of the shop. He wears black-rimmed glasses that anchor a cloth mask covering his nose and mouth. A stained apron protects a white shirt, rolled at the cuff. As he approaches, he removes the mask and runs a hand through his hair. Harry sees him glance at their clothing, draw a conclusion. In accented German, he says,

"How can I help you?" He adds, "My English is poor. We can speak German, if you wish."

"Suits me," says Mick, acknowledging the man's observation. "You are Tamás Sándor?"

From behind the counter, the man nods, a slight smile on his lips. "Yes, of course. Who else would be in my shop?"

"I'm Mick MacLeod. This is Harry Douglas. We represent a London magazine called *Burlington*." Mick sets down a photograph of Tennyson Neale. "Do you know this man?"

Sándor's eyes sweep the street. It is a subtle scan, one that comes from years of practice. Harry notes the peeling blisters on his hands. "Why do you ask?"

"He was murdered two nights ago," said Mick.

"Murdered?" Sándor studies the picture, sighs, his face pale. "I wondered where he was."

"So you worked with him?" asks Mick. Harry steps back, watches Sándor's reactions.

"Worked with him?" Sándor pauses for a moment. "You could say that. For the last few months. He buys film. He brings film. It becomes habit, a daily event. Sometimes he finds a chair and waits. We talk about the photographs. How to take the pictures, how to develop the pictures. He wants to learn. I show him my studio." Sándor points to the narrow door from which he emerged. "A nice fellow, exceptionally kind to my wife."

"What did he want to know about processing film?" asks Mick.

"What every photo processor wants to know. The chemicals, the timing."

"Anything special? Just for him?"

Once again, Sándor's eyes search the street. He reaches around, unties the apron from his middle, folds it once, then again, and sets it under the counter. "He was interested in high contrast. At times, black-and-white film is not able to reproduce the image perfectly. If overdeveloped, the image is lost. The longer the developing chemical works, the darker the image. There is a point at which the image is too dark, unusable." Sándor twice pats the hair on the back of his head, a nervous gesture. "Why do you come here?"

Mick withdraws a card from his pocket, holds it up. "Tennyson Neale was a colleague. We found this card in his flat."

"A colleague?" Sándor lowers his voice. He walks to the door, locks it, pulls the shade. "Did anyone follow you here?"

"Not that we're aware. We have not come to bring trouble to you or your business. Mr. Douglas is a solicitor representing the interests of Mr. Neale's employer." Mick hurries on. They were about to lose the man's cooperation. "When did you last see Mr. Neale?"

Sándor eyes Harry. "A solicitor," he repeats. "For his employer, you say?"

Harry nods. *"Burlington Magazine."*

Sándor appears to relax a little. "I saw him three days ago. Late afternoon, 31 May. He came into the shop, asked what time I would close. Nights, the shop is open. I have a late supper with my wife. But that night, my daughter was coming to dinner. I said I would close at six o'clock."

"Any idea why he wanted to know?" asks Harry. "About the time, I mean."

"He seemed happy, smiling, said he needed photos developed late. For his editor, he said. Would that be you?" He stares at Mick.

"No," says Mick. "I work for the editor's assistant. Scheduling, that sort of job."

Sándor continues. "I offered him the studio. Told him to clean up afterward."

"How did he respond?" asks Mick.

"He thanked me, paid in advance. Said he'd let me know what time, but I never heard from him."

"Do you suppose he came in and used the studio without telling you?"

"It is possible. The key is available. If he did, he cleaned up. There was nothing out of place."

"Did Neale leave film with you for development? Anything he hadn't picked up yet?"

"In fact, yes, the photographs in the envelope there, on the third shelf."

"When was this?"

"The end of last week. Night scenes of Budapest. A fine eye for shadow and light, he had. Others may be more recent."

"My editor will need them." Mick searches the shelves.

"I have no use for them. There is one roll I could not develop. The film is damaged. You will see the images are blurred. They were taken in a dark place, the film not sensitive enough. I wondered why he would make such a mistake."

After a few brief inquiries, Harry and Mick, impatient to depart, thank Sándor and leave the shop with an armload of photographs, a roll of undeveloped film, and answers that didn't add up.

"Not too curious, was he, about the murder," says Mick. "No questions."

"More nervous about who might be watching the shop," says Harry. "And anxious to get rid of these." Harry rearranges the envelopes under his arm.

The aroma of fresh pastry wafts from the small bakery next to the Kádár café where a host with thick black brows seats them at an outdoor table, a blue umbrella tilted to block the setting sun. They order beer and a plate of pork sausages and settle back to watch the string of sidewalk artists selling watercolors of the steeples on Castle Hill. Across the street, a balladeer strums his guitar.

"What have we got so far?" asks Mick, slathering a pork sausage with mustard.

"Missing pieces," says Harry.

"The work would go faster if you perked up. You're in a vile mood," says Mick. "Any more posturing with government types, we'll get thrown out before we find anything."

"I'm bothered by this morning. Not surprised, mind you, but bothered all the same. They handed us a coroner's report and sent us on our way," says Harry. "Did they think the report would satisfy us? They're hiding something."

"That's all we'll get from them. They don't like the idea of foreigners nosing around. No use dwelling. I had my say this morning. Lot of good it did. We can't be too rough about it. We represent a magazine, for Christ's sake." Mick drains his beer, orders another. "From the flat, we have the diary, photos, the odd list, and a film roll. All seemed important enough for Neale to secure. Near enough to get to, when necessary. From Sándor, we have Neale's interest in film development—not unusual, given his cover—the damaged roll of film, these photographs." Mick taps the brown envelopes on the table. "And the probability that Neale used Sándor's darkroom the night he was murdered."

"You believe Sándor's story?"

"No reason not to. At this point."

Harry pounds the table. "The watch. The watch doesn't fit. At least three people aren't telling everything they know. Gaska. Sándor. Savic." He ticks them off, pausing after each name. Harry is certain both Tamás Sándor and Laura Savic possess information to help unravel the puzzle of Neale's death.

"I doubt we'll get anything more from them," says Mick. "I'll ask about this restaurant bill." Mick waves the waiter to the table and hopes he speaks a bit of German. The waiter does not, but returns with the broadly built host in tow.

The host adjusts a pair of reading glasses, inspects the bill, and strokes the goatee on his long chin. "An Englishman—tall, thin, dark hair, blue jacket, gray trousers, two ales, goulash—meets a lovely companion. They talk, they laugh, then a lover's spat. One minute, they kiss. The next, she shouts and leaves him standing alone." The host shrugs, gestures with open palms.

"What time?" asks Mick.

"Before midnight, as I recall."

"Is this the man?" Mick produces Neale's photograph.

The host and waiter exchange looks. "It may be," says the host, clearing his throat. The waiter stares at the picture for some time. He shakes his head a little. He is not sure.

"And the woman. What was she like? Hair? Height? Dress?" asks Harry.

"I cannot say," the host says. "The light was dim. She did not stay long."

Chapter Seven

4 **June.** As Brinkley predicted, Harry and Mick are summoned. It is one of those spectacular Neo-Renaissance mansions designed in the grand style that lines Andrássy Boulevard. The entryway to Number 60 conveys a clear message of power. A massive chandelier casts shadows at their feet; a wide curving staircase is carpeted in red plush. On the right and left stand thick double doors of rosewood with polished brass hardware.

A security officer, smelling strongly of hair wax and wearing a suit a size too small for his generous frame, meets them in the foyer, checks their identification, and directs them down a long hallway. At the end of the corridor, a grim-faced guard opens a door, ushers them inside, and pulls it closed behind them.

Harry's eyes roam the cavernous room. A luxuriously carved desk holds the center. A long dining table of polished mahogany set for three—crystal goblets, china place settings, gleaming silverware anchors the far end. Above the table hangs a large rectangular mirror. Matted pastoral landscapes in subtle shades of brown and green line the paneled walls. Drapes, a brilliant shade of royal blue, frame the full-length windows.

Harry and Mick register the form sitting behind the desk. The man sits back, head straight, elbows resting on the arm rails of an imposing black chair, a look of amusement on his face. He removes his eyeglasses and lifts the lid of an inlaid cigar box. The man pauses to choose one for himself, and then offers the box to his guests. Cheap Burmese cheroots. Harry expected more. Successful men are known to flaunt their cigars. He wonders where the expensive Presidentes are stashed. Mick declines. Harry selects one.

The man behind the desk says, "Douglas and MacLeod, agents of the British Foreign Service." The big deep voice might have echoed off canyon walls. The man stands, walks around the desk to shake their hands, firm two-handed clasps designed to swallow lesser men. "I am Colonel Laszlo Vací, chief of the Hungarian Secret Police." He enunciates each word in slow, precise English, as if he has practiced the phrase. He does not ask them to sit down. There follows a long silence. Vací spends a goodly amount of time examining them.

Harry has encountered the Laszlo Vacís of the world. He recognizes his tactics. The initial distance. The exaggerated voice. Silence, followed by an amusing expression, conveys that he knows more about his audience than they know about him. Elements of intimidation. Designed first to unsettle. Later, to coerce. Here is a man who enjoys watching others squirm.

Vací takes a slow walk around the room, a slight limp in his gait. Harry sniffs his cheroot and studies the man. Vací wears a business suit, no colorful medals. From the ill fit of the coat, Harry concludes that he must buy his suits off the rack, an error on the part of a man with arms as long as Vací's. His wrists are visible below the ends of his sleeves, leaving one to stare at the size of his hands. He smokes languidly, blowing great puffs upward to the ceiling, pausing at each ashtray. Like many Hungarians they have met, he has dark eyes and a thick head of hair slicked straight back from a low forehead. A full mustache fills the space between a prominent nose and a mean mouth. He reminds Harry of a taller, less handsome version of the actor Paul Muni. About the same age as Muni.

Mick breaks the silence, "Colonel Vací, we are in your debt for inviting us to meet today. We have a few questions about the death of Tennyson Neale, a British citizen."

Vací smiles a humorless smile, but says nothing. He stubs out his cigar, finds a chair and sits down, hands folded loosely in front of his chest, his glance level. He looks from one man to the other with thinly veiled hostility. "There is a connection between us, as intelligence officers, a trusted relationship. Indeed, Mr. Neale was a British citizen." Harry thinks he sees Vací's lips twitch. "Also, a British agent gathering information. We were aware of his activities."

"Were you acquainted with Neale?" asks Mick.

Vací shows no sign of having heard the question. "How long do you plan to stay in Budapest?"

"Were you acquainted with Tennyson Neale?"

Harry watches Vací's calculation, debating for an instant. "I met Neale. A function at the embassy, I believe."

"When, specifically?" asks Harry.

Vací's face goes blank, the room silent. In Vací's world, Harry knows, others dare not question him.

Vací looks at his watch, rises to his feet and says dismissively. "I have no definite recollection. I frequent the British embassy."

It is plain Vací is playing with them. Enjoying the game. They could provide Vací with some fiction about their departure date, thank him for the audience, leave. Harry knows they need to play, too, to prolong the encounter. He catches Mick's eye, then walks to a sideboard tucked neatly between two upright wooden file cabinets. From a decanter on a silver tray, he pours out two fingers of whiskey into three glasses, hands one to Mick, one to Vací, and keeps one for himself. Vací does not seem surprised, but Harry notes a tic under Vací's eye.

Still standing, Harry throws back the whiskey, feels the warmth in his chest. He walks to a window overlooking the courtyard beyond. He gazes out for a moment, turns back to Vací's desk where he places the empty glass. "We'll be in Budapest until we find out more about Neale's murder. His murder may not be your concern, but it is ours."

Vací sips at his drink. "In my country, the murder of a political figure or the representative of a foreign power leads to serious reprisals. I trust your journey will not be wasted."

卌

Half past one. Andrássy Boulevard teems with café patrons hurrying to luncheon appointments. On their way to Erzébet Square, Mick stops to admire the fine facade of a turn-of-the-century townhouse while Harry relives their encounter with Laszlo Vací.

Mick seems to read his mind. "There's a chap who prospers in good times and bad."

"Your point?" Harry pushes back the brim of his hat and looks up at the second floor of the townhouse.

"A very active cellar at Number 60, I'm told," says Mick. "No reasons necessary."

"An uninviting place to be sure. I wouldn't like to think on it too closely," says Harry. "It's a long way to Chain Bridge from that cellar. All the same, he knew Neale was up to something."

Mick says, "Sándor has reason to squirm."

"What did you make of that last remark about serious reprisals?"

"I wondered about that phrase. Is he expecting the Crown to take after the murderer?"

"That's not the way it works in our business. He knows that."

"With all that crystal on the table, I figured we were invited to a sumptuous last supper," says Mick.

"That table was set for three. Who is coming to dine?"

"Likely not the woman who's been following us since we left his office." Mick nods in the direction of a woman wearing a fashionable olive plaid dress and matching broad-brimmed hat worn low over her brow. Low enough to obscure her face.

"She is unmistakable. Shall we back her off?"

"Not yet. Let's see how far she's willing to follow."

At the next corner, Harry and Mick abruptly cross the roadway. They circle the square. She circles the square.

"Do you suppose she's the woman Neale met the night he was killed?" Harry checks his reflection in a window. A split second later, the broad-brimmed hat disappears into a doorway.

"If that's the case, we need to be following her. You go meandering off somewhere. I'll fall back, see how she plays it."

Harry tips his hat and sets off in the direction of the railway station. "Meet you at the Gellért."

Harry's stroll provides opportunity for reflection on the morning's events. They had been interrogated—mild by industry standards, but all the same an interrogation—by one of the most powerful men in Hungary. Harry understands that Vací is not so much interested in questioning them as wanting to communicate what he knows about them. He said as much. He knows Neale was an agent. He suspects Mick and Harry are in Budapest for more than retrieving Neale's body. He wants them to know their covers were exposed. The question is, why? Why did he share such information with them? Then there is the woman in the olive hat. Does she work for Vací or someone else? If she is part of the secret police, she must be a raw recruit. Her crude surveillance techniques would not measure up at Six. Then again, maybe she wants to be seen. Could she be the woman at the Kádár café? She seduced and subsequently knocked off Neale, and is now on the hunt for more British spies. Not so fanciful, that. Neale was always keen on the ladies. Budapest is rife with foreign spies. Why pick on Neale?

Chapter Eight

4 **June.** After a late dinner, while they walk from the restaurant to Zsolt Csárda, a tavern at the south end of Dorottya utca, Mick details his observations about the woman in olive. "I doubt she works for Vací's lads. She kept up your pace for a couple of blocks, then sat down at an outside table. You had gone from sight. I left her there sipping a cup of tea. Don't know what she was up to. If we see her again, I'll stick with her."

They wait for Brinkley, Mick nursing a pint of pale ale, Harry a whiskey. Brinkley promised an update on Neale's whereabouts—at least what he could piece together—the day before Neale's death.

Mick leans in, speaks low in Harry's ear. "You'd think Brinkley couldn't afford to be seen with the likes of us."

"Could be he's a regular here. If we are who we say we are, Brinkley has reason to communicate with two Englishmen who work for a classy art magazine. Obviously, this place is a government watering hole. A place like this, Reuters can pick up a story now and again." Harry signals the bartender for another whiskey.

It is true. This is a bar for establishment types. Diplomats, politicians, the like. The crowd mingling throughout the bar—well-trimmed men in tailored suits, stylishly dressed, high-heeled women in seamed stockings—look to be business and government workers anxious to shed their routine and share the day's stories with friends. The smoky haze makes it difficult to distinguish one individual from another, so they do not catch Brinkley's arrival until he motions them to a private table in the back. A heavy curtain separates them from the rest of the patrons.

"Nice little setup," says Mick, taking the chair facing the doorway. "What time does the game start?"

"Check with Zoltán. This side of the river, Zoltán's king. He decides who sits at his table." Brinkley lights a cigarette, shakes out the match, and orders a Manhattan, giving the waiter an extended list of instructions.

Mick digs in, "What have you got?"

"A timeline of sorts," says Brinkley. He retrieves a notepad from his coat pocket, flips a few pages, and reads aloud. "The morning of 31 May, Neale seen taking photos around St. Stephen's Basilica, afternoon at Dohany Synagogue. Afterward, he visited a film developer named Sándor on Arany János utca, stayed no more than twenty minutes. From there, he returned to his flat, arrived at seven. Nothing after that." Brinkley sits back in the fat leather chair, satisfied, it appears, with his report. Harry listens to Brinkley and thinks about the elegant dining table set for three. And what a lousy journalist Brinkley must be.

Annoyed that Brinkley summoned them at this hour for such paltry intelligence, Harry jumps in. "Later that night, around eleven o'clock, dressed in the clothing in which he was found, he was seen at the Kádár café in the company of a woman. Conveniently, no one recalls a description. According to the host, they carried on as possible lovers, then had a falling out. The woman left in a hurry. She was on foot."

"That leaves four hours between seven and eleven," adds Mick. "From Sándor's comments, we know Neale changed clothes at some point, probably at his flat. Give or take a few minutes, he left the café around midnight. The time of his murder is estimated between three and four in the morning. Therefore, we have seven to eight hours unaccounted for. Four before midnight, three to four after midnight, the café stop in between."

"Time and place," muses Harry. "Where was he and what was he doing during those hours? One possibility is Sándor's darkroom. How long to develop a roll of film?"

"Not my area." Brinkley watches the smoke of his cigarette. "From working with our photographers, I'd say at least an hour for the roll, then drying."

"Let's say it can be done in two hours, start to finish," says Harry. "Let's say that's how and where he spent two hours of his time. Which leads to more questions. Did he develop the film before or after midnight, and where are those photos?"

"Given the way he was dressed after eleven, I'd say before midnight. He may have passed them off to someone," says Mick.

"Or hidden them in a spot we've yet to find," says Harry.

Mick adds, "It's conceivable, but I don't buy that. Why hide the photos if he was set to dispatch them that morning? Why not pack them up and be done?"

The image of the Cartier occupies Harry's mind. Maybe the woman in the olive hat made it a departure gift. More than one woman had paid handsomely for Neale's time. Still, Harry cannot shake the possibility that the watch was payment for something. Payment for what?

In any case, he is not going to share such speculation with Cephus Brinkley, and he steers the discussion in another direction. "Do you have any notion where Neale went after he left the café?"

The question hangs, unanswered. Brinkley rises from his chair, distracted by a loud clatter from the bar. Parting the curtain an inch, he says, "You gentlemen are in luck. In a single day, you've been in the presence of two of the most powerful men in Budapest."

From Harry's perspective, Brinkley's normally pink face whitens a shade.

Brinkley positions himself behind the doorframe, holds the curtain back far enough for Harry and Mick to get a glimpse of the new arrival. A handsome man in an expensive dark gray suit struts across the room and stops at the center of the bar. Curly black hair tops a youthful face and a muscled frame, Magyar roots evident in his thick brows and high cheekbones. Late thirties, Harry guesses. An inch over six feet, about Harry's height. A cigarette dangles from one corner of his mouth. An air of carelessness. Or arrogance. The barman hands him a drink. The crowd makes room.

The man stands with his feet apart, taking up more than one man's share of space, and holds his glass up to the light as if inspecting its color.

In a solemn voice, Brinkley announces, "Kristof Balas of the Arrow Cross." Brinkley takes two steps back and retrieves his hat from the peg. He is still speaking as he slides out the side door. "You'll excuse me if I don't stay. I will be in touch. At the Gellért perhaps."

"There's the Brinkley we know," says Harry. Brinkley's hasty exit may be necessary for his cover in the world of Hungarian politics, but it does not sit well.

Mick stands at the half-open curtain, measures the man. "Balas is skilled at attracting an audience. Shrewd, from the looks of him. Might as well meet him."

Harry scans the crowd, not sure he wants to meet Kristof Balas, given the hour and the place, a bar on Balas' home turf. Other than Brinkley's brief information about Balas' less-than-stellar reputation, Harry and Mick know nothing about the man. If anything troublesome should occur, they are not on the warmest of terms with the Budapest police chief.

Harry shrugs, "Why add another complication?" He grabs Mick's shoulder, ready to turn around and call it a night.

The sight of Laura Savic on Balas' arm stops him cold. Stunning in an off-the-shoulder white blouse and long black skirt, she gazes up at Balas in apparent admiration. Balas pulls her close. When she tries to pull away, he grabs her wrist, holds it fast, and then gives it a jerk. Harry sees her wince. She stares down at the large hand that encircles her wrist, then up at Balas, a look now akin to disgust.

"Let go," she says, enunciating each word, eyes narrowing, mouth set.

Above the din of the crowd, Balas speaks in a commanding voice, drawing attention. "Let go. Did you hear her?" He raises her wrist to his lips, kisses it, squeezes it harder. "Shall I release the bitch?" He lets loose a grating laugh, drawing low murmurs from those closest to them.

Laura does not take her eyes from his. "Let go of my wrist," she repeats.

"Did you not hear my question? It is up to them." He gestures at the bar patrons, many of whom shake their heads and turn away.

In response, Balas drops his hold on her, raises his arms wide, plays to the crowd, talking to no one in particular, "She's a bitch of a woman."

Harry's first inclination is to reach for the knife strapped to his ankle. He watches Laura's face redden, wonders what reason she has to be in Balas' company.

Harry steps through the curtain. Mick follows.

Laura sees their approach. She places a hand on Balas' arm and directs his attention to them. "Kristof, meet Mr. Douglas and Mr. MacLeod, our British visitors." She turns in Harry's direction, though she does not meet his eye even when she introduces Balas to them. She lifts a hand to her collarbone, toes the floor with a delicate shoe, turns away and stands behind a table nearby.

Balas steps from the bar and stares at them, cold-eyed. Cold enough to dispel the smallest doubt that Balas knows exactly who they are. "What brings you to Budapest?" he asks. "Our warm springs? Our famous boulevards?"

Harry says, "A bit of business."

"Government business, I assume," says Balas.

"We're in Budapest on our publisher's request, the death of a colleague." Harry tries to swallow his seething anger at the man, and tells himself to redirect the exchange. He does not wish to draw attention to the encounter. "It is possible you can assist us."

Balas blinks languidly. "Why would I?"

Harry lessens the distance between them. The stench of Balas' aftershave cannot mask the whiskey that oozes from his pores. The bar crowd has stopped to watch. It would be wise to back off, Harry tells himself. Nothing good will come of confrontation.

He is not one to retreat, the image of the beautiful interpreter's assault fresh in his mind. "Decency."

Balas pulls back his shoulders, cocks his head, his chest forward. A rooster in full alert. "Hah. An Englishman who talks of decency." He claps his hands together. "Where was your English decency when you carved up my country? Where was your English decency when you gave away our land?" Balas' voice booms throughout the room. "In 1918, where was your decency?"

The crowd edges away. Experience has obviously taught them the signals of Balas' anger. Harry sees them, too. A spasm at the left side of the mouth, hooded eyes, the persistent opening and closing of fists. Harry takes a step to his left, a stool between himself and Balas. Not exactly a weapon, but at least a safe distance from the table where Laura stands.

"You chose the wrong side," says Harry. "And couldn't finish the job." He hears the crowd's gasp and waits for Balas to react. Men like Balas are easily insulted, and men of violence know one response to such injury. Their raw vanity increases with an attractive woman in their audience.

Balas lays one hand on the stool. "What are you calling me?" He begins a menacing dance, feet moving back and forth behind the stool, hands tightening around the stool's legs, eyes on the floor.

Harry catches Mick's eye, aware he has shifted to a position off Balas' right, prepared to intervene.

"I'm simply pointing out—"

Harry is interrupted by Balas' bellow.

"Goddamn English cowards. I come to Zoltán's to drink, to enjoy my friends. I am insulted by a goddamn English coward." Balas picks up the stool and hurls it.

Harry tenses. The man is out of control.

It is not Harry who attracts the brunt of Balas' ire. Balas lurches toward Laura. His big hand grabs her arm and shoves her hard. She makes a sound as if to resist and tries to tear his hand away.

Harry's blow catches Balas across the jaw, and Balas staggers. With the back of his hand, Balas wipes a thin trickle of blood from his mouth. He pushes the table over and lunges for Harry. Harry grabs Balas' collar, lifts him off his feet, and slams him against the bar. A hammering punch to the sternum finishes it. Balas doubles over, coughs, droplets of blood spat onto the floor. He stumbles his way to the exit, and stops, leaning on the frame. Clutching his chest and gasping for breath, he points a finger at Harry. "You English cowards will regret this."

Chapter Nine

5 **June**. Brinkley will have heard by now. Harry suspects Brinkley plotted the entire scene. Who directed Mick and Harry to the Zsolt Csárda and then sneaked away? Brinkley knows where Balas spends his late nights, that a crowd is present, that Harry and Mick would immediately dislike the man. Brinkley was right about that. There are plenty of men Harry can't stomach.

Harry holds a chunk of ice to his red and swollen knuckles. He cannot remember the last time he hit a man with his bare hand. He grapples with reasons for this lapse in judgment and arrives at only one. Laura Savic. He cannot blame Brinkley for that. He grabs his coat, leaves a message for Mick to meet for an early lunch, and sets out for the Zsolt. He will apologize, cover Zoltán's damages, and, with a bit of luck, wrangle a seat at his poker table.

〸〸〸〸

When Harry arrives at the lunch café, Mick already is seated at an outside table with an exquisite view of the Danube. After a hard morning rain, the sky is a clear blue, and the summer sun blazes above them.

Harry removes his jacket and settles back to relax in the shade of the umbrella. "We have a new friend in Zoltán Zsolt, an invitation to drink any hour day or night, and a chance to win a few quid this evening," he says.

"And a new enemy in Kristof Balas," replies Mick. His disapproving tone is clear. Mick rarely passes judgment. Not since the early days of their service.

"Out with it," says Harry.

"Not my place."

"You have an opinion that's not likely to change. I want to hear it." Harry leans forward in his chair, folds his hands on the table.

"Balas had too much to drink. You could have walked away." Mick downs his beer. Harry waits. "Instead, you had to attract her attention. So you baited him."

"Came to a similar conclusion myself. Not my best hour."

"She didn't need you acting the gallant gentleman," continues Mick, still aggravated. "The lovely translator looked like she could handle whatever was going on."

"You saw it, too, did you? Something peculiar in that exchange," says Harry.

They sit silent, faces blank, staring at Mick's empty beer glass. Then, simultaneously, they break into fits of boyish laughter.

"Right or wrong, I enjoyed that chest thump," says Harry.

"All the same, we're an easy target. We do not need anyone questioning our credentials. Get us thrown out," says Mick. "Or worse."

"An empty threat, that parting remark."

"You hope as much. The Arrow Cross doesn't stand for foreigners interfering in their business. We're not worth Balas' time. In any case, we're wise to decipher what we've got, make the most of it, and close the case. I read a healthy bit of Neale's journal this morning and looked at the photos we found in his flat. The enlargements of Horthy and his son and the ambassador in Berlin bother me. I can't say why, except there must be hundreds of similar shots out there. Why would Neale keep those specifically? They can't be of any intelligence value."

"Identification, maybe. For someone who doesn't know them on sight." Harry changes the subject. "I don't trust Brinkley."

"Why involve him?" says Mick.

"He seems to know everything."

"If he did, there's no need for us," says Mick.

"I've no interest in playing his fool," says Harry. "Or being his diversion."

"Nor have I. He may know more than he's saying, but he doesn't know who Neale's murderer is. Otherwise, we'd be on our way."

"Politics is his primary game, and we've landed in the thick of it," says Harry. "I don't like it."

ﬞﬞﬞﬞﬞ

After lunch, they return to the Gellért, gather the evidence into Mick's hotel room, and set to the tedium of sifting small pieces of information, settling timelines, sketching webs of acquaintances and contacts. Harry rigs up a light box, suitable to examine the roll of seemingly damaged film retrieved from Sándor and the film remnant from Neale's shoe.

"You said you worked with Neale." Mick thumps a pencil on the table.

"One case. We shared data, discussed possible theories, results. If you're asking what I know about Neale's habits, he was thorough. Kept detailed records. Nothing fancy, but logical, practical. Got the job done, but saved his energy for the field. Worked his cases on foot. Followed every lead. Met every source."

"That's what puzzles me," says Mick. "We've been shown a limited picture. Brinkley says he had little contact with him, didn't interact much."

"Neale was an affable sort. A performer. Liked to impress. I remember once he caused a mighty ruckus over a woman he met in Hastings. Told her a tale about his family estate. Wanted her to know he was important, His Majesty's secret agent. Rented a smart sports car at the weekend, drove to the Epsom Derby, and convinced her he was a personal friend of Aga Khan."

Mick's eyes brightens at the topic. "In '36? The year the Aga's fast gray took it?"

"Right, June of '36. Charlie Smirke orchestrated a fine race, that beautiful finish. Mahmoud set the track record, but Neale nearly got the boot over it."

"You're saying he could be reckless," says Mick.

"I'm saying he was capable of doing something unauthorized. Outside the rules. Particularly if it involved a woman."

"We've all been in that muddle. What else?"

"I'm still surprised at the watch. Can't explain it."

"Turned?"

"That's not the Neale I knew."

"Greed's a deadly game," says Mick carefully. "Maybe he filled his pockets at someone else's expense. That someone thought he'd gone too far. On the other hand, the watch could be a plant."

"Hadn't seen it that way." Harry is certain Neale would not trade reputation or mission for a Cartier watch. "We passed a couple of jewelry stores yesterday. Let's take a visit."

⁞⁞⁞⁞⁞

At seven o'clock, on a side street off Kossuth utca, they catch a jeweler as he is removing the stock from his window and setting down the metal grille for the night. The jeweler remembers Neale, assumed he was a British tourist with money to spend. For cash—pounds sterling—Neale purchased the Cartier on 30 April. The jeweler produced a receipt that listed the sale price at fifteen hundred pounds.

Neale had found an extra source of income.

"A gamble that scored big?" Mick speculates.

"I'll check with Zoltán about wins the last week in April," says Harry.

"If not, that leaves a couple of possibilities, none of them good," says Mick.

They turn their attention to the envelope found hidden in the carpet seam. Three pages of lists that appear to be sequences of dates, then three to seven letters, then a series of numbers beside them, all written in Neale's careful hand. On the first page, the numbers in the left-hand column move along in an orderly fashion, leading them to conclude that, in the past year, Neale recorded twenty separate dates. The corresponding letters, however, have no apparent pattern, albeit some repetitions.

After they scanned, counted, and recounted, Mick steps back. "You said he did things simply, thorough but nothing fancy. From Sándor's comments, we know Neale was fond of habits and routines. Here's a date, 20–3, 20 March, with four letters in the next column, MGCB. In the journal on that same date, he has notes of meetings with Marton Gaska and Cephus Brinkley."

Harry runs a finger down the column. "Take a look. This second column is a record of his contacts on that date. That explains the repetitions. TS, Támás Sándor, appears on at least half these dates. The journal should tell the full names for the other initials. It should verify whether Brinkley and Sándor are telling the truth about their contact with Neale."

Harry is near certain they will find discrepancies. "These sheets look to be an abbreviated version of the journal. In case the journal is lost, he still has a record." Harry remembered his early trainer's warnings. *Keep nothing incriminating on your person. Hide it in a place no one will think to look.* "What are the numbers in the third column? They seem random. No pattern." Harry points to one near the end, a string of zeros.

Mick selects two open envelopes scattered on the floor. "The photos. Do the photos have numbers?" He parcels out the stack of photographs. "By God, they do." Mick reads off the first two.

"They're on the list," says Harry.

"I'll nail it down," says Mick. He hunches over the paper. "You're due at Zoltán's. Find out what you can. I'm keen to know the players."

On Harry's exit through the lobby, a messenger hands him an envelope, cream-colored with a thick green line around the edge. He is late, and starts to stuff it in his pocket until he catches the name on the back fold. Inside, a brief note.

Harry Douglas,
I have information regarding Tennyson Neale. If you please, meet me in the Gellért breakfast lounge tomorrow morning, ten o'clock.
Laura Savic

His eyes sweep the street. He gives serious thought to cancelling his appearance at the poker game, losing the secret police, and tracking her down. But he has not the first notion where she might be or how to begin such a search. He does not want to call attention to himself or to her. Vací's men will be nearby, hidden behind a newspaper or a shop canopy. Again, Harry wonders how Vací discovered their identities.

The night is still. Headed east across the Erzébet Bridge, he stops to lean against the rail and admire the white moon, stark amidst deep shades of purple sky. He studies the dark Danube beneath him, and wonders what it can tell him about Neale's last hours. His eyes are tired from reading the small print of Neale's handwriting. His mind turns to Neale's purchase of the watch. A crucial fact he does not want to believe, but there is no mistake. Fifteen hundred pounds sterling. A small fortune. The note from the interpreter surprised him. He is not at all sure he wants to know what she has to tell him.

Out on the river, he hears the low steady rumble of a passing barge, spies a faint light in the window of the pilothouse, and contemplates the barge's destination. Thus engaged, he almost misses the slight motion in the periphery of his vision. Coming up the bridge behind him is a man in a heavy overcoat on a warm night, hands in his pockets. Faster than normal. There is nowhere to go, the walkway narrow where Harry stands. In an instant, the man is upon him. Pinned against the rail, Harry finds himself standing toe-to-toe with the taller man. A black cloth covers the man's head and neck, exposing only hooded eyes and hooked nose. The eyes are dark and flat. He has a deep crease across his brow. Harry smells the man's sour breath. The man gives a sullen grunt and pulls something from his pocket. A silver blade, the end curving up into a deadly tip that will push through flesh with little effort. Harry reaches for the man's wrist, squeezes hard and digs his fingers into the base of the man's thumb. The man's weight sends Harry's spine against the iron bars. He tries to wrestle with the man. He pushes against him, but can find no advantage. The man shoves back, forcing Harry almost over the rail. Harry feels the heaviness of the man's chest pressing hard against his own. In a low rasp, the man spits out a word in Hungarian. Then he speaks in accented English, "Harry Douglas. This is for you."

Harry sees the glint of the knife against the black cloth. He feels a small point of pain at the base of his throat. His mind flashes to Neale's bloodless face on the morgue table.

The man snorts, his mouth an inch from Harry's ear. "Go home."

He eases away, slides the knife into the pocket from which it came. His eyes glare. The man stands back, waits.

Harry reaches for his throat. A warning. Nothing more. No deadly intent. Unless he and Mick ignore the threat, of course. Harry says nothing, matches the man's cold-blooded glare, and nods once. Message received.

卌

Harry knocks on the second door off the street, turns the knob. A smoky haze greets him, the air heavy with the smell of men and tobacco. Harry is the last to arrive. Across the room, fat cigar in one hand, whiskey in the other, Zoltán Zsolt hollers, "We feared you have forgotten us."

"A slight delay." Harry forces a smile. "My apologies."

With an exaggerated flourish, Zoltán pulls out the chair on his left and addresses the gathering, "Meet Harry Douglas. He wishes to study the Hungarian way for taking other people's money. I tell him, it is always simple. First, we study the man's pockets." Zoltán holds his glass of whiskey aloft and waits a beat. "Then we steal his wallet." He laughs outrageously.

Harry manages a small laugh. The scene on the bridge stays with him. The swift man in black knew his name, knew where he would be. The man is merely a loyal follower, a menacing messenger with a knife. Dispatched to persuade a reluctant subject. Budapest is famous for heavy-handedness, the blood-stained handkerchief in his pocket proof of Harry's first encounter with the truth of it. He has no doubt that in this same moment, the arranger of the intimidation—Vací, Balas, Gaska, which?—is receiving a full report. The question for him and for Mick is what to do about the warning.

Harry shakes hands with each player and registers their faces. The last is surprisingly familiar. Jan Nagy puts a hand on Harry's shoulder. "When we met, you failed to mention your fondness for the cards."

"A recent interest," says Harry. "How is it you're in this game?"

"Zoltán and I conduct regular business. I supply the glassware for his tavern. On Monday, I take his money. On Wednesday, he takes it back." Jan shrugs and smiles. "Good to see you again. Your business progresses well, I trust."

"Progress is occasionally slow," says Harry, grinning.

"At least you have found the best Csárda in Pest," says Nagy.

"Sit, sit," commands Zoltán. "Get your drinks, your smokes. We begin."

The group removes coats, loosens ties, rolls up sleeves, counts chips. Harry sets his place in order and observes each man. When the game grows tense, they will reveal, as all men do, their eccentricities, their habits.

Host Zoltán Zolst, round faced, full bodied, big fisted, black curly locks—everything about the man louder and larger than life—directs the action.

Joszef Kovacs, on Harry's left, is the opposite. There is something mole-like about him, the pale skin and watchful eyes, the layer of fuzz on cheeks and chin, tension in his slight shoulders, light brown hair falling forward onto his forehead. He pushes up a pair of wire-rimmed glasses that slips down his nose.

Next to Kovacs, Nagy is the picture of the graceful gentleman, chiseled jaw, streaks of gray in carefully trimmed hair and mustache, the most stylish of the group. Nagy leans into the table, hands folded one over the other, quietly attentive.

In the chair on Zoltán's right sits Peter Toth, youngest player, the first fair-haired, blue-eyed fellow Harry has seen since arriving in Budapest. A local resident or regular visitor? The freshly scrubbed Toth and Zoltán seem well acquainted. Zoltán rearranges the young man's chips, playfully steals one from his pile. Toth busies himself shuffling and reshuffling two decks of cards, his hands fast and loose as he laughs at Zoltán's tricks and watches Harry's eyes.

Across from Harry sits Polish Count Oszcar Bychowsky. He is square shouldered and long necked, the shadow of a beard meticulously shaved along his jaw. Thinning hair tops a bony frame that nearly shows through translucent skin. There are pouches beneath his eyes. The tips of his fingers wear a yellow nicotine cast. He seems more interested in ordering another martini than in the cards.

They may be easy reads, Harry thinks. Then again, this is a local bunch, apt to have their own manner of exchange. They play a preliminary hand of five-card stud. No bets involved. Casual, easy. After Zoltán signals the waiter to refill everyone's glasses, Harry feels the mood change. Zoltán grinds out his cigar, unwraps a new one, sets it unlit between his teeth. His face is now a frown. Rapid-fire, he speaks, "Seven-card stud. Two down, one up, then opening bets, next three cards up, last one down, bet after each card. Your deal, Mr. Harry Douglas."

After several rounds of aggressive betting, Toth makes a show of lifting the edge of the seventh card, turning his head a fraction, lifting his chin to display a wicked smile. He produces a straight on the first hand. Harry, holding a pair of fours, has folded when he observes the young man push away from the table, cross his legs, and nod ever so slightly, a mere twitch of his head. Although winning or losing is no matter this evening, Harry is not about to go broke before the night is done.

Kovacs prepares to deal. He swipes a hand through his hair, looks sideways at Harry, wild-eyed. "It doesn't matter, you know."

"What's that?" Harry is unsure whether Kovacs is referring to the cards or some other topic.

"The way one dies," says Kovacs.

Harry tries to keep the surprise from his voice. Has the man drunk too much or is he being intentionally morose? Harry has heard stories of the legendary tormented Hungarian psyche. "Of course it matters."

Harry feels the weight of Zoltán's foot on his own, a message. "Joszef," Zoltán reaches across Harry to pull on Kovacs's arm. A tender touch, it seems to Harry. "Deal the cards, my friend. What shall we play?"

Harry watches the nervous flutter of Kovacs' hands. There is an odd expression on Toth's face.

In a hushed voice, Zoltán, moving closer, speaks in Harry's ear, "Pay him no mind. Joszef is not himself. He witnessed a disturbing sight. A dead man strung up. On the bridge. One night when he was leaving our game."

Harry nods, keeping himself in check. A dozen questions leap forth. Did Kovacs see Neale's murderer? Did the police question him? He wants to ask Kovacs why he did nothing to stop such a crime. This is not the time for such inquiries.

Before Harry can focus, Zoltán sets off on stories of last season's track winnings. He is intent on brightening the mood, distracting Kovacs. "Joszef, remember last season your winners? Such beautiful beings, these thoroughbreds. When does the season begin? We shall go on the first day." Zoltán pounds a fist on the table.

Kovacs deals the first and second cards. At the upturned third card, the game grows serious. Harry expects fast play from Toth, and gets it from Bychowsky. The Count, on his third cocktail, seems to catch fire. Over the next three rounds, amidst bouts of painful hacking, the Count bets, raises and re-raises—leaving the other players fumbling to interpret the cards and manage their bets. Apparently, it does not occur to Bychowsky that slow play builds the pot. Perhaps, Harry reasons, the Count wants to win as much as he can before his lungs fail. Mostly, Harry plays it tight, gets out early and observes, without seeming to look at the other players and their give-away mannerisms. Particularly Toth's. Harry judges him a young player with little patience and a high tolerance for risk. Happy feet and jittery legs mean the strength of his hand increased with the last card. A scratch on the back of his neck means the cards are not going his way. A nibble on his thumbnail signals he is going to raise.

Well past two in the morning, after each man has dealt at least three hands, Harry's stack shows a reasonable, albeit small, profit. He is bone-tired and wonders how much longer the game will go on.

"A break?" suggests Zoltán. "More whiskey?"

The waiter brings a tray from the barroom, clean glasses and a full bottle of eighteen-year-old Jameson whiskey. The men stand in place, rotating the tightness from their shoulders, moving their necks side to side. Toth walks once around the table and stops at the chair next to Harry. "Zoltán tells me you are a solicitor. You have business in Budapest. Have we met at the Embassy?"

Harry turns up his glass and finishes what remains. With a nod, he acknowledges Toth while he selects two empty glasses from the tray. The waiter pours generously. Harry hands one glass to Toth, then swirls the gold liquid in his own. *"Egészségedre*, to your health."

Harry lifts the glass. "My business in Budapest regards my client, *Burlington Magazine*. You may have heard of it." Harry pauses, drinks. "No reason why you would. Unless you're an art collector."

"We have art in Budapest." Toth has not drunk from his glass. He seems to be staring at the base of Harry's neck.

When Harry sees Kovacs step outside into the alley, he eases away and follows Kovacs.

Kovacs lights a cigarette, inhales, and walks a few steps into the alley. He turns back in Harry's direction and squints through the smoke. Harry rests one shoulder against the wall, says nothing. He wants the man to feel at ease. Kovacs speaks first. "Douglas, what brings you to Budapest?" He holds the cigarette between steady fingers, his earlier anxious state gone.

"Business," replies Harry. "A project to complete."

"Ah," says Kovacs, "Budapest is becoming a difficult place for business. At least certain parts of Budapest. The city used to be more open, more alive."

"So I'm told. What kind of work do you do?" Harry isn't sure he wants to follow that line of questioning, but the subject slips out before he can call it back.

"I own a business on the Buda side. A shop on the west end of the Chain Bridge. My wife sells teas and spices. In the same building, I manage an export business." That explains his walking across the bridge in the early morning, thinks Harry. "What time do you usually finish your game?"

Nagy steps into the conversation. "Depends on who is winning. Isn't that right, Joszef?"

"Or when Zoltán tires of us." Kovacs smiles. "And throws us into the street."

Harry tries again. "Just trying to get a feel for tonight's schedule."

"We never play past three," says Nagy. "Magda begins to worry. Unless, of course, she decides to sit in. She will play until the sun comes up. She loves for Zoltán to take her money. Mostly, she loves to pretend she holds a winning hand. Bluffing, as you say. It's the actress in her."

"Bluffing is an art I haven't mastered," Harry says. "So I need to prop open my eyelids until three, then." Harry wants to steer the conversation back to Kovacs. "Any transport available at that hour?"

Nagy says, "No taxis in the early morning. I have a car. I'll give you a lift."

Harry nods in Nagy's direction. He turns to Kovacs. "Don't suppose there's much traffic at that hour on the bridge. For getting back to my hotel, I mean."

Kovacs looks at him closely, pushes his glasses up higher on his nose. "There is little traffic on any bridge in the early hours."

"So it's safe enough to walk, then?" asks Harry. "No bandits about?"

Harry watches the color die from Kovacs' face. He gazes at Harry, no doubt unsure how much Harry knows. Kovacs opens his mouth to speak, closes it without uttering a sound. The cigarette falls from his fingers. He does not notice the burning tip ignite a slip of paper next to his shoe until Harry stomps it out.

"You all right, chap?" Harry reaches for Kovacs' elbow, but Kovacs has already rushed inside.

Chapter Ten

6 **June.** "Are you questioning my word?" Laura Savic sits calmly, breaking her bread without eating it, sipping now and then at her coffee, long ago turned cold.

Harry suspects she is baiting him, so he merely raises his eyebrows. He can wait her out, at least until he hears what else she has to say. So far, she's brought him nothing new, nothing he and Mick haven't already determined.

She tries a different tack. "Are you surprised by what I've said?"

"Surprised? No. You've given me a few stray details. We won't ignore them." Harry focuses his attention on her hands. "I must admit I have a poor understanding of why you're here."

She looks out at the street and absently stirs her coffee, as if deliberating an unanswerable question. She did not explain her lateness, just crossed the room toward him, hung her umbrella and raincoat on the hook beside the table and sat down. Then proceeded, without ceremony, to tell Harry what he has already guessed. That Neale made frequent visits to Gaska's office. That she suspected Neale was into more than travel photography.

That Gaska put out a statement that Neale was killed by a gang of street thugs—though no evidence existed to support such conclusions.

"The reason is simple. I liked Tennyson. We were friends. I'd like to know what happened to him." She folds her hands in her lap and looks down. "What I can do to help."

"So, it's personal," says Harry. "What else should I know?" He wonders about the extent of her friendship with Neale and then remembers she had been with Balas two nights before. He will ask about Balas, too.

A police car goes by, siren blaring. He watches her face change. At the same time, the waiter comes and stands just behind her. The waiter clears his throat and stares at the back of her head. Immediately, Harry rises, pulls out her chair, "Let's take a walk," he says.

"But it's raining."

"All the better." He places her raincoat on her shoulders.

They cross the hotel's courtyard with its colored glass windows and statues, past the domed hall and conservatory and out into the street. The rain is warm, nothing more than a steady drizzle. Harry turns up his collar, holds the umbrella for them. Their shoulders touching, he catches a waft of perfume—a light lilac—from the nape of her neck.

The street follows the right bank of the river, turns toward the base of Gellért Hill, then up to Castle Hill. With no compulsion to chatter, they walk for ten minutes, find a small café with dark interior and shaded windows, and settle into a high-sided booth. They are among the café's few patrons.

Laura shrugs off her coat. "I've never been to this part of the Hill. It is splendidly quiet."

Harry orders ale. She spreads her napkin and orders a red wine, Egri Bikávér. Bull's Blood, she calls it. He says it is an odd name for a glass of wine.

"Do you know the story of this wine?"

"I'm a whiskey and ale man. Not much experience with wine."

"The Hungarians have a legend about it. In 1552, the invading Turks staged a siege of the medieval town of Eger. Seeking to control Western Europe, the Turks sent 150,000 troops to overtake this tiny fortress town. Two thousand soldiers defended Eger. During the siege, the citizens of Eger and the soldiers drank red wine to give them strength for the fight. Story has it that the wine spilled onto their beards and armor and covered their bodies in the deep red color of blood. Word went out that these Hungarian soldiers were drinking the blood of bulls to make them strong and fierce fighters. The Turks, as you might know, are a superstitious people. They became afraid to fight soldiers who dared to drink the blood of bulls, and the siege was broken. The winemakers of the Eger region honour the legend by producing this red wine."

"Intriguing story. You talk about the Hungarians as if you were not one of them."

"Several years ago, after I completed university, I came to Budapest to work. I was born in a small village. It is now part of Czechoslovakia."

"Which used to be part of Hungary?"

"At one time, yes. Before 1918, my village was within the Hungarian borders."

"I understand the Hungarians want it back," he said.

"The Germans want the Sudetenland. No one is satisfied with what they have."

"People with power wish to keep it or add to it," said Harry. "People like Kristof Balas." He looks at her when he says this, gauging her reaction.

"Your questions have motive, don't they?" she says, unsmiling. "Kristof drinks to excess. When he does, he is volatile, occasionally mean. All the same, he is a popular man in Budapest."

Harry hears steel in her voice, but her face says nothing.

"I saw a hard man, interested in himself and his own needs. Popular, did you say? When I was a kid, I knew a hockey player like Balas. People pretended to like him because he was a very good hockey player, aggressive, brash, scored lots of goals for the team. When the game was over and we had won, nobody liked him much. I'd stay far away from Balas, drunk or sober." Harry can use a few other words to describe Kristof Balas and his Arrow Cross Party, but decides he has said enough.

They listen to the rain outside. The waiter comes to deliver their drinks and they wait until he is gone before either of them speaks. She sips from her glass and smiles at him.

Over her raised glass, she says. "You have a scar on your left cheek, high on the bone. Do English barristers perform dangerous work?" Her voice is almost in a whisper.

He rubs a finger across the reminder. "Now your questions have motive," he says, smiling. "A bad memory. Nothing much to tell. Dull story."

"An accident, then?" she persists. "A childhood fall?"

"Neither," he says, not wanting to revisit a dark tunnel to the past—the enormity of war—nor divulge the nature of his work.

"You're being mysterious," she says, her attempt at intimacy failing.

He detects a flirtatious note in her voice. "I'm an English solicitor, not a barrister. There's a difference." He pauses. "At the hotel, you were about to tell me something about Neale. Since then, you have avoided it with legends of red wine and questions about my insignificant scar. It's safe here. There's no one to overhear."

She gazes at the ceiling, then clears her throat. "I'm an obstacle to your business. Is that what you're saying?" She pauses, starts again. "Tennyson was, supposedly, a travel photographer."

"A travel photographer for an art magazine." Harry tries to remember more of *Burlington's* mission. "Why do you say 'supposedly'"?

"We'd known each other for a few months. Tennyson asked me to pose for him. He wanted to use the photos, he said, for his articles, in his work. He would pay a small fee. I said no. We quarreled. I never saw him after that. What kind of travel photographer takes pictures of nude women?" She raises her eyebrows, stares at Harry across the table.

Harry coughs, incredulous. "Tennyson Neale was taking nude pictures?" Unprepared for this absurd disclosure, he tries not to laugh, but cannot keep the smile from his face. Nude pictures. Wait until Mick hears this. Harry attempts to recover his professional demeanor. "*Burlington* has been known to devote an issue or two to artistic nudes." He hopes this is not far from the truth. "You think that's what got him killed?"

"The women he tricked do not find this in the least humorous," she says, "including me."

"There were others?" Try as he might, Harry cannot picture Neale snapping pictures of nude women. Then again, one often derives unanticipated benefits from cover assignments.

Laura nodded.

"I'm not laughing at them. It conjures up all nature of possibilities." He pictures the pinched faces at MI6 and the astonishing speed of the gossip when he and Mick report that news. Ever the analyst, Harry has serious doubts whether a woman, even a group of women, would have the strength to string up Neale on that lamppost.

"Do you have any idea what Neale did with these pictures or how many women were involved?"

"I asked for the photos to be given to me. I can't say how many women were so involved with Tennyson." She does not seem embarrassed by her revelation.

"Did he give them to you?" He and Mick found no such photographs. Those, he would remember.

"No," she says simply.

"So you think these women would kill him? Producing a few photos is motive for murder?" Too late, he realizes his voice does not carry the solemnity she requires. But what black comedy it is. Tennyson Neale murdered by a bunch of angry women in the nude.

"These women have reputations. They have families and husbands. They would suffer grave consequences if these pictures surfaced."

"No intent to trivialize them. But they did, after all, take off their clothes and allow themselves to be photographed. What did they expect?" he asks, annoyed at both her defense of them and the notion that they might be justified in murdering the man.

He gathers himself. "I suppose these women don't want to be questioned."

"Probably not," she laughs gently.

"Well then, I hope they all have alibis." He grins to himself, imagining the embarrassed conversations. "Let's have some lunch."

They eat the beet soup in silence. The waiter delivers a basket of bread, then two plates of smoked sausage and sauerkraut. She takes a piece of bread from the basket, closes her eyes and chews it slowly.

Harry waits while she cuts the sausage on her plate into bite-sized slices. "You're not working today?" He may glean a bit of information about Gaska's reasons for covering up the circumstances of Neale's death.

"I work when I am needed. Chief Gaska speaks only Hungarian. My Hungarian, German, and English are quite good, and in demand at the station, particularly when foreign visitors, usually tourists, are involved. Tourists have a variety of police issues, some of them routine—stolen passports, lost automobiles—some of them unique. There are others at the station who handle the Slavic tongues. Slavs tend to understand each others' languages."

He tries not to interrupt, but she stops her explanations, puts down her fork and drinks her wine almost to the bottom of the glass. Curious about her Slavic connections, he asks, "Why is it, given your home, you don't do the Slovak and Czech translations?"

Her smile flickers a moment. "In the eyes of Chief Gaska, I am Hungarian."

Harry is not sure what to make of this. If she is trying to tell him something, it is not plain enough. "Do you have family in Czechoslovakia?"

"My brother has a trade there. He is a carpenter." She says this without glancing up from her plate.

"Anyone else?" he asks.

She shakes her head, almost imperceptibly. He waits for her to say something, but she does not. It crosses his mind that she is protecting someone close to her, possibly herself. Perhaps she sees him as a threat. Then why invite him to breakfast?

He tries another approach, "How long will you stay in Budapest?"

She looks at him quizzically. "You ask many questions."

"That are none of my business, you mean?" He gives a thin smile and a small laugh.

"Something like that." She wipes her mouth with the napkin, takes one last swallow of wine, and stands up. "Let's walk again. The rain has stopped."

They walk along the avenue, scarcely speaking, then find a quiet bench and sit together for a long time. She leans back against him, tilts her head, and smiles. He feels the heat of her next to him. It is a long time since he has found a woman this attractive. Longer still since anything has come of it. She sought out his company, he reasons. He takes her hand, and she rises to her feet.

Her third-floor apartment is small and bright, three rooms and a bath, a set of double doors leading to a balcony that over-looks the street. As she locks the doors and draws the shades, she offers him coffee, then takes his hat and coat and hangs them on a polished stand by the front entrance. He stands very still, aroused as he watches her remove her shoes—low black pumps—and unbutton the top two buttons of her blouse, fanning herself with her fingers as she apologizes for the heat. She takes a step toward him, stops and looks at him, waiting, he supposes, for some action on his part.

The aroma of her perfume and the close warmth of her body excite him. "I'm not sure this . . ." He does not finish his sentence.

"That won't matter," she says, wrapping her fingers around his wrist and leading him to the bedroom.

His arms enclose her slender body, the warmth of it over-whelming him. She arches her back, leaning into him. He bends to kiss her neck and shoulders. Their passion, easily awakened, grows heated. When she slips out of her skirt, he is surprised to find that she wears nothing beneath it. He lifts her up, carries her to the bed, conscious of her lightness—a beautiful hollow-boned bird. She is not secretive about her desires. For the next hours, he feels like a lost thing finding itself, unaware of time and place.

Chapter Eleven

6 **June.** Mick spends a long time poring over the three large photographs. He arranges them vertically, then horizontally, mixes the order and repeats his inspection. There must be a connection. Neale stored them together, separated from the rest, in a safe place. The handwriting on the attachments, in German, did not belong to Neale. All three have the same grainy quality, as if someone took a photograph of a photograph. Unlike the others he and Harry retrieved from Sándor's shop, these have no numbers nor are they listed in Neale's journal or summary pages. Thus, Mick makes several assumptions. The photos were taken recently—the originals probably replaced so as not to appear to have been disturbed. Likely, they were taken within hours of Neale's death so that he had no time to number or record them. Mick suspects they were meant to be part of Neale's intelligence dispatch, the one that never arrived.

In the first photo, he recognizes the Hungarian Regent Miklós Horthy strolling on a sun-drenched, gravelled path that leads to a residence set back among a stand of trees. A younger man, perhaps in his thirties, accompanies him. Two girls not yet in their teens, swinging hands and laughing, walk a few paces behind. The men's heads are slightly down. They are dressed in business suits, hands in pockets. The two resemble each other in demeanor and features. Due to the upward angle of the photo, all four faces are identifiable. Mick decides the taker had been kneeling to one side of the path as the four walked by. A circle is drawn around the younger man's face, a faint line visible. Attached is a smaller photo, a notation written in German in a hand very different from Neale's with the words *Horthy, sohn Miklós Jr, zwei tochters Zsófia and Nicolette, 23 Mai 1400*. Thus, the photo was taken two weeks ago, on 23 May at two in the afternoon. A week before Neale's death. Why had Neale taken a photo of this image and a photo of the notation on the back? Why bother to capture yet another picture of the Regent when there are hundreds from any number of sources? With a magnifier, Mick verifies the circle around Miklós Jr.'s face and another line, slightly smudged, coming from the stand of trees. A small note next to the line reads *80 meters*.

In the second photo, Mick studies the face of a familiar-looking British diplomat in discussion with Hitler's newly appointed Foreign Minister Joachim Ribbentrop and Hitler's German watchdog in Budapest, Ambassador Edmund Veesenmayer. The two men and diplomat Sir Geoffrey Knox stand on the curb outside the Carlton Hotel, apparently waiting for a taxi. Mick notes a faint circle drawn around Veesenmayer's face. A small attachment identifies the men. The date and time are noted: *23 Mai 1300*.

The third photo shows an American diplomat, Ambassador Hugh Wilson, entering a meeting in Berlin. He is accompanied by a man Mick does not—due to a shadow over his profile—recognize.

Mick knows little of the American ambassador. In the Milan office, his reputation is controversial. A recent arrival in Germany, Wilson emphasizes, unlike his predecessor Dodd, the positive aspects of Nazi Germany. Further, he publicly accuses the American press of being controlled by members of the Jewish faith, and he praises Hitler as a leader who pulled his people out of economic despair. These are not isolated views in the UK or in America. The attached notation, hard to decipher, reads *US Botschafter Hugh Wilson, UK Botschafter Sir Nevile Henderson, 23 Mai 1400.* Henderson has served as British ambassador to Germany since 1937. Like Wilson, Henderson believes Hitler will cooperate with England and repeatedly advises accommodation of Germany's ambitions in Czechoslovakia and Austria. Two like-minded peas in a pod. Other than the common date, what do the two ambassadors have to do with Horthy's son and Edmund Veesenmayer? Oddly, no one is circled. Could it be that they are both targeted?

Mick puzzles over the photographs, wondering again about the connections among the men. About the circles around their faces.

Where the hell is Harry? He's been absent most of the afternoon. While Mick does not necessarily mind—he enjoys the time to examine evidence in detail—it is not like Harry to skip out and expect Mick to do the heavy lifting, particularly without telling him. A year ago Mick would have known to search the bars around Milan's racecourses, but Harry's been clean, at least under control, for a good eight months.

Alone, Mick runs through possibilities. Among the three photos, the date and the German notations are commonalities. Mick feels strongly that Neale had shot the photos the very day he died. Hence, the reason Neale asked to use Sándor's darkroom. So the photos would be ready for the next day's dispatch. Surely he meant to send out more than these three pieces, with, at the least, a message to explain their inclusion.

What else did they find in Neale's flat? The undeveloped roll of film in his shoe. Mick is not finished analyzing the photographs and their notations. So far, he's come up empty. He needs a fresh set of eyes. Where the hell is Harry? A dinner break and a brisk walk along the river might sort things out. It looks to be a long night.

ⅠⅠⅠⅠⅠ

The early evening sky, a magnificent array of orange and gold, is the perfect backdrop for Mick's stroll. An hour ago, he had marched in and out of three restaurants until he found a cool refuge from the hot evening and ate his fill of a rich veal stew.

A few blocks from the hotel, he comes upon the sound of soft jazz, a Sidney Bechet clarinet, a Tommy Ladnier trumpet, and a woman singing the weary blues at an open-air club that looks out on a medieval church and a statue to soldiers fallen in the Great War. He orders a cold beer and settles into a comfortable seat on the terrace to watch the night unfold. The fragrant air reminds him of Edinburgh, the Queen's Gardens in summer's full bloom. In the distance, the Chain Bridge traffic ebbs and flows, and he wonders about Neale's last moments. Had Neale known his killer? Had he known why he was to die? Had he felt the arms that lifted him up? Was he mercifully unaware as his life drained from him? There had to have been more than one person at that lamppost. Likewise, more than one person had taken the photos. If the noted times are correct—the photos were all taken on the 23rd day of May—there had to have been at least two people, possibly three, clicking the cameras.

Mick is certain Neale's death is tied to those images.

Chapter Twelve

6 June. "There's a rich question. Where have I been? You're the chap who disappeared for the better part of the day." Mick has rarely seen Harry Douglas at a loss for words. Harry's behavior this evening is plainly singular. He fidgets with his pipe, tamping and retamping the tobacco. He paces aimlessly about the room, grunts an indistinct word in response to Mick's observations about the case as if he scarcely hears him. Long ago, Mick promised himself never to take issue with Harry's idiosyncrasies, but Mick has had about enough of Harry's distant meditations.

"Are you working this case or shall we pack it in and go home?" he asks.

"You're not serious," says Harry.

"Bloody serious. We are here to bust this case. If you're not up to it, say so. We need a bit of concentration." Mick sets up the light box on the table, inserts the roll of film, and hands Harry the magnifier. "Make yourself useful."

"What am I looking for?" asks Harry, still not fully present.

Mick eyes him curiously, but plunges ahead. "I'm certain Neale shot that roll the day or night he was killed. Later, he developed the first three photos and their notations. For some reason, he didn't entrust the roll to Sándor. I found only the three developed and enlarged photos. Identify others we want for a further look, ones that can tell us where the photos were taken and why. That roll was valuable enough for him to hide. There's something significant there."

"Where is the damaged roll Sándor gave us? I'll have a look at that one," says Harry, alert at last. Mick has finally penetrated Harry's fog.

Through the night, they work and doze, awake and work again, rising from their chairs to stretch. A few hours before the sun comes up, Harry has regained his composure and given his usual level of serious concentration to their task. By midmorning, they decide a shave, a change of clothes, a breath of fresh air, and the services of Tamás Sándor's development lab are in order.

"After we finish with Sándor, I'm off to buy a tin of tea," says Harry.

"Now you're a heavy tea drinker," says Mick, teasing now.

"An excuse to run into a poker companion. I keep seeing the chap's face when I asked him about river bandits the other night," says Harry.

"Startled, was he?"

"More afraid than startled. Rather than answer my question, he fled. Name is Joszef Kovacs. His wife runs a tea and spice shop on the Buda side. According to Zoltán, Kovacs witnessed a crime on the bridge." Harry pushes his hat back from his forehead and removes his jacket. He is sweltering in the heat of June.

"Need some company?"

"Better I go alone. Kovacs' wife might be willing to talk if she thinks I'm her husband's poker pal. Besides, we need to persuade Sándor to develop those rolls straight away. Preferably while you wait."

"He won't be eager to see me," says Mick.

"Well, then, it's in his best interest to get rid of you sooner than later," says Harry. "In any case, I'll meet you back at the hotel after I talk to Kovacs' wife."

꿢

"What a pleasing surprise," says Joszef Kovacs. "My wife, Julianna." Kovacs stands beside his wife, his arm resting around her shoulders. Harry notes anew the slight stature of the man. Kovacs looks at his wife. "This is Harry Douglas. Two nights ago, we met at Zoltán's. A fine gentleman. A solicitor. I mentioned our shop." Kovacs smiles, directs his next comment to Harry. "It is kind of you to remember. What can we get for you?" His arm sweeps the shelves in front of the counter.

"I've come for a tin of tea," says Harry. "I understand you import teas from the Far East and from Africa. I have a friend who likes to try the exotic." His mind conjures the image of Laura Savic's body, the sweet taste of her in his mouth.

"We have just the right thing for your friend. A wild tea called rooibos. Its tiny seeds are grown, inch by inch, on a Dutch farm in South Africa, then delicately sifted. The leaves are cured, fermented, and packaged by hand. It is quite a process and a new taste for tea drinkers." Julianna Kovacs selects a small green cylinder from a shelf behind the counter, holds it up. "We have a limited supply and many who covet the taste. This makes it a bit expensive. Dear, as the English tourists like to say." She raises her eyebrows, a silent query of his intentions.

Did Laura offer him tea or coffee? He cannot remember. Regardless, it will be a gift for her. "If you'll allow me, I'll take what you have in hand." He hopes the miniature container of African tea leaves will not make a sizeable dent his wallet.

While he waits for Julianna to wrap the gift, Harry follows Kovacs out to the river walk. On the railing, gazing up at the underbelly of the Chain Bridge, Harry offers Kovacs a cigarette. "Perfect location for a tourist shop," Harry says, lighting Kovacs' and then his own. This time, he chooses the more direct approach to the topic he has come to discuss. "The other night, I noticed you were disturbed at the mention of river bandits. The comment was meant to be my weak attempt at humor. Sorry if it upset you."

Kovacs cocks his head, stares at Harry for a long moment, and blows smoke from his nostrils. He shifts his focus to the entryway to the shop. "I do not want Julianna to hear of this," he says, the eyes watchful, the thin brown hair falling forward. His voice drops to a whisper. "She is not involved." Harry waits, but Kovacs does not elaborate.

"Is there a place we can discuss it further?" asks Harry. "I'm interested in finding out what you know about the death on the bridge. It's important."

With his free hand, Kovacs pushes the hair from his face. His shoulders tense, and his eyes blink rapidly behind his glasses. A barge laden with crushed rock glides past on the smooth surface of the river, the tricolored flag of Romania flat against the pole, no late-afternoon breeze to lift it free. A seaman standing at the helm waves; Kovacs waves back. Harry waits, knowing Kovacs is deciding what to tell him. "Tomorrow, the entrance path to Margaret Island, six o'clock. We will go to the spa. You will need a suit for the baths."

"A suit for the baths," repeats Harry. The look on his face must have thoroughly amused Kovacs. It is the first time Harry hears him laugh, a big belly laugh that does not belong to a man the size of Kovacs. There is more to the man, Harry thinks.

"Margaret Island lies in the Danube between Buda and Pest," Kovacs explains, still chuckling. "Named for the daughter of a king, Margaret spent her life in a convent there. The island is limited to pedestrians only, no automobiles, bicycles, trams. It is home to more than one hundred hot springs, some that come up from great depths, the most in Europe. It is a favorite spot." A smile lifts the dark corners of his eyes. "There are visitors who choose not to wear a suit. It is your choice, of course."

〜〜〜〜

"You've got to see this," says Mick. "We may have found our connection." He pulls out two large photos, lays them side by side. "Two official reports, the first one dated 21 May, regard those two Germans who were killed in Sudetenland."

"I spotted the article in the Berlin paper the morning I arrived," says Harry, picturing the black ink of the headline. "Something similar in the Budapest paper, too, but I wasn't able to translate it."

Shoulder to shoulder, the two men lean over the table, studying the small print of the first report that Neale photographed. Harry moves the lamp closer and sits down to examine it through the magnifying glass.

"Publicly, the Reich announced the two were killed by Czech police, denouncing the Czech government for its hand in the killing," Mick continues. "This report, however, clarifies that Nazis in the region were told to provoke trouble. For months, security in Sudetenland has deteriorated into many small-scale clashes between pro-Nazi followers and Czech police. This latest propaganda is designed to accuse the Czech government of atrocities on innocent Germans." Mick hands Harry the photograph. "This second report is more inflammatory. Dated 28 May. Three days before Neale was murdered, Hitler called together his senior staff and announced plans to erase Czechoslovakia from the European map. His exact words, apparently. He instructed Keitel to draw up the plans."

"We're sure the reports are official?" asks Harry.

"Can't be absolute, but the marks look right—stamps, initials, the works." Mick points them out.

"Did Sándor get a close look at these?" asks Harry.

"Not so I could tell. I was with him the whole time in the darkroom. Acted as if the faster he saw my back, the better. He worked quickly. As soon as he'd hung up the last one to dry, he grunted and left them to me."

"You were right. Based on that last report date, the document photo was taken right before Neale died," says Harry.

"We can make an educated guess at the purpose of the photos of Horthy, Veesenmayer, and the two ambassadors. Hitler needs a clear motive to invade—a big event to convince the world that the Czechs are the aggressors, and that Hitler is only defending his people. Importantly, he needs Horthy's support, his vocal support," says Mick.

"I can see using Horthy's son to get him to cooperate. But killing him wouldn't make sense. Kidnapping," says Harry, "holding him until Horthy acquiesces. Just the threat of it—showing him this photo—would do the job."

"Horthy's son is a public figure, a politician. An easy snatch," says Mick.

"Veesenmayer is something else again. He's one of Ribbentrop's boys. You can't mean they'd sacrifice him." Harry's voice trails off.

"It's been done, laddie," says Mick. "The propaganda machine has to have somebody worth oiling it. Not the head man, mind you, but important enough to matter."

"Otherwise, the two ambassadors will turn against the Führer," says Harry.

"That's why there are no circles on that picture." Mick snaps his fingers. "They're not targets for violence. The Reich needs those two as sympathetic supporters, convinced of justification for invasion. Another piece falls into place."

"Neale might have discovered this conspiracy."

"Without realizing he had. Kidnap Horthy's son to blackmail him into compliance. Bump off the German ambassador. Blame the Czechs so the US and British ambassadors side with the Germans when they invade Czechoslovakia."

"We're closing in on motive," says Harry. "Neale's dispatch would have blown that plot wide open."

"Brinkley said Neale's missing dispatch was likely to do with an immediate event. Something soon to occur. Hitler was pressuring Horthy to appoint a new cabinet." Mick chews his bottom lip.

"The photo of Horthy's son makes me think that Brinkley—newsman Brinkley—knows more than he shared. How do you suppose Neale came across this intelligence? You have to believe it was in a secure—very secure—location. Maybe he was caught stealing it."

"If that were the case, we wouldn't have the photos," says Mick.

"He could have secured one batch. Gone back for more," says Harry.

"But then, we'd simply hear of his disappearance. Or never hear at all," says Mick, raising an eyebrow.

"How many more photos on the roll?" Harry asks.

"Several, but I can't make them out," says Mick. "A few words here and there at the top and bottom of the pages. Makes me think they were deliberately smudged. But I don't know if it happened before or after they were developed."

"I'm betting after. Sorry to say, our theory of events may fit in with what we learned about the watch." Harry is still reluctant to accuse Neale, but cannot discount the possibility.

"How do you figure?" asks Mick.

"Sell these photos," says Harry, "disfigure the rest of the roll before anyone sees the images."

"But he bought the watch a month ago, before these photos were taken," says Mick. "Could be he inherited family money. It's possible." Though not likely.

"Improbable. His sister Martha lives in a small cottage in Folkestone, nothing to brag on. No. I'll bet he bought the watch with payoff money. He was working off the clock. Maybe he was killed when the side job went awry. Maybe the purchaser of the information welches on the deal. Neale threatens to walk—no cash, no deal."

"Why leave the watch, then?" asks Harry.

"Traceable. Hard to get rid of. Not interested. Didn't see it. Any of the above," says Mick. "What's your guess?"

"Can't say. I'd have to know more about who's interested in the deal. Who needs the information? That's the question. Who stands to gain from knowing? Who's willing to pay?" Harry pushes his chair back, too restless to sit down. "It wouldn't be anyone in Hitler's inner circle. They already know. Someone else then. The Czechs maybe." He scratches the back of his head and adds, "The other question is where Neale acquired these documents.

Did he just stumble upon them? Doubtful. Who keeps this type of intelligence?"

"You think Neale was killed in retaliation for the theft?"

"I'm not saying that." Harry shakes his head.

"What do we know? Laszlo Vací and Kristof Balas. I can see where Balas and his Arrow Cross buddies would be interested. A German invasion of Czechoslovakia could lead to a power grab for them. Hungary regains its territory, and Horthy is overthrown. Balas knows this possibility; he works himself around to be first in line for the Regency." Mick considers the scenario. "I'm not so clear about Vací."

Harry stops pacing. "Vací has access. His secret police enter homes and businesses, tap phones, search mail and packages. He has created a police state under his direct control, locked down power for himself. Unlimited power. There's something to hold on to."

Mick whistles. "You think Neale was daft enough to deal with these chaps?" He shakes his head. "For a few quid and a watch?"

"Maybe he didn't know who he was dealing with." Harry sits down. "Kovacs has something. If I can get him to talk, we may have a lead. We're wandering from one detail to another. At the bottom, there's still a gaping hole, things that do not add up. Do we have a plot to unseat Horthy? An imminent invasion of Czechoslovakia? A power cabal?"

"Whatever it is, looks as if Neale paid the price for knowing it," says Mick.

Harry rubs a hand over his eyes, yawns. "I'm beat. Let's sleep on it. See you in the morning. By the way, where do you figure I can pick up a bathing costume?"

Chapter Thirteen

8 **June.** It is too early to knock, streetlights still on. A solitary jaybird's rasping screech alerts others of his kind to Harry's presence. The street empty, a light mist at his feet, he looks up at the small balcony he determines is hers. Pulled in, away from the edge, a wooden stool lay on its side, red pots brimming with leafy geraniums arranged to catch the morning sun. He recognizes the floral curtain behind the French doors. Under his arm, he carries the parcel of tea and, inside his coat, the Budapest newspaper he purchased the day he arrived. He wonders how long he should wait before he disturbs her. Perhaps she will refuse to answer a knock, fearing an intruder at this early hour. It occurs to him that he might be an unwelcome visitor.

He sees a rustle of curtains, decides to take a chance, and enters the building, making a clatter on the stairs. Before he raises his fist to knock on her door, he straightens his tie and checks the smoothness of his jaw. She answers on the third tap, cracking the door no more than an inch or two, one eye peering along its edge. He clears his throat, holds out the tin of tea.

"Care to share a cup of tea?" He wears his most hopeful grin.

"What are you doing here at this hour?" Her tone contains a mild rebuke.

"I was in the neighborhood?" he says, a lilting question mark at the end.

"Why should I believe that?" She is teasing, not ready to allow him to enter, yet widening the opening and stepping forward so that he can see her dressing gown, diaphanous against the light, a green ribbon tied at the waist. Her feet bare.

"I'm an honest fellow and mean no harm." He bows slightly, staring at her toes. She laughs a little, as he'd intended.

"In that case," she says, "you may wait in the parlor." With a loud creak of the hinge, the door swings wide. She keeps him at a distance, points to the chair across the room, reminding him that her world does not include him, and disappears into the bedroom.

Ten minutes later, she emerges fully dressed, a red silk jacket over a slim gray skirt that hugs her figure. Black suede heels add three inches to her height. She smells of the same lilac perfume. She places her warm hands in his cool ones, her widening smile urging him to explain his arrival. Her scent and warmth stir him in places he thought he'd locked up and hidden away. She pats his tie into place.

"I don't know what's wrong with this tie," he says, groaning softly, conscious of the unexpected warmth of her skin, the thin silk of her jacket. "It's constantly crooked."

"It's fine," she murmurs. "I've fixed it for you."

"I need a favor," he says, trying to concentrate on the reason he's come. He had a passing notion they would make love. It is not to be.

"If I can do it, I will," she replies, her eyes upon his.

Reluctantly, he steps back from her, rummages inside his coat and pulls out the folded newspaper. "Can you translate this for me?"

"All of it?" She sounds somewhat dismayed.

"The article under the picture," he says, "and anything else to do with the same topic."

"You're interested in German politics now?" she looks down at the paper.

"I'm interested in whatever killed Tennyson Neale," he says. "We think there may be a connection between Hitler's plans for Czechoslovakia and Neale's murder."

"We?" She stares at him, her eyes now intense with interest.

"Mick and I," he says.

"You're not just two Englishmen sent to recover a colleague's body, are you?"

He tries to ignore the question. "As I mentioned in Chief Gaska's office, our publishing house must find out as much as we can about Neale's death. That's why we're here."

Her eyes narrow. "I'll see to the translation," she speaks abruptly. "I told you I would help. Can I get it to you this evening?"

"It'll have to be later this evening. I have an appointment on Margaret Island."

⚏

"Why the bloody hell would you do that?" Mick slams his fork on the table, pushes his food away.

"I didn't want to trust anyone else," says Harry. "We know her."

"I'm beginning to think you know her too well. Or maybe not well at all. Get your mind straight, man. This is not smart. We don't know her."

"It's just a translation, for Christ's sake," Harry argues.

"There are warning signs all over this. We can get that translation any number of ways, for whatever it's worth. Now you've blown it. She—and whoever she cares to tell—knows we're not two *Burlington* representatives here to collect a body. I'm telling you now, I don't like it. She works for the police department, for bloody sake. No matter how taken you are with this woman, let it go."

"And I say there's no problem. We'll have the translation tonight. Then it's done. All of it." Once he has said it, he wonders how he'll live up to such a promise. How he'll deny his feelings for Laura Savic.

"You've got that right." Mick throws his napkin on the table and scrapes back his chair. He's had just about enough of Harry Douglas.

Chapter Fourteen

8 **June.** At the entrance to the small island in the middle of the Danube, Joszef Kovacs rests against an ancient stone pedestal and uses a thin pocketknife to swipe the dirt from beneath his fingernails. As the young Canadian draws near, Kovacs raises his hand and waves. Ah yes, hatless, he is carrying, as Kovacs instructed, a package of suitable bathing clothes.

Like most residents of Budapest, Kovacs frequents the thermal hot springs to share stories with neighbors as they float, blissful, in the warm waters, and afterwards to gather around the chessboards that line the perimeter of the pools. He has decided to introduce Douglas to the old Roman pool on the west side of the island. There, the custom is males-only. They will not be distracted by women in their tiny swim costumes.

Kovacs knows Douglas has a motive for meeting him this evening, that Douglas wants information Kovacs can give. All the same, he aims to take pleasure in the outing. After the soothing springs clear his head, after he determines what kind of man Douglas is, after he is certain no one is listening, he will choose whether to tell Douglas what he saw that night on the bridge.

"The ground is hot," observes Harry as he extends his hand to Kovacs. "The closer I came to the island, the warmer it seemed. Strange phenomenon."

"Poke a hole in the ground, and you'll find hot burbling water. Budapest sits on a thin crust over thermal springs." says Kovacs.

"Makes for interesting planting seasons," says Harry.

"And warm winters. You feel it most here on this island. For more than two thousand years, since before the time of Christ, men have come to these baths. The waters are said to cure many ailments. Illnesses of the heart and lungs. I have no reason to doubt. In the winter months, we warm ourselves on the hot rocks of the circle of rapids. Within a haze of steam, I feel as if I am floating on a warm cloud. I forget time. The Roman bath measures 30 degrees. We will go there."

They walk across the narrow bridge, down a wider hard-packed dirt path. On the way, they talk about Kovacs' business. For the last ten years, he has exported textiles to European markets, and small manufactured goods to large cities in India and South Africa. These activities have secured a high standard of living for him and his wife. He runs a reputable, profitable operation, he explains, and is thankful his fellow citizens regard him highly.

"Do you know Jan Nagy?" asks Harry. "Outside of Zoltán's poker table, that is."

Kovacs opens his arms wide. "Of course, Nagy and I have done business for years. We export his beautiful glass. We ship to France, Italy, Britain. Our biggest client is Germany." He pauses, looks out across the river to the far bank. "The politics, always the politics. Business and politics are entwined." He laces his hands together, holds them out. "It is worrisome, this political situation. I don't care so much for myself, but others like Nagy can be harmed by these madmen."

Harry remains silent. Before Kovacs can continue, they arrive at the entry to the bath; the clean scent of freshly laundered towels hangs in the air. A bath attendant in a white apron, exuding an air of old authority, directs them inside. Throngs of men, a plentiful mix of citizens and tourists, crowd the subtly lighted interior, anxious to shed the restrictions of clothes and cares. After they change into their bathing suits, Harry and Kovacs emerge into the night, the twilight sky lit in shades of scarlet and gold. A haze of steam, an eerie extra presence, hovers over the octagonal pool. Near the shallow end, they find a warm place, isolated from the crowd, sheltered by piles of white rocks. They ease in until the soothing liquid envelopes their bodies. Healing waters bubble up from deep within the earth. For the next hour, Harry allows body and spirit to drift on the edge of consciousness. He remembers the Tennyson Neale he revered. The handsome rascal who laughed easily, the expert operative, the admirable man.

卌

Dressed once again, they find a small café some two hundred yards from the bath and sit down at a table along the edge of a broad terrace, trees above, river below. Soon the waiter brings their beer, and they linger over it, swapping stories of card games and characters they have encountered. Kovacs searches his pocket for a cigarette, Harry lights his pipe.

"Beautiful evening," says Harry. "I've not felt this relaxed in years."

"Each time I come, I further understand why the Romans and the Ottomans travelled so far to restore themselves," says Kovacs.

"Restoration. We don't always realize the need for it." Harry has been out of sorts with Mick. A small voice tells him to find Mick and set things right.

Kovacs swirls what remains in his glass. He raises his eyebrows. Shoulders hunched, he looks around. The café is half-full, there are no diners nearby.

"You are curious about what happened on the bridge." Kovacs keeps his voice low.

"More than curious," says Harry. Mindful of his cover, he adds. "It is necessary that my client learns what happened to Mr. Neale."

Kovacs pauses to light his cigarette. "You must understand. At first, I did not know what I was seeing. Otherwise, I might have."

"Might have what?" Harry asks softly. He thinks he knows what Kovacs will say. He takes a draw on his pipe and waits.

"I might have been able to stop them. What they were doing." Kovacs places his elbows on the table, hangs his head, and smokes his cigarette.

In Harry's experience, men like Kovacs—good men caught in difficult situations—harbor guilt at their own inaction, their inability to come to the aid of a fellow human being, ashamed of what they perceive as cowardice. They are reluctant to talk about what they have done nothing about. Harry knows better than to insult the man with empty words of reassurance. He is not interested in Kovacs' courage or shame or in assuaging feelings of guilt. What is done is done. He needs information.

"It must have been quite dark," Harry says, hoping to start Kovacs talking.

"Yes, that night we started late at Zoltán's, after midnight. The game broke up around three. It is a habit of mine, at that hour, to walk to my home across the Danube. The bridge is silent. You hear the water running hard beneath. A rare and beautiful time, this early hour when there is nothing to disturb."

Harry nods in agreement. "A good time to think things through. As you're walking."

"That night, there was a sliver of moon. Even the bridge lights were subdued, all was quiet," says Kovacs, eyes fixed impassively on the river. "Everything in shadow. That's why at first—" Kovacs opens his mouth to speak, but stops when a man on the terrace passes near their table. The man stops, looks around, intense eyes landing on Harry and Kovacs. He moves on when the waiter appears, deposits a basket of dark bread, informs them they can stay if they plan to order dinner.

When the waiter is gone, Harry prompts Kovacs to continue.

"I heard a series of grunts. No talk, sounds of physical effort, men working. There were two of them carrying a weight between them. It crossed my mind they were stevedores, loading a barge. I almost called out to them, in good humor, to ask how they were the lucky ones to work this early morning shift. How much extra pay? I almost hollered. They would have laughed. You make a joke, they might have said." Kovacs scratched his forehead above the bridge of his glasses. "By a stroke of luck, I hesitated."

"What was it? What caused you to stop?" asks Harry.

"Some detail seemed wrong. They were dressed alike, perhaps wearing uniforms. They were coming up from the steps, not going down to the river. Still, I did not know what they carried."

"Where were you?" asks Harry.

Kovacs struggles to explain. "I had stepped back behind the lion, the base of the statue, and crouched there, trying to remain quiet, not to breathe. You said it the other night. There are bandits who steal from the boats anchored in the river. They are ruffians. Dangerous." He sighs and looks away. "I was afraid. While another man died, I was afraid."

Harry now understands why Kovacs retreated so hastily from his remark about the bandits. Harry plunges ahead, "You said they wore uniforms. What can you remember about them?"

"I cannot say. There was so little moonlight. The uniforms, if they were so, were dark, the same on each man. No hat. I would have remembered a hat." Kovacs lets the cigarette burn to ash in his hand.

"How long did you stay by the statue?" Harry avoids any word that might imply a lack of courage.

"Until I heard them leave, scuffle down the steps, their voices fade away. I could not hear what they were saying."

"So you heard them running away," says Harry.

"Not running. I heard a boat. That's why I thought they were thieves. Until I saw him." Harry hears a hitch in Kovacs' voice.

"You mean the man hanging on the post?"

Kovacs' white hands are clenched. "I ventured out slowly, listening. Not fifty meters in front of my eyes, I saw this odd form, not sure what it might be." Kovacs removes his glasses and buries his face in his napkin. He stares up at Harry, the experience vivid on his face. "The head was slumped off to one side, ropes wrapped around his arms, looped around the cross bar of the lamppost and pulled tight. There was this strong smell. I remember thinking that his legs were overly long, Christ-like in his pose. I saw the dark oozing stains on his shirt and trousers. For a moment, I thought he was alive."

"Was he?"

"No. I moved in closer and took his hand. It was warm, but I felt no pulse. I wanted to check his mouth for breath. It was out of reach."

Harry and Kovacs sit smoking, saying nothing, comforted, perhaps, by the lively bustle of the café.

"What could I have done?" Kovacs' voice is almost pleading.

An unanswerable question, in Harry's mind. He pictures the scene. Neale died a close and violent death. Harry hoped him dead before the hanging began. Likely not, if he were still bleeding from his wounds and his hands warm. Why risk exposure by hanging him from the post? A public signal to show he was dead? A means to assure he would be found? A distancing from the place he was stabbed? A warning to someone?

To Kovacs, he says, "You could have done nothing to help the man. You did what anyone would do. You reported a crime to the proper authorities."

The relevant question is why these facts did not appear in Gaska's report. Harry wants to know the extent of Gaska's cover-up. "Did the police question you about what you saw?"

Kovacs nods.

"And you had no reason to believe these were common thugs?"

"No. Why do you ask?"

"That's what the police report stated. That Neale was killed on the bridge by a gang of street thugs."

"A gang? No. Definitely not. Only the two I saw. These local thieves do not commit murder. Malicious mischief? Yes. Protests against the wealthy? Of course. Not murder."

"Did you tell the police investigators what you told me?" Harry knows he may be crossing the line of Kovacs' trust, questioning his truth-telling.

Kovacs shakes his head, a few more times than necessary, and looks away. "I did not mention the uniforms."

"Why not?"

Kovacs gets to his feet, shouts for the waiter several tables away who gives him a cold gaze and raises his hand in response. I am a busy man, wait a moment. From his pocket, Kovacs removes the sufficient number of forints to cover their drinks, the bread and the use of the table. He signals for Harry to follow him onto the terrace. "Behave normally. Laugh. We are having a good laugh at my joke," Kovacs instructs him.

They walk down a set of steps onto a gravelled path and toward a tall water tower. Halfway there, Kovacs places a hand out, stopping Harry in mid-step. Kovacs scans the area, then guides Harry to a bench set apart from the rest, no trees nearby.

"I've heard rumors," Kovacs says, almost in a whisper.

"What do you mean?" asks Harry.

"They know he is being coerced. They're going to get rid of him."

"Who?"

"Horthy. The Regent," he adds. "They will accuse him."

"Of what?"

"Hungarian politics are poisonous. Horthy has opposition. He is not conservative enough. He protects the Jews. They all say this."

"Who are they?" asks Harry.

"Contemptible extremists."

"This is the reason you did not mention the uniforms?" Harry tries to put it together with Horthy's enemies. He is not clear how Neale's death and Horthy's political demise are connected.

"Yes," says Kovacs.

Harry waits for more. Finally, he asks, "When will this take place? When will Horthy be removed?"

"The time is not yet right."

"You mean there's a plot against him," says Harry.

At first, Kovacs does not respond. He hangs his head and wrings his hands. "In Budapest there are many plots. Some are real. Some are empty conspiracies. You've heard of the Arrow Cross."

Harry tries a different question. "Arrow Cross is organizing this?"

"With Horthy gone or accused of wrongdoing, their leaders will gain power," says Kovacs. "There are others, of course, who want power. To gain, to keep."

"I don't understand what this has to do with the death on the bridge," says Harry. "Are you telling me there's a connection?"

"I've said enough." Kovacs rises from the bench, inclines his head briefly, and nervously rubs the crease on his pant leg. "Your colleague knew more than he should." Kovacs turns on his heel. Before he walks away, he says, almost to himself, "There is a point in telling lies."

Harry wonders at that last remark. What has he missed?

Chapter Fifteen

8 **June**. There is nothing more Mick can gather from the photographs, film, and diary. He has analyzed every number, read every word, scanned every inch. In the past five days, he and Harry reviewed the items repeatedly, trying to find links among them. He is increasingly less confident in their conclusions.

They know there is a plot to assassinate a high-ranking German official and blame the Czechs. They know Hitler needs an excuse to invade, that he needs the British Parliament's support, at least no interference from it. He needs the United States to remain neutral. Someone wants Horthy out of the way and is willing to use his family to accomplish it.

It seems incredible that Neale was involved. What impulse possessed him?

Every night, Mick goes to bed pondering possible connections. Instead of becoming clearer, the pieces remain muddled. He and Harry are missing something. Something significant. Unlike Harry, he had no personal bond to Tennyson Neale. He is not reluctant to consider Neale a turned agent. More than any piece of evidence, the smudged film bothers him most. He is beginning to think those few indecipherable images are the key to Neale's murder.

Dinner and a long walk, he reasons, may work out the loose ends or pop free an inspiration that lingers below the surface. At an outdoor café close to the Vörösmarty Square—one of Budapest's more upscale areas—he finds a small table and settles in to observe the evening sightseers. A genial waiter—thin, middle-aged, in a spotless white apron—brings a plate of *paprikás*.

A light-haired, clean-shaven man of Mick's age, dining alone, occupies an adjacent table. He presents none of the physical attributes of Hungarian men Mick has encountered in Budapest. Rather, he has the high cheekbones of a Slav, a cordial manner, a smile on his face. The man leans over and introduces himself, in heavily accented English, as Erik Drucek.

"Mick MacLeod," Mick says, extending his hand. "Are you in the city on business or holiday?"

Drucek wipes his mouth on a green napkin, the flag of Budapest in its center. "A beautiful night," he observes in a strong voice. "Some would say business," he adds and places his napkin on the table. He takes up the glass of red wine, holds it aloft.

Distant church bells peal nine o'clock. "Long live the king," Drucek says, laughing.

Mick raises his ale in response, "Long live the king." Curious of Drucek's business interests in Budapest, Mick eyes the man for a moment, plays a mind game with himself, and tries to guess Drucek's nationality. A hint would help. "To which king are we raising our glass?"

"Not many left to choose, are there? A scarce profession these days. Scandinavia and the Balkans still intact. And your George, of course."

"You're forgetting Leopold of Belgium," says Mick, smiling. After days of grim detective work, here is a rare opportunity for banter, to ponder something other than murder.

"How long will Leopold be in place? Until the Belgian Army falls." There is obvious sarcasm in his tone. "Like the rest of us, the great Leopold—the third and last great Leopold—will answer to the Führer." Drucek gulps the last of his wine and sets down the glass purposefully, a note of finality.

"That's the future, as you see it?" asks Mick, bothered that the conversation has taken a decidedly cheerless turn.

"See it. Hear it. Feel it. Taste it. Smell it. Mark this day. Unless the British and the French intervene soon, we'll all speak German within five years."

"Where do you come from?" asks Mick, surrendering himself to the direct question. "What country, I mean?"

For a moment, Mick assumes Drucek has ignored him. Then, the man rises to full height, his eyes narrow, mouth resolute, chin in the air. Drucek is a big, broad-shouldered man with a surprisingly soft voice, "I was born in Prague. My country is Czechoslovakia."

Mick watches Drucek walk away. Where has life's lightness gone?

卌

Mick rambles along Budapest's fashionable streets seeing, but not taking in, shop windows, outdoor diners, passing bicycles. His earlier argument with Harry sits heavy on his mind. As he turns it over, he understands Harry has a point. He also knows that Harry Douglas can rarely resist—indeed, he has always known Harry to be a sucker for—the attention of a beautiful woman. Laura Savic is undeniably that. There is something about the way she looked at them that first day in Gaska's office. He cannot put his finger on it. A feeling, though, that needles the edge of his brain. Given what they've learned thus far about Neale's death, he is not sure she translated Gaska's comments accurately. Otherwise, how can a police department that covers a city the size and scope of Budapest perform in this slipshod manner when dealing with the murder of a foreign national?

Though he has never said it aloud, Mick is concerned about Harry's excesses. His drinking. His need to come to the aid of attractive women. The knight, the rescuer. Not such a dangerous flaw, is it? There are those with worse. Up to now, Mick has refrained from locking horns with Harry. Who is he to judge him? In Mick's experience, anger and fear are wasted sentiments. He has no time for either. Unless one's life depends on them.

Lengthening shadows tell him it is later than he imagined. He has lost track of time and place. The street is deserted. No murmur of voices. No scuffle of shoes. Alone in the middle of a block, dark and silent buildings on either side, he stops to get his bearings. He realizes he has ignored the first rules of his profession. Attend to your surroundings, know where you are, what is around you, who is nearby.

It strikes him that those very rules are what gnaws at him about Neale's death. An agent with Neale's training, experience and size allowed himself to be overtaken. The man had been stabbed at close range. Seven times. In whatever situation Neale found himself, he had been comfortable. He had been there before. He knew where he was. He knew his attackers. He and Harry have found camera equipment and the odd bit of clothing, but no stash of money, no collection of letters, no personal items one accumulates over a year. Where are Neale's possessions?

Mick begins to walk briskly to the corner, some hundred meters away. Across the street, a car pulls out. He glances over his shoulder, increases his pace, and realizes the car has done the same. He moves closer to the building. A screech of tires causes him to turn. Lights from the headlamps bear down, closing fast. He raises his hand to shield his eyes. The car has not altered its path. Surely, the driver will swerve.

Ahead and to Mick's right, he spots an alleyway and sprints toward it, reaching its entry as the car speeds past. With a shower of sparks and the sound of grinding metal, the car swipes the building just as Mick dives headfirst behind a barricade. The ground falls away beneath him. He is face down in a shallow drainage culvert, choking on stench. He hears the car slow, then gather speed and drive off.

Struggling to his feet, Mick is ankle deep in decaying trash. Underfoot, the crunch of broken glass. Legs wobbling, ears ringing, he brushes bits of dirt and paper from his shirtfront and wades through the stinking debris. At the other end of the alley, he finds a reeling drunk urinating against a wall. The man shies at Mick's approach, the arc of his urine suspended as he scrambles to reassemble himself. Mick raises his hand in greeting and keeps walking. No harm, my friend. Finish your business. When he reaches the main street, he turns right and leans, chest heaving, against the nearest wall. Dizzy, he crouches beneath a thick concrete sill until his heartbeat slows. He tries to remember what he saw of the car. He checks the street for traffic.

The driver's actions were not accidental or negligent. That driver meant to run him down.

He did not get a good look, recalls only that the car was light in color, cream maybe, and boxy in design. One of those sedans with the wide running boards. Probably what he heard against the building. The scrape would make it recognizable.

This street, too, is empty. No tourists. It is late, the curfew strictly enforced in this district. Mick stands and walks cautiously, wishing to make no sound. He wonders if the car has gone. More likely—not having fulfilled its purpose—it waits in ambush around a corner, idling, ready to race forward at the sight of him. Wisely or not, he turns his attention to the next block.

Searching for a good vantage point, he spots the hanging steps of a fire escape and heaves himself up to a narrow ledge that marks the top of the building's ground floor. One step at a time, nose against the building's facade, he sidles to the corner and peers down at the street. A cream-colored car is parked on the opposite side. From this angle, Mick has a clear view of the car's interior. The driver slumps, drumming his fingers on the steering wheel, hat pulled low so Mick cannot see his face. The man's other hand rests on the gearshift. The car's engine growls. Mick is deciding whether to approach the car, when he sees the driver reach out and adjust the mirror, a quick up and down movement. A signal. Far down the street, a gate slaps shut. A dark figure emerges and heads to the car. From the look of him, the man outweighs Mick by at least a stone. He wears a topcoat and carries a revolver down by his side. Mick watches the man climb into the passenger door and speak to the driver, the voice a long way off so that Mick cannot hear what he says. The hair rises on the back of Mick's neck. He draws a deep breath, calming himself. His gun, strapped above his right ankle, is no easy reach. He has to trust they do not look up and discover him.

As he grips the narrow ledge, the muscle in his leg begins to twitch. He has to move before the leg gives way, and he tumbles into the street. He inches back to the fire escape stairs, and eases himself down the metal stairs to the platform. He rests on his knees, gathers his strength, assuring himself that both legs will respond when called upon. In a single gliding motion, he swings down onto the street and begins to run south, away from the car, aware that the sound of running feet will attract attention.

Ahead lay a long stretch dimly lit by a zigzag pattern of streetlamps, broken intermittently by narrow alleyways on the left and right. Farther on, at least a quarter mile in the distance, he sees the lights of a bridge. He picks up his pace, glancing into each alley for an open door or stairwell that might lead him to safe haven.

Behind him, he hears the acceleration of the car, the tires squeal. This time, he knows they will not miss. There are two of them, the driver concentrating on the road, the shooter on Mick's back. Mick veers from side to side, hoping to spoil the shooter's aim. At a critical moment, he races recklessly across the street in front of the oncoming car, its lights blinding him for an instant. Swallowed by a covered passageway between two buildings, he tears down the alleyway, sucking in air, sweat blurring his vision. Midway, he encounters a set of steps that descend into a walled courtyard, a slimmer passageway off to the left. The car cannot follow. Mick flees down the steps and into a tapered corridor. Out of sight from above, he stops to catch his breath.

Moving in silence, he rushes farther into the passageway of broken cobblestones. Little more than a meter separates the walls of the two tenant buildings. Lights from the curtained windows cast soft shadows. He hurries along in search of darkness. The fragrance of baking bread and two neon eyes cause him to slow. A bird swoops down, flutters in front of him. He hears the clink of milk bottles placed on the stoop, the tinkling of bells, and a deep voice singing what sounds like a Scottish lullaby. He harbors false hope that he has eluded his pursuers. The next instant, there is a clacking in the alley behind him, the scuff of boots on pavement. Running feet.

Sheltered between the buildings, he rounds a corner and sprints for the blackness of an open door. A moment before he reaches the opening, his ankle strikes a pipe that juts from the wall, and he goes down hard. Stunned, he wills himself not to cry out. A wounded animal knows enough to keep silent. There is a bone-deep pain in his left shoulder and a wild sense of outrage at himself. For an odd instant, he feels his defenses unravel.

Steady, man. They'll not find me strung on a lamppost. Or collapsed in a littered alley.

He pulls the pistol from its ankle holster and staggers to his feet, thankful for the wall's support. Head ringing, he steps over the guilty pipe and through the open door. An odor, dank and strong, fills the room. He inches inside and finds a corner of obscurity—absolute darkness—at the base of a set of stairs, and props himself there, gun close to his gut and aimed at the entryway. At the least, I'll make a fight of it.

He listens for the smallest sound. The man following him will have a devil of a time maneuvering the narrow corridors. His boots will squeak. He will slosh through the water below that pipe. Mick's hand twitches. He inhales and blows it out soundlessly through pursed lips. An odor of human sweat makes his nostrils flare. There is a scuffle outside, then the thunk of shinbone meeting pipe, a deep grunt of pain. A broad shadow fills the doorway. Mick's body tenses, and he squeezes back into the corner to find a firm footing, to make himself invisible. He watches his hunter cross the threshold, the man's profile turning left then right, hair hung limply to his shoulders. The man scans rapidly, strides forward, favoring the newly injured leg. Within arm's reach, the man stops, gun poised to fire. Mick hears the pin set, the click of the revolving cylinder.

A quick move will knock the gun away. What then? Mick's own gun lowered, the larger man would be upon him before Mick can have him by the throat. Wiser to wait, fire point-blank, drop to the floor, fire again. Mick's brow drips with sweat. He licks it away, prays the barrel of his gun gives no reflection. The man is past him, peering into the emptiness of the long room, his back a broad target.

Mick has never knowingly shot a man in the back. Face-to-face is another matter. Hands gripping the gun, the tip of his finger caressing the trigger, Mick considers the outcome. Two shots, maybe three, before the man turns and fires at him. Then, a hail of bullets, one after another, impossible to gauge from which direction, Mick unlikely to dodge them all successfully.

Any moment now, the man will turn. When his eyes adjust to the darkness, he will discover Mick standing there. When their eyes meet, in the split second before it dawns what is happening, Mick will fire two bullets into his chest. No time to think. Afterwards, he can determine who the bloody hell is trying to kill him.

Headlights flash, two quick reflections on the opposite wall. A horn sounds, a long blast followed by a shorter one. Mick's hunter looks once over his shoulder, backs out of the room, and runs toward the sound.

Chapter Sixteen

8 **June.** The breeze off the river is unusually dry. Laura wraps the shawl around her shoulders and settles herself on the wrought iron bench, comfortably warm, a remnant of the sun's heat. The Gellért's cone-shaped towers loom above the enclosed courtyard. A long colonnade leads to a broad expanse of stairs, up to the stunning Art Nouveau entry doors. She might have waited in the lobby, but breathing the fresh scent of the night and watching the dream-like display of lights slide over the water hold more appeal. Inside, she would be obliged to acknowledge the concierge's inquisitive stare and feign interest in the lonely bar patrons.

In the low light of the garden lantern, she studies the statue of the famous horned stag, and recalls the old Hungarian legend of the two princes and their chase for life outside the limits of their realm.

Limits. She dares not examine the jumbled nature of her own. When Marek was alive, she could state her limits, justify them, put them to practice when the need arose. When Marek was drawn more deeply into the resistance, they held grave discussions about the limits each would endure in pursuit of their cause. What was too far? Not far enough? She no longer knows the woman who believed in such restrictions. The world has changed. Desperately so.

She stands, checks her watch. Ten-thirty. No telling how long he will be. She sits down again and reaches into her bag to assure herself that the newspaper and page of translation still reside there. Another twenty minutes, she concedes. Then, she will make other arrangements.

Thirty minutes later, she spies the familiar figure approaching at a fast pace along the river walk. She watches until he is directly across. He stops to stare at the bridge, his back to her. The urge to confide in him is strong, but she cannot. She rises from the bench and calls his name.

Chapter Seventeen

9 June. "Two of them that I could see." Bare-chested, Mick sits on a corner of the bed, his face buried in a towel while he swipes at his freshly washed hair. It is his second attempt at removing the alley's filth. He smooths the hair into place. "One driver, one gunman. To my mind, the car came out of nowhere. More likely, they followed me for a distance, biding time, waiting for a deserted roadway."

"I should have been there," says Harry.

"Don't be daft. Your meeting with Kovacs had to be done. Otherwise, we'd have learned nothing. Now, we have more details. We know at least two men were involved. Three, counting the boatman. That's something."

"A flair for trouble, that's what you've got," says Harry, a forced lightness in his voice. "Budapest is a bit more hostile than we've been led to believe. This was not a chance encounter, I'll tell you that. Did you tell anyone where you were going?"

"I didn't know myself, did I? After dinner, I wandered street to street, going nowhere." Mick examines his fingernails, unwilling to disclose the reason for his inattention. "There was this odd chap at dinner. Sat at a table nearby. Struck up a conversation. Exchanged a bit of light mockery. Out of the blue, he turns serious, harsh even, goes on about Leopold's army and announces he's from Czechoslovakia."

"Czechoslovakia." Harry repeats it to himself. "Where was this?"

"Not far. Outdoor place across from Vörösmarty Square. Hung with those showy gold lamps the locals favor. We were out in the open. Nothing covert about it."

"Did you get the chap's name? Anything memorable?" asks Harry.

Mick stares at nothing, trying to recreate the scene. He shakes his head. "Bloody son of a gun," he mutters. "He introduced himself straightaway. In English. Erik Drucek, he said. Waited for me to do the same. Somehow knew I was from the UK. Made a remark about the King and Britain needing to get involved with the Czechs. Light haired, broad shouldered."

"What else?"

"When I asked why he was in Budapest, he said, 'some would say business.' Wore a bit of a smirk. I remember thinking it was an odd way to phrase it."

"A bit dodgy, then?"

"Evasive. Don't want to make too much of it. Could be he was a lonely chap out for dinner."

"You didn't recognize him as the driver?"

"Nor the gunman. I got a decent look at them."

"The real question is why. Why stick a knife in my throat? Why try to run you down?"

"More than anxious to get rid of us. One way or another."

Harry paces, hands in his pockets. None of it makes sense. Who, besides Vací, has guessed their identity? His was hardly a guess. "We're missing something. I got the same feeling tonight when Kovacs left me. He made a comment about the usefulness of lies. Made me wonder if we're on the wrong path altogether. Now this. Who else?"

"There was the threat from Balas. Possible. Unlikely, to my mind. The fellow was drunk. Maintaining his pride for the crowd. I doubt he even remembers it." Mick throws the towel onto a heap of clothing. Suit, shirt, tie crumpled on the floor. "I don't suppose the hotel laundry picks up in the wee hours," he says, wrinkling his nose. He reaches for the reception telephone, sending a shock of pain through his left shoulder.

"Much as I hate to do it, we need to brief Brinkley." For the first time, Harry notices that Mick carries his body carefully. "What's the trouble with your arm?"

"No trouble," says Mick. "Brinkley won't know anything."

"Maybe not, but I want to see his reaction." says Harry. "Kovacs provided details about Neale's death, ones that didn't show up in the police report. All well planned, the way it was done. Kovacs also revealed a plot against Horthy. Arrow Cross, that bunch. I thought about it more. We need to know what Brinkley knows."

"It's almost midnight," says Mick.

"We'll roust him from his barstool." Harry waits while Mick, left shoulder lowered, left hand fumbling, slowly buttons his shirt. Quicker for Harry to do it, but he knows Mick will balk. Best to let him work it out. "Throw me that smudged roll of film. Brinkley won't know it's indecipherable."

Chapter Eighteen

10 **June**. The search begins as soon as the early light allows them to see more than shadow. There has been a report from the captain of a barge passing downriver. Six uniformed officers are spread out in fifty-meter intervals, three on the west bank, three in the same formation on the opposite side. Heads down, hands behind their backs, they walk along the river wall, scanning the water's edge as well as the grassy slope that rises slightly above. After they have walked nearly a kilometer south, those on the west bank stop and gather around a barefooted young woman in a wrinkled pink dress. She slouches on the damp stairs that drop down to the water. In one hand, she clutches the neck of a brandy bottle, in the other, a pair of red high-heeled shoes. Clumsily, she rises, the red shoes falling as she clings, teetering, to the sleeve of the officer's outstretched arm. Unwilling to release the bottle, she sways, points with it in the direction of Csepel Island, home to the industrial plants that lie on Budapest's extended southern border at the confluence of the Soroksar

River, a long-armed branch of the Danube that defines the opposite edge of the island.

"There," she slurs, averting her eyes from the spot. "It's washed up down there. I choked when I saw it." She brushes at the vomit that trails down the front of her dress.

A whistle's shrill blare pierces the morning quiet. At the commander's arm signal, the three officers on the opposite bank turn and make their way toward the wall of industrial smoke. The sharp smell of chemicals grows stronger as they approach the shallows, a small marshy inlet at the tip of the island. Out of the swift current, the water stands tranquil and silent.

From where they stand, they cannot reach the body. One officer steps down; the knee-deep water is oily and strangely warm. He clears away a clump of river grass. With both hands, he grabs the trouser legs and drags them shoreward. The skin is blotched, mouth and arms stretched open, eyes glassy and wide to the sky, the beginning of bloating on the face and limbs. The other men gawk and grimace.

"Not dressed like a factory man."

"Must have fallen somewhere upstream."

"Likely from the steps."

"Hard to tell how far he drifted with the current."

"Check the pockets."

"A pair of wire spectacles. Nothing else."

"A slight fellow."

"It's good we found him."

More men gather. The waiting boat, the one that has followed the officers on their walk downstream, eases near the shore. Commands are given. The four largest men find solid footing in the shallows. Others stand by to steady the boat. Quiet in the presence of death, the four lift the body to a height sufficient to clear the side of the boat, hand it up, shoulders first, then hips and legs, to four more who place it with care upon the deck, a blanket as cover. When it is done, they wipe their hands and stare away, silent, at the distant shore.

Chapter Nineteen

10 **June.** Not yet fully awake, Cephus Brinkley rummages through the night table drawer in search of a tin of aspirin. He had gotten to bed after three. They had interrupted his nightly routine, caught him by surprise with their questions about missing photographs and film developers. He has a devil of a headache.

"One hears of film that's damaged or doesn't appear from the developer," he had heard himself say, anxious for them to leave him to his whiskey.

"Not in this case," Douglas had said. "Neale and the shopkeeper were well acquainted."

"I wouldn't know about that," he had said, evading their questions. "After a time, I didn't keep up with Neale. He had his assignment. He used a different developer, perhaps. There's more than one shopkeeper in Budapest who owns a room without windows." Finally, he had sent them away. He had not concealed anything from them, merely protected his position.

He had to ask himself who else Neale had enlisted in this business. Brinkley has Tamás Sándor in his pocket. For a price, Sándor kept him apprised of Neale's work. With Neale's death, the film developer will not be necessary. If another developer is involved, if another set of eyes knows of the photographs, therein lies a source of exposure.

Now these two.

He is weary of Douglas and MacLeod, their craving for action and answers. They have no tact, no notion of what it takes to navigate the political back alleys of Budapest. For almost twenty years, from when he'd first arrived in 1919, he's managed these treacherous maneuverings. For all their analytic exuberance, Douglas and MacLeod know nothing of the outcomes of war, defeat, honour lost, collapse of empire. They cannot imagine the hatred for the new Czechoslovakia or the subsequent spike in nationalism. Hungary's radical groups are determined to reclaim—by whatever means—their losses.

He understands this climate of national mourning and anger. Within it, he has learned to move skillfully, speak humbly, win trust, even admiration—if he so acknowledges—from the aristocracy and extremists on both sides, even Gaska and Vací. He has become, after all, one of the best journalists at Reuters. He dines with Regent Horthy, for Christ's sake. Of course, Horthy is in danger. Arrow Cross, his greatest threat.

Brinkley catches a glimpse of himself in the mirror. No longer young, he is not about to relinquish his place, to lose it all, because two impatient young men possess a keenness for solving puzzles. Now this damned drowning in the river. An exporter, Gaska said, name of Kovacs. Joszef Kovacs. Brinkley has heard the name before.

Chapter Twenty

10 **June.** An insistent jangle interrupts Harry's dream. "Douglas here. Who's calling?"

Harry searches his brain for the voice. "Nagy. Of course. Sorry, old man, you roused me from a sound sleep."

Harry listens to what Nagy has to say. "No, it can't be. I was with him last night. We had a drink, left each other a little after nine."

He listens a moment longer. "Julianna. Where is she?"

Harry dresses hurriedly. In the street, he hails a cab to the Kovacs' teashop. On his way there, he realizes he does not know exactly where Kovacs and his wife live, but surmise they occupy quarters adjacent to the shop and Joszef's export office. He recalls Kovacs' remark about walking to the end of the bridge. When he exits the cab, he spots two uniformed officers descending a set of stairs on the north side of the building. The officers are bidding goodbye to a woman—Julianna—silhouetted in an open doorway. She stands, one hand over her mouth, the other holding a small object in her hand that she slips into a pocket. She stares after the men, then out at the river. After a long moment, she sees Harry and waits in the doorway as he climbs the stairs. Her hands grip the waistband of a blue apron.

"Let's go in," she says.

From the outside, the building looks plain, ordinary. Inside, the high-ceilinged reception room is decorated with oriental vases and statuettes, handmade Turkish rugs, fine furniture and rich garnishes. A marked contrast to the small, shaken woman. She leans into him, hands flat, face buried in his chest. Having met the woman a mere two days ago, Harry is surprised, but wraps her in his arms, feels her body shudder and listens to her high pitched wails of sorrow. He stands silent through bouts of weeping and sobbing.

She wipes her face and steps back, briefly holding his hand. "Stay," she says. From the pocket of her apron, she brings forth the wire spectacles, holds them out flat in her palm. "They brought them."

Harry follows her into the kitchen. She asks what he would like for breakfast, where he would like to sit. He protests that he mustn't trouble her. She insists, brings out the bread, sausages and cheeses, and turns up the water kettle for boiling, the pan for the eggs.

"Did your friend like the tea?" she asks in a distant voice.

"Yes, I think so."

"Joszef was joy in my life. Always, I tell him. Be careful walking on the bridge, along the shore. The water is cold and swift." She shakes her head. "So pleased, he was, to show you the baths, to share them. With you, he was comfortable. Unlike him, really. You were a friend of Zoltán's, he said. The cards were good to you, he told me, and so you must be a good man. Joszef was superstitious in that way. When he left me last night, he was happy." She smiles a little. "What could have made him so careless?"

Harry shakes his head. "After the baths we drank, shared a slice of bread, sat on a bench in the park under the tall tower." He does not tell her of their conversation or that Joszef Kovacs was far from happy when Harry left him. "So, you did not see Joszef again last night?"

"No." She fixes a plate of eggs and sausage, places it on the table, and pours two cups of tea into blue Nippon cups. While Harry eats, she drinks her tea.

"He told you," she says.

"What's that?" Harry chooses not to guess at her meaning.

"The bridge. The murder. What they did." Absently, she stirs a tortoise shell spoon round and round, does not look up at him.

"We talked of it. Yes." Not enough, he wants to say.

"They did not trust this man Neale."

Careful. There's more. He wonders who "they" are.

"Did you meet him? Neale, I mean," asks Harry.

"Only the once. He came to deliver a package for Joszef."

"So Joszef and Neale did business together?" Harry doesn't know where this is going.

"Business," Julianna scoffs. "Is that what Englishmen call it?" This time she looks him in the eye. "You see how we live." She sweeps an arm around the room, out beyond the entryway. "One must pay a price for such luxury." She lifts her head, dabs with her apron at her cheeks. "I do not know the nature of Joszef's interactions with this man Neale. Only that, in the spring, Neale began to bring packages. I asked Joszef about them. He pretended this was nothing out of the ordinary. Said Neale required a way to send his packages, quicker than the Hungarian post. Last week, Joszef took the cash from my shop's register, said he had to change the forints into English pounds. I assumed Joszef needed it for Zoltán or his games. That same night, very late, Neale came with a package. It was the only time I saw him in this room. He seemed surprised I was here. Joszef took the package, counted out the English money. Neale said he would see Joszef tomorrow to 'finish it' as he said. When he left, I asked Joszef what was going on. He said he would explain when he returned from Zoltán's."

They sit in silence. Harry eats a cold sausage. Julianna sips her tea. A puzzle piece clicks into place.

"These packages, what happened to them?"

Julianna says, "I assumed Joszef took care of them. Sent them as he usually does. They were not my concern." She shakes her head. Her shoulders sag. "One dares not interfere in the fierce world of Hungarian politics."

Harry persists. There is always a chance. "The last package. The one Neale brought that night. Do you know where it might be?"

"Perhaps in Joszef's office. If he has not sent it off. There are many things there. In the safe, maybe. I cannot say."

"So you think there's a political connection." Harry thinks about which questions to ask, ones that will not shed negative light on her dead husband. He replays Brinkley's explanations of the various parties at play.

Julianna folds her arms. "Joszef is not a revolutionary, if that's what you mean. He has no regard for the Arrow Cross. Any radical group, for that matter."

"He was a nationalist, then," says Harry, staring at his saucer.

"Hungarians are nationalists. Some more extreme than others. For eighteen years, we have suffered. And been unwavering. We will never accept the 1920 Treaty. That document seized our territories, changed our borders." Julianna's eyes take on the hard look of determination, her chin set in defiance. "Hungarian soil is eternal. No one has the right to give it away."

Harry nods, suspects he, too, would take matters in hand if a group of foreign politicians ceded parts of Canada to the Americans or, worse yet, the Russians. "I understand there are factions, some violent, at work trying to reclaim the territory."

"Joszef did not believe in taking up arms." She gazes once again at the spectacles that lay on the table between them. "He was a slight man, but he was not a coward. Neither was he the first to be brave."

Hungarian nationalism and its political intrigues. Harry is woefully unclear on its many variations. He plunges forward, feeling he is closing in on the reason for Neale's death, and invariably Kovacs'. "The new country of Czechoslovakia is building its defenses." The newspaper translation he received from Laura lay on the table in his hotel room. "Hitler seems to think he can use the German military to help the Hungarians take back what was theirs."

"That presents another problem, does it not?" She gathers up the dishes, sets them in the sink to soak. "The warnings are clear. Hitler is at home in the fields of war and acquisition. No one is safe. Already, he is dictating what Horthy must do."

"Your husband was aware of this?"

"He talked of little else. In this room, he, Zoltán and Jan sat with their whiskey, spoke of it for hours. They hold great admiration, adulation even, for Horthy. To them, he is a great warrior, high in the sky. Still, they asked, what will Horthy do in the face of such pressure? How far will he go?"

"You know Nagy well, then?"

"Of course, Jan and Magda are frequent visitors."

"It was Nagy who called me this morning," says Harry.

"Yes." She sits down opposite Harry, her face lined with fatigue.

"Did Joszef explain why he gave Neale money for the package that night?" asks Harry.

"No," she says. "He did not want me to know. And I, the family coward, did not ask." She shakes her head. "You think it is important."

"I think it has to do with his death," says Harry.

"You must excuse me," she says, taking Harry's hand across the table, squeezing it in hers, pressing a small object into his palm. "I need to rest. You will need the key to Joszef's office."

༈

Harry wonders if he had been wrong to seek out Kovacs. Did their conversation lead to his death? It might be so. At the same time, he now knows Kovacs withheld information about his relationship with Neale. Kovacs' guilt over Neale's death meant more than abandoning a stranger. Rather, out of fear, Kovacs abandoned a colleague or friend. At the least, a conspiratorial partner. Kovacs' remarks about Neale knowing too much were based in fact, not speculation. Kovacs likewise knew too much and was killed for it. Harry puts the key in his pocket, still puzzled by the last sentence Kovacs said to him, "There is a point in telling lies." In his work, Harry regularly confronts contradictions. What is truth and what is a lie? These are real people. He likes Julianna and Joszef Kovacs, Jan Nagy, Zoltán. Which of them is lying? Why? Aside from any personal motivation, there is a larger scheme to Neale's death, and now Kovacs'.

Chapter Twenty-One

10 **June.** In Mick's room, they finish a cup of strong coffee. Harry taps a pencil on their worktable.

"Broadway wants an update," says Mick. "We've got forty-eight hours."

"Doesn't leave much time. I thought we'd have a handle by now. Kovacs' death complicates it. Strikes me we don't see the wood for the trees." Harry draws ten lines on the tablet.

"First, our victims: Tennyson Neale, murdered in the wee hours, at least three men involved, two wearing uniforms. Joszef Kovacs, murdered ten days later, received and paid for packages delivered by Neale. There's one connection."

Mick nods. "Then, the Budapest chap. Regent Horthy, caught in the middle between Germans and extremists."

"Kovacs said there's a plot against him, soon to be evident." Harry jots a note.

"Photos indicate his son, who may be the target of a kidnap scheme to force Horthy to appoint members of his opposition to leadership positions," says Mick. "The camel's nose under the tent."

"Kovacs insinuated Arrow Cross is plotting Horthy's fall. That photo seems to bear it out," says Harry. "Neale had the photo, suggesting Neale knew about the plan."

"Add Kristof Balas to the list," says Mick. "Leader of Arrow Cross, hot-headed, threatening, ambitious. Indications are that both Neale and Kovacs knew about Horthy's downfall and that Balas is involved. A tighter connection between Neale and Kovacs."

"Tell me again how you met Kovacs," says Mick.

"Zoltán's poker game."

"You got an invitation to that game from Zoltán. We met Zoltán through Brinkley. Brinkley knows Balas and Zoltán."

"And Neale," added Harry.

"Who sat around the table?" asked Mick.

"Zoltán Zolst, tavern owner. Joszef Kovacs, exporter. Jan Nagy, manufacturer. Oszcar Bychowsky, serious drinker. Peter Toth, young, aggressive player, occupation unknown."

"All Hungarians?" asks Mick. "All well acquainted? All regular players?"

"As much as I know, yes to all three questions," says Harry. "Julianna Kovacs said Zoltán, Jan and Joszef spent a lot of time together. She knows the Nagys well. From all appearances, Horthy supporters."

"Horthy supporters." Mick scratches his chin. "They'll want to keep him in power. Neale and Kovacs have evidence of plans to depose him. Would Kovacs be the only one doing business with Neale?" Mick muses. "Just a thought." He stretches, pours another cup of coffee. "Add their names. We don't know much about the other two players. Bychowsky and Toth, you say."

"Toth and Zoltán were well acquainted. Bychowsky looks to be old aristocracy. Either could have an agenda. Or not. Nagy told me there's a game tonight. Zoltán's idea of a tribute to Kovacs," says Harry. "I'll find out what I can about them. Some pointed questions during a break."

"Anyone we're missing?" asks Mick.

"What about Vací?" asks Harry. "Head of secret police. He'll have a lot to lose if the Germans or extremists come to power."

"So, the status quo is best for him," says Mick. "Keeping things the same is top priority. If leadership changes, his future is bleak."

"A potent personal motive, that. What might a man do to preserve his power and position? He wouldn't have any use for border quarrels or kidnappings. As long as Horthy is leader, Vací is in a good spot. Otherwise, uncertainty. I'm seeing that elegant table service for three. Who was coming to lunch? He was more than anxious to see our backs before company arrived."

"Good question. Vací has, at his disposal, the means to discover and inform Horthy of potential danger," says Mick. "No qualms about using force. If Neale had clear information about a plot, Vací found a way to get it."

"To sum up, as far as we know, everyone on our list is backing the existing power regime," says Harry. "Except Balas."

"That's how it looks," says Mick. "He's there by himself. We don't know if he knew Neale. Or Kovacs. We need to find out."

"Any others?" asks Harry.

"Sándor," says Mick.

"He saw Neale almost every day. We can't say if he knew the others. Let's see if his name pops up again. A tense little chap. Always looking over his shoulder. Must have a reason for it." Harry scribbles, looks up, pencil poised. "That wrap it up?"

"Not quite." Mick hesitates, gulps some coffee, directs his gaze to the window, then back at Harry. "What about Laura Savic?"

"What are you thinking?" Harry tries to keep the edge from his voice.

"We're looking for connections," says Mick. "She figures in with Balas. She knew Neale. She said Gaska was fond of Neale."

Harry frowns, but has to agree. "Connections to all three men." Harry writes Laura's name, then Gaska's on the next line. "Gaska's a player, I'd say."

Mick, reminded of the scene in Gaska's briefing room, paces. "Gaska definitely botched the investigation into Neale's murder. Intentional or brainless?"

"Brainless," Harry announces.

"I'm not so sure," says Mick, folding his arms across his chest. "Kovacs gave information to the police that never showed up in the report. That was intentional."

"So we'd give up and go home," says Harry.

"If that was his motive, he's as dumb as he thinks we are," says Mick.

"My point exactly." Harry laughs, gestures toward the paper, now full of names and lines. "Is this getting us anywhere?"

"It's led us to our next steps," says Mick.

"Which are?" Harry waited.

"Kovacs' office, Kristof Balas, Zoltán's tavern tonight, and Laura Savic. In that order."

Chapter Twenty-Two

10 **June**. The key turns easily in the lock. Harry and Mick survey the room, awash in shafts of light that dapple the dark wooden floor. From a distance comes the monotonous whine of a boat engine. The scent of Eastern incense permeates the air. Twenty feet square, the room is devoid of decoration save a delicately carved desk that faces four massive windows, bare of window dressing, a stunning view of the churning waters of the Danube. Shelves of ledger books line the walls. The office might have housed a successful accountant.

Julianna assures Harry and Mick no one has entered Joszef's office since his death, not even herself. She has not volunteered its location, she tells them, to the police who came in the late morning inquiring about Joszef's workplace.

The uniformed officers cited official policy, insisted on the address. She offered them tea and explained that she had not recovered from the shock of viewing her husband's body. Tomorrow, she told them, when she was rested and calm, she would answer their questions, find the key, and go with them to her husband's place of business.

Harry and Mick set to work. The room is tidier than Harry had imagined for a man who could not know he would never return. In the center of the desk sit two stacks of papers, requisitions and invoices, corners perfectly aligned. Between them, a heavy-handled metal date stamp. A blank pad of yellow paper. A fountain pen and ink bottle. Here is a man careful to settle his accounts. Promptly billed. Promptly paid. Surely, then, Kovacs kept a record of his transactions with Neale. Receipts, transmissions, payments. A specific place for Neale's packages. Hidden but accessible.

By midafternoon, Harry and Mick have searched every nook, filing cabinet and account ledger, their only revelation a secret drawer in the desk that contains four hundred US dollars. Nothing that passes for a secret exchange, no package. The trash can yields a torn page of notes, written in German. The only place they have not searched is a small hallway behind the rear door. They find a stepladder leaning against the wall.

"Close at hand, no dust. Used on occasion," Mick says.

"To climb where?"

"There's nothing in here," says Mick. "The office is more likely."

Mick carries the ladder into the office. Harry scans the walls, bottom to shoulder height, feels for seams, ill-fitted panels. Mick climbs four steps of the ladder, studies the room from the heightened angle.

"If I sat behind this desk, what would I see?" Harry moves to sit in the swivel chair Kovacs occupied each day. "Windows set deep, an alcove where a man could sit and watch the river run its course." He gets up and points to the planks that frame the top of the windows.

Mick notices a screw on the underside of one of the planks, a different color, a rise above the rest. He unscrews the horizontal panel and reaches inside. To Harry, he hands down two round cylinders, each no larger than a tin of soup, lighter in weight. They are bound in the same white paper, a flap loose at the end. When shaken, they sound like a baby's rattle. Tucked into the side of the frame is a flat sheaf of papers, folded over and clipped.

"What do you make of these?" asks Mick.

"Both cylinders addressed to Miss Martha Neale in Folkestone," says Harry.

"The sister. Let's have a look."

Mick lifts the flap of the first container. Three metal spools tumble into his hand, on the top of each a different date in May written in thin black digits. The second contains two spools labeled 31 May. "By jove," Mick says, his voice rising above a river barge's whistle. He passes the containers to Harry. "These are written in Neale's hand."

"Neale delivered them to Kovacs the night he was killed," says Harry, examining each in turn. "Julianna said she saw only one package change hands."

"Maybe she was mistaken." Mick stares out at the water. "So Neale was here after he shot the film and before he was killed. That same night Neale met a woman at the Kádár café, around eleven. Afterwards, he came to Kovacs. Then, Kovacs left for the poker game. Is that the sequence?"

"Kovacs left for the game after midnight, according to Julianna," Harry confirms.

"After the game ended—three or four hours later—Kovacs sees Neale killed on the bridge." Mick turns to Harry.

"More specifically, he sees Neale hung on the bridge. The rest sounds right," says Harry.

"That means, at some point before he met Kovacs—before midnight—Neale wrapped these packages and developed the photos we found in his apartment," says Mick.

"That's a tight timeline from the Kádár café to Kovacs' home. Enough to develop film? I don't know," says Harry. "How much time was involved? Neale might have developed the photos after he and Kovacs met."

"Which means he shot several rolls, passed these to Kovacs, held on to the rest. After their meeting, he developed the negatives, hid them in his apartment, the strips we found. He also developed a few actual photos," says Mick.

"So, he'd already wrapped these packages before he met the woman at the café," says Harry, "knowing he would leave her and get them to Kovacs around midnight."

"A busy evening," says Mick. "Why wouldn't Kovacs have mailed them?"

"Maybe he never meant to. If Kovacs was mailing a package to Neale's sister, wouldn't Neale have paid Kovacs? But it was the other way round. I think Kovacs never intended to mail these packages to Miss Martha Neale. If the packages were confiscated or fell into the hands of authorities, both men could say Neale was brightening his sister's dreary life by sending these travel photographs of Budapest. Kovacs was simply helping a friend. When we develop the film, I'll wager the first few photos are pretty little pictures of Buda Castle. Kovacs paid Neale for these photos. Let's find out why."

⁂

Mick and Harry squeeze into the development room next to Tamás Sándor. Though Sándor is not pleased to see them again, a payment of fifty US dollars and a promise they will be gone in a few hours ease his anxiety. The first roll holds eight images. Sándor switches off the light. The three stand in pitch-blackness. Harry and Mick wait.

Finally, Sándor speaks. "For the beginning, the room must have no light. The film is light-sensitive at this stage. Listen only."

Harry and Mick hear Sándor mumble, then a small popping.

"The film spool is open," says Sándor.

They hear a fluid sound, as placing one's hands in water, a gentle lapping of water. After a few minutes, Sándor announces, "Now the rinsing."

"Hang this strip on the clips behind you." He snaps on a low intensity red light. "The film is no longer light-sensitive."

Harry follows Sándor's instructions. An instant later, the room is dark once more, the process repeated.

"These strips must dry twenty, thirty minutes," says Sándor.

"Then what?" asks Harry. This is new science to Harry, one he finds useful. Moreover, he wants to know how Neale spent the last night of his life. Timing is critical to the reconstruction of events.

"Then the photo paper is used. It is a different process. One uses an enlarger, places each negative on a tray. A lamp and lens project the image from negative to paper. The light-sensitive paper captures the image. The paper is exposed ten seconds, and then developed by placing it in trays of chemicals. Rinsed between the first and second chemical. The paper is washed thoroughly with running water, hung to dry. Then the picture can be seen clearly."

"A lengthy process." Harry checks his watch as he watches Sándor work.

"The negatives, as you experienced, take little time. It is the paper enlargement that moves slowly. If the chemicals cooperate and one's hands are swift, a strip of negatives can be transformed to paper in thirty minutes or less."

Harry calculates. Mick interrupts. "So two spools of eight can be done—photos on paper that is—in a little more than an hour?"

"Closer to an hour and a half. One cannot rush the drying," says Sándor.

#

An hour later, photographs strewn on the bed, Harry and Mick are certain Neale hit upon crucial information the night he died. The first group of photos proves their earlier assumptions. Pages of a recent report spell out increasing pressure on Horthy to appoint Arrow Cross members to his cabinet and change the Jewish laws to correspond with the harsh German and Austrian measures. Horthy is getting demands from the Germans and his fellow citizens to permit the removal of Hungarian Jews. A plan, to be carried out in midsummer, involves kidnapping Horthy's son on the day he visits his father's residence. Junior to be released after Horthy appoints extreme nationalists to a majority of his cabinet and Jewish race laws pass. Within six months, the scheme continues, Horthy will be overthrown, power transferred to Arrow Cross party leaders.

"Who authored the plan?" asks Harry.

"My bet's on Balas," says Mick. "At the very least, he's a major contributor."

"Christ. Take a hard look at these." Harry hands the photos to Mick.

More alarming than the first group, the next series contains news of a larger plot, all related to the overthrow of Czechoslovakia. Detailed scenarios for the assassination of German Foreign Minister Joachim Ribbentrop and German Ambassador Edmund

Veesenmayer will place blame on the Czech government, giving the Germans reason for retaliation and invasion.

Photos of three British Parliament members—apparently paid to influence colleagues to support Hitler's Third Reich and advise an isolationist approach regarding Germany's ambitions in Czechoslovakia—accompany a short listing of names and payments.

"Very similar to what we pulled from Neale's safe deposit." Mick points to the third name from the bottom. "A wee bonus. Hansford Brinkley. A relation? Brother? Cousin?"

"Explains why Neale preferred to use Kovacs as an alternate method of transmission. Uncommon name, Brinkley."

"Interesting twist," says Mick. "What do you make of it?"

"Tells me Cephus Brinkley left out a few details in his lesson on Hungarian politics. His family's stance on Horthy's leadership, for a start." Harry makes a mental note to check out both Cephus Brinkley's and Hansford Brinkley's backgrounds the next time he is in London.

Harry works through the remaining photos. The last piece of the plot, bold in its premise, is incomplete. Along with a survey map of Hungary's northern border, there is a front page of an operation called Case Green, apparently an invasion of Czechoslovakia. The plan's author is General Wilhelm Keitel, Commander-in-Chief of the High Command of the Armed Forces of the Third Reich.

"Where's the rest of it?" asks Mick. "We developed all the negatives."

"Details have to be on another roll. The text stops abruptly at the bottom of the front page," says Harry.

"Neale was careful with the other documents. Unlikely he'd cut this one off," says Mick, "without the gruesome details."

"Those details would bring a high price," says Harry, "a lofty fee from somebody who needs them."

"Note the author of the plan," says Mick.

"Keitel wields exceptional power," notes Harry. "Three months ago he issued orders to exterminate Germany's Jews and execute communist party and labor union officials."

"Critical documents to the Czech government."

"And to Britain and France and the US. More than enough motive for murder," says Harry. "Either to get hands on these documents or keep them from leaking out."

"I'm wondering how Neale came across these. Christ Jesus. It's highly classified material, released not a day or two before he died. He must have known the value of what he had."

Mick checks off the major players they have encountered in Budapest.

Harry recalls Kovacs' words, "Your colleague knew more than he should." "Someone else knew its value, too," says Harry. "Aware of what Neale knew, he—or they—killed him for it. The almighty question. Who?"

Chapter Twenty-Three

10 **June.** Feet propped on the ancient oak desk, Kristof Balas puffs on a cigarillo and gazes at the seven mounted Magyar chieftains in silent watch beyond his window. In a foul mood, he reaches for the file of newspaper clippings. The one on top catches his eye, and he thumps a finger on it. The article has been on his desk for weeks. He's read it countless times. Rumors. Nothing specific, but evidence is mounting. The Germans will move when they are ready. He sits back, angles his head and sends the smoke upward.

I cannot afford to wait longer. I must move soon. The future of Hungary is in play. Horthy's political elite neglected to pass the most basic reforms, their indulgent attitude toward Jews worst of all. If Hungary is to triumph, to regain the purity of its roots and exalted status among the great nations of Europe, it must be free of Jews. The entirety of Jews. Then, we will regain Slovakia and Ruthenia. We will establish a common border with the Carpathians and Poland.

The Czechs are in the way, of course. The Germans are not the answer. The Germans will bargain; they will promise to expand our territories. In the end, once they bring the Czechs to their knees and make Czechoslovakia disappear, the Germans will exploit us, turn on us, take the land for themselves, principally our industrial cities. Already, there is talk that Poland is on the Führer's list.

Hitler and his ruffians do not intend to allow Arrow Cross to govern our own country, especially if led by the likes of me. They consider me unfit and unstable. Ill-suited for leadership. Hot tempered. Veesenmayer said as much.

I know my party is loyal. I demand loyalty. I evoke loyalty. Others are eager with their goodwill. The vodka, free and flowing. The women, easy with their favours. Szálasi's imprisonment came at the right time. I've made a good front, talked of assuming temporary leadership until Szálasi returns. For this, I have received Szálasi's blessing. I must make the most of the time left. I must seize and establish power before Szálasi's release. Szálasi is not easily deceived. He will learn of my moves soon enough. Luckily, he is behind bars. Another three years behind bars. Even if Szálasi hates me for it, he cannot doubt my devotion, my desire to avenge Hungary's honour. Szálasi understands this. He will not be pleased, but he will understand.

Slowly, Horthy's support is eroding. So far, the elections next year favour Arrow Cross. The constant bickering and clashes among the parties, always scrapping for position, weaken them all. The other parties will no longer prevent Arrow Cross from gaining power. Arrow Cross soon will win more seats in the parliament.

I cannot wait that long. The others are vicious. Anything can happen. I can lose my position, pushed out by scandal, innuendo, slurs. We Hungarians rely on power of the strongest. A ruler must be feared.

Ambassador Veesenmayer is known for arm twisting, black-mailing. I suspect he is hammering out an agreement with Horthy. One that will bind us to the Germans. Hungarians, those I trust and respect, will never be agents of German imperialism. I will preserve our independence.

The telephone bell interrupts. Balas reluctantly sets his feet on the floor and looks sideways at the telephone, unsure whether to answer. On the fourth ring, he crushes the cigarillo and reaches across the desk, "*Igen*. Yes."

He listens. "Zoltán's, ten o'clock."

Balas replaces the receiver, glances at the clock. He will reschedule his dinner with Laura.

Chapter Twenty-Four

10 **June**. Balas looks around for a table. Zoltán's smoky interior swarms with patrons lingering over their drinks and cigarettes. He expects Brinkley has arrived before him.

Years ago, Balas decided he did not like Cephus Brinkley. Always too pleased with himself. Fiercely pro-German, some old connection in his family. Nevertheless, after Brinkley interviewed him for a story on "peaceful revision," Balas discovered that he and Brinkley understood each other. A professed anti-Semite, Brinkley much favours the Jewish laws. Unlike others in Britain who are strikingly ignorant of Hungarian issues, Brinkley is a long-time observer of Hungary's political scene. Brinkley appreciates Hungary's position, its need to regain territory and power, to avenge its honour. He recognizes the importance of Hungarian independence. Brinkley has come through for Balas, though Balas doubts that Britain—or France for that matter—supports Hungarian causes or will assist in restoring its territories. They turn their backs on Eastern Europe's tangled affairs. He does not trust them.

In a recessed alcove, at a corner table near the back, Brinkley nurses a glass of Irish whiskey, absorbed by something on the other side of the room.

"Those two," Brinkley gestures with his glass as Balas approaches.

Balas stops beside the table. Across the room, Harry Douglas and Mick MacLeod, with a nod, acknowledge his gaze. "I thought they'd gone."

"I did my best," says Brinkley.

"You failed," says Balas, suddenly annoyed at everything about Cephus Brinkley. "Why are we here?"

"A development. Are you going to sit or stand?"

Balas shouts to the bartender, "Vodka and tonic. Two doubles." He sits down and sighs. "Why meet here for the world to see?"

"Precisely the reason," mutters Brinkley. "What do you know about the Kovacs' drowning?"

"Drowning?" asks Balas. "I was not aware the cause of death was determined."

"So goes the story," says Brinkley. "The official ruling."

"Intriguing. What else is there?" Balas upends the vodka, drinks it down.

"How do you know him?" asks Brinkley.

"Export business. A good front, in any case. Kovacs has done business in Budapest for decades. Conservative, not extremely so. A nationalist all the same." Balas starts on the second vodka.

"Anything else?" asks Brinkley.

Balas shifts the second vodka from right hand to left and back again. In a flat tone, he replies. "Faithful to his wife. The occasional game in Zoltán's back room. Never a big winner. A solid Hungarian. Though a Horthy supporter, from what I'm told. Why these questions? You know this."

"In truth, I know nothing of the man. Only that our foreign friends uncovered classified information in his possession," says Brinkley. "I want to know how he got it."

"What classified information?"

"Film, negatives, photographs. My source is not clear about their content. He got a quick look, noted a few names: Horthy, Arrow Cross, Veesenmayer, Keitel." Brinkley stared at Kristof Balas across the table. "Douglas and MacLeod now possess this information. It could already be on its way elsewhere. I don't need to tell you what that means."

"How would they get it out of the country? You control the transmittals." Across the room, Harry and Mick make their way through the crowd. They are joined by another man and woman. Balas recognizes the actress Magda Nagy. Balas rises from his chair to see them pass into Zoltán's private rooms. "You do control the transmittals?"

"Of course," says Brinkley, too quickly.

"But not these," says Balas, easing back into the chair, folding his arms, smiling at Brinkley's discomfort. "With these, there is a problem." Balas now realizes why Brinkley has called him. "A problem that requires fixing."

"We've come this far. Horthy must fall, Arrow Cross take control. The Jewish laws must pass," says Brinkley.

"Have they come to you?" asks Balas.

"Not yet," says Brinkley. "I expect they're putting together a report. Six gave them forty-eight hours."

"There's no other method of transmittal? Nothing except the wireless in that storage locker of yours?"

Though Brinkley is beginning to wonder, he cannot allow Balas to doubt it. "None."

Balas calculates. "We must assure all is destroyed, nothing left behind, not a hint of it."

"You have the rest of it? The other pages, the details of the invasion?" Brinkley asks.

"In the safest of places," says Balas.

#####

"What do you make of that meeting in the corner?" asks Mick.

"Odd pairing. Looks friendly enough," says Harry. "Not sure it's mutual. From the looks of his whiskey glass, Brinkley's been here awhile. Balas just arrived, stopped at his table. Maybe a simple exchange of pleasantries."

"I didn't see him sit down," says Mick. "Pretty obvious, they saw us."

"And not too delighted about it."

#####

In the largest of Zoltán's private meeting rooms, a dozen fiddlers, flautists and drummers perform the distinctive rhythmic patterns of Hungarian folk music. A pair of dancers emerges, first moving slowly to the music followed by a faster dance, clicking their heels in cadence. The audience—men in business coats and ties, women in stylish evening dresses—claps in time.

In a far corner Harry recognizes Peter Toth and Count Bychowsky. Next to Zoltán, his arm around her shoulder, Julianna Kovacs appears fragile, dwarfed by the man's size and spirit. Dressed in a simple dark dress and choker of pearls, she nods solemnly at each passerby, acknowledges their words of sympathy.

"Joszef's clients," she whispers aside to Harry and Mick. "Zoltán directs them to the bar to forget their sorrow." She smiles, a mix of gratitude and mischief in her eye. "As if it were so easy. After the drink is gone, the grief is here, waiting."

Jan and Magda Nagy—by far the most handsome couple in the room—stand together, cocktails in hand. She in an emerald-green satin gown, the bodice tightly fitted, the long skirt in sway at her slightest movement. Tight curls of blonde hair are swept away from her face, her earrings a shower of stars against a swan-like neck. Before Jan has a moment to introduce them, Magda turns to Harry and Mick. "The dances you see—slow and fast—show the dual expressions of Hungarian character. We are miserable. We despair. We are joyful. We rejoice." She makes a face and poses her body, pretending each emotion. Then, she laughs and takes Harry's hand in both of hers to draw him close. She smells of roses. Over the music, she says, "Mr. Douglas, you have been very kind to Julianna and to my husband. We must repay you somehow."

"No need," says Harry.

Before Harry or Magda can say more, Zoltán signals. The music stops. "We gather to honour Joszef. Among us still. First we eat." Arms spread wide, Zoltán points to a table laden with sumptuous offerings—sausages and potatoes, chicken stew, cabbage rolls and peppers—and great carafes of red wine. For more than an hour they eat and drink and talk of the late and departed Joszef Kovacs.

Soon after, the crowd disperses, leaving Harry and Mick, Zoltán and Julianna, Jan and Magda, Toth and Bychowsky in a tight circle in the center of the room.

"We have one more tribute," says Zoltán. "The cards."

Julianna speaks, "Forgive me, Zoltán. I am very tired. If he were here with us, Joszef would play for hours. I must go home."

"Let me find a taxi," says Zoltán, searching the room for a waiter.

Mick nods to Harry. "I'm going that way myself, Julianna," he says. "Poker's not my game. May I escort you home?"

"Safe at last. With a strong handsome man," she says, looping her arm through his. "I prefer to walk on summer nights."

Julianna finishes her goodbyes, gives Zoltán an affectionate hug before Mick guides her through the rear door, the evening light fading to dark across the river. Zoltán leads those remaining into the smaller room, directs them to their usual places.

"As if he were never here at all," says Zoltán, heaving a great sigh, settling his body into the oversized chair reserved for him alone.

"How cruel," says Magda, sweeping her arms in a giant arc over the table. "Joszef, friend and citizen, gave his talents to our beloved Budapest which is now richer, better for his life. We must remember this. We must acknowledge this."

"Cruelty is not what I intended," says Zoltán. "Nor that Joszef's life had no value. You misunderstand my words. I say only that his chair—here, next to my right hand—will not be empty. Another soul moves to fill the space. Another heart beats in his place. It is the way of life."

Silence falls among the group.

"A quiet man," says Jan Nagy. "One of principle."

Harry looks around the table. How is it that a quiet man of principle regularly paid a foreign agent for political information, became rich because of him, then watched that man die, unwilling to come to his aid? In the brief time Harry spent with Kovacs, he liked the man. He likes Julianna. He respects Nagy and his opinions. But Harry cannot reconcile his afternoon discoveries with the man they describe.

"Enough serious talk," says Zoltán. "The night leaves us. The cards."

Harry sets his place in order. As usual, Zoltán stacks his chips and directs the action. Next to Harry, Nagy leans back, says something to Magda who has placed herself behind him. Toth once again sits directly across from Harry, his youth, fair hair and blue eyes in striking contrast to the other men at the table. A thought nibbles at the edge. Harry remembers Kovacs telling him Toth worked with the government service, as an aide at the German embassy. How closely, he wonders, does Toth work with Ambassador Veesenmayer?

Toth shuffles the deck, his fingers loose as Magda Nagy settles into the chair on Zoltán's right. Between her and Toth is Count Bychowsky, a happy expression on his face, his bony frame angled toward Magda. A serious chain-smoker, the Count has somehow decided not to smoke this evening, though a cigarette lays within easy reach and Harry notes the Count's glances in its direction. Likewise, he shows no interest in refilling his ale glass. Apparently, the nearness of Magda Nagy more than satisfies his addictions.

Zoltán unwraps a new cigar, sets it between his teeth. "For my friend Joszef, we will begin with seven-card stud. Your deal, Toth."

Magda proves the most difficult read for Harry. As Jan pointed out nights before, she takes great pleasure in bluffing. Though she often possesses no winning cards, she runs up the bet—alternately chewing her lip in despair, sitting tall in her chair, smiling broadly at the ceiling or the cards in her hand. After several rounds of her behavior, Toth throws up his hands and his cards, and pouts for the remaining hour of play. During a later round, Harry, supremely confident with three jacks in his hand and certain of Magda's bluff, matches her final bet. Astonishingly, she produces a full house, fives over tens. For his part, the Count seems content to sit next to Magda and sniff her perfume.

It is clear, after another round, Magda has taken the greater part of everyone's money and that she has grown tired of the game. "You know I must sleep, check on the boys, and pack for my trip to London," she says to Jan.

Harry repeats. "London. What takes you there?"

"The Palace Theatre. A performance of Countess Maritza," says Magda. "Rehearsals begin next week. The play opens on 6 July. I'm to be the lead."

"Congratulations. I'm surprised I've not heard of the play. Then again, I haven't been in London in quite a while," says Harry. "Tell me about it."

"It is a romantic play, three female and three male roles. The Countess lives in a large country estate on the Hungary/ Bulgaria border. My accent is, of course, perfect. The strong-minded beautiful young Countess does not wish to marry the suitor her father has selected for her, and she resolves to avoid the marriage."

"That's it?' says Harry.

"There is more, but you must come to the performance and learn the rest." She throws back her head and laughs. "Do you suppose the ending will be happy or sad?" asks Magda.

By then, Toth, Bychowsky and Zoltán have drifted outside to stretch their legs and light their cigarettes. Harry, Jan, and Magda rise together and walk down a short hallway. A single overhead light shines above the front entrance. The darkened tavern is quiet, save the intruding sounds from the river.

"The happiest ending will be if Magda remains in London instead of returning to Budapest," says Jan. "Horthy cannot hold off the push for further Jewish laws. You must stay away, darling."

The icy look on Magda's face tells Harry such a decision has not yet been made.

"When will you leave?" asks Harry.

"In two days, the twelfth of June on the evening train. I will travel north to the coast to board the Harwich ferry at Hoek van Holland," she says. "I will arrive in London the following evening."

"You're not taking the Paris route?" says Harry, surprised at her lack of caution.

"Indeed, the southerly route through Zurich is more scenic," she says. "But it adds many hours to the trip. The extra time will be tedious."

Jan says, "The extra time will provide hours to study your lines and sleep." He turns to Harry, lowers his voice. "For days, we have discussed the more cautious route. I cannot convince her. The train she prefers goes through Linz, then crosses into Germany. Five hundred miles with checkpoints at the borders of Austria and Germany. God knows how many in between."

Magda pretends not to hear. "I must pick up a costume in Cologne where it is being completed. A special fabric for the hemline. I assured the costume designer in London I would bring it with me," she says.

"I'll get it for you, send it in plenty of time," says Jan.

"You've no time for such things. It is my responsibility. The seamstress will bring it to the station in Cologne. From Linz, the train goes through Frankfurt to Cologne, then into the Netherlands and the ferry port," she says. "The timing is much better. The train arrives in Hoek van Holland before the morning ferry leaves for England."

"You will travel hundreds of miles and spend many hours within the German Reich," says Jan, arms folded across his chest, voice hardened. "They will question you, search your things. It is too dangerous. How will I know you're safe?"

She takes a step forward, caresses his cheek. "I will be perfectly safe, dear husband."

"I'll go with you," he says. "Just to the ferry port."

"Don't say ridiculous things. You must stay with our children."

"Then I forbid you to go." He pounds his fist. "You are my wife. You will stay in Budapest."

Harry assumes Magda Nagy will be angry at this declaration of spousal control. Instead, seeming to understand her husband's desperation, she takes his face in her hands, lightly kisses his nose and forehead. "They will not control us. I am an actress. They will not keep me from my work. Their laws, no matter how they wish to humiliate and destroy, cannot make me who I am not." She lowers her eyes, turns slightly away from him. "My travel papers are in order. There will be no questions. If they search my things, they will find stage costumes and makeup. I'll send word to you from the ferry port before I depart for London."

"The matter appears to be settled," says Harry, retrieving his hat from the peg by the door.

"So it would seem," says Jan, a weary smile upon his face. They shake hands, mumble their goodbyes.

Harry starts to ask Jan about his conversations with Kovacs, but the time is not right. He can see in Nagy's face he is frightened for his wife. "May I call on you tomorrow, Jan? It's important."

Jan responds quickly, "Of course. Anytime after noon, I'll be in my office. You have my card."

Harry has neglected to bid Zoltán good night. He strolls to the back of the building where he knows the three men are smoking. Maneuvering around the trash cans at the entrance to the alley, approaching from a narrow pathway, he sees two silhouettes, partly visible against a side partition. When he hears Toth's voice, Harry stops and waits for their conversation to end.

"It's clear Veesenmayer is the target. The plan is to wait until Ribbentrop arrives. The two of them will meet together, go out for an early dinner, later have drinks at the casino," says Toth.

Soundlessly, Harry removes his hat, steps back against the building, out of sight.

Toth continues, "I am to accompany Ribbentrop back to his hotel. This will leave the ambassador alone. Most likely, from what I am aware of his custom, he will be slightly drunk and not know his way home. A taxi will come. It will take him to his death. The following day, the Czechs will be blamed and Horthy will be discredited for faulty security for the German ambassador. Adequate reason for Hitler to seek revenge against the Czechs and depose Horthy. Due to the circumstances, Britain and France— and truth be told, the United States—will withhold support for the Czechs. Czechoslovakia will be left to survive on its own."

Another voice, muffled enough that Harry does not recognize it. He dares not move closer, but inclines his head to concentrate on listening. "How can the Czechs be blamed?"

"A paper left with the body. Threats from the Czech resistance," says Toth. "There will be no doubt."

"A brilliant plan. It cannot fail." The unknown voice, then a long pause. A cough. A scuffle of feet. "When?"

Toth's clear voice again, "I cannot be sure. Ribbentrop's visit is scheduled next week."

Another cough, a deep hacking that lasts a full minute. A wheeze. A spate of inaudible words. Then, "Timing's not right. Too soon. Not now. Early fall, it was to be."

"Tuesday," says Toth.

Thinking back, on his way up the steps off the Gellért lobby, it strikes Harry that Toth and his ailing companion spoke German. Did anyone at the gathering appear ill? He cannot remember. Certainly, no one at the card game. The date hangs in the air: 14 June, Tuesday.

Chapter Twenty-Five

10 **June**. A mile away, across the city, Laura Savic waits for Kristof Balas. She looks out the window, marks her own reflection in the glass. Dressed in a low-cut blue evening dress, she moves to the sofa. Propped against two pillows, she flips pages of the latest issue of *Theatre* magazine. Outside, the street is quiet. An occasional taxi passes. She has left the door ajar, so her neighbors will not be awakened by his knock. Still, they might hear him on the iron stair. She suspects they spy on her. An attractive woman, alone, coming and going at any hour. A prime target for gossip and suggestion. After one neighbor discovered, she knew not how, that Laura works for the Budapest police department, the whispers subsided. She even discerned a slim smile from the women she passed on the landing, laundry baskets in hand. She would like to invite them for a cup of tea or to discuss the latest movie or fashion, but she dares not reveal too much of herself. They will ask, naturally, about her family, why she has not married, if she knows this one and that one.

When Erik once banged on the wrong door in search of her apartment, she lied and called him brother. Since that incident, they ask each week when her brother will return, why he does not visit more often, where he lives. While she is not fond of pretense, it is not possible to tell the truth.

It has been ten days since she and Erik met face to face, their communication now through notes and intermediaries. She warned him about Douglas and MacLeod, assumed he would proceed carefully. No one else thinks the two Englishmen matter, but she is convinced the group must be cautious. The last thing she said to Erik was, "If there's a problem, I'll make sure you know."

Her thoughts return to the magazine. She spots a review of a recently staged play at the National Theatre she wants to see.

I Married An Angel, based on a Hungarian fantasy by Janos Vaszary, features love-weary, wealthy Budapest banker, Count Willie Palaffi, who ends his engagement to Anna Murphy, swearing the only girl he could marry would be an angel. Soon, a real angel flies into his life, and he marries her, only to discover she has no human failings. In particular, she is unable to lie. Her honesty alienates Willie's acquaintances and his customers and causes a run on his bank. His sister saves the day by teaching the angel about the real world. She bribes taxi drivers to make Willie's creditors late, so that he has time to save his bank. Willie and his now-earthier angel live happily ever after.

If only life were so. In her world, living happily ever after is the farthest thing from truth.

She does not want to see Balas this evening, or ever again for that matter. In the beginning, she found him handsome, charming, powerful, and occasionally brooding. His ambitions for the future of Hungary were enlightening. Soon enough, she saw him clearly. Arrogant, selfish, cruel. When he had drunk too much vodka and she refused to sleep with him, he hit her, a hard slap on the side of the head. He laughed, said it was merely a tap to show her a man could do what he wanted, that he could do worse, break her arm if he chose. It was the night Harry Douglas and Mick MacLeod foolishly intervened on her behalf. The next morning, the scene was the talk of the police station. Gaston had invited her into his office, questioned her.

She wanted to flee Budapest, take the first train to Prague. But a slap from a swine like Balas will not keep her from their mission. This evening, she will make sure he has something useful to say. He cannot stay the night. She does not want Vací's surveillance teams reporting late-night visitors. She has been careful.

She had arranged, that morning, to meet Balas at the Halaszbasta restaurant near the Fisherman's Bastion side of the castle, and had anticipated a long evening on the romantic roof terrace. Wildly pleased, Balas told her of the magnificent views of Budapest. He expected, as head of Arrow Cross, to be treated as a VIP guest. For her part, she intended to flatter him, learn what she needed, then feign a bout of nausea and hurry home, as far from Kristof Balas as it was possible to be. In late afternoon, however, he cancelled their dinner, citing an urgent meeting. To her ears, he sounded anxious, evasive. Given the insistence of Erik's desperate message yesterday, she, too, is anxious. There is a problem with their plans.

For the first time, she invited Balas to her apartment. She toyed with renting a room at the Gellért for the night, but decided it was too risky. Visitors in the lobby or elevator might lead to an unwelcome encounter. Instead, she iced a platter of fresh oysters, opened an expensive bottle of French wine, lit a dozen candles, and selected a suggestive neckline.

It is nearly midnight when he arrives, smelling of liquor and cigarettes, bathed in aftershave. For over an hour, they eat, drink, and listen to Benny Goodman's clarinet on the phonograph; she shamelessly praising Balas' masculine prowess, his intellectual supremacy, he loosening his tie and his tongue. She feeds him oysters, prepares a hot perfumed bath and then leads him into her bedroom. Afterward, they lay naked together, he talking lazily, intimately, she laughing softly. Balas boasts a fount of information and delivers what she needs.

Erik will be pleased.

Chapter Twenty-Six

10 **June.** Harry does not recognize the clerk at the reception—a ruddy-faced man of uncertain age—who with a grim nod hands him his room key and a folded slip of paper. Harry reads through the translucent page with the red, white, and green embossed emblem and the heavy dark signature:

Harry Douglas
Gellért Hotel
10 June
Your presence is requested in my office on 11 June at 09:00 to provide information regarding the death of Joszef Kovacs.

Laszlo Vací. What could he want? Probably discovered they searched Kovacs' office. Why is the Hungarian secret police, rather than the Budapest police department, investigating Kovacs' death? In any case, there is nothing subtle about Vací's summons.

Mick has received the same note. Harry finds him awake, adding details to their report.

"I've included the bit about the watch. What about Sándor's shop?"

"All of it," says Harry. "Don't send the report until we see what Vací has to say."

"I doubt he's going to share anything with the likes of us. What about Brinkley? When shall we turn this over for transmittal?"

For a long moment, Harry ponders the slats on the floor then folds his arms. "I say we find another way."

"He's going to expect something." Mick rubs the stubble on his chin. "I can see him salivating for it, like an old dog on a hot day."

"I'm not certain he'll transmit the report. One look at that name on the list of parliament lords on the take, he'll scratch the whole of it. Make Six think it was our mistake." Harry crosses the room, checks the window curtain. "Our assignment is to bring Neale home and his documents to Broadway. All of them. I'm not clear why we have to go through Brinkley."

"We'll keep a copy," says Mick. "Could be our copy is a few pages longer."

"What about the photos?" Harry asks.

"I'll throw in a few, none of any consequence. We'll hold back the significant ones."

"We need to get the full report to Six before Tuesday," says Harry.

"What about the diplomatic pouch?"

"Possible. We may have another option. Find a safe place to stash the original until I'm sure." Mick nods and Harry continues. "Give me four hours of sleep. Then I'll fill you in on the conversation I overheard in Zoltán's alley. After that, we'll have our trip to Vací's cellar."

"Something to look forward to. Don't forget Laura Savic. No missing pieces. She's next on our list."

Now, there is something to look forward to. Harry smiles.

卌

"I am pleased you could join me." Vací points out two chairs for them.

"We were in the neighborhood," says Harry. Join him? Harry looks pointedly at Mick.

"I trust you've had a worthwhile visit." Vací directs this comment to Mick.

"Ups and downs," says Mick, examining his fingernails. "You wouldn't be acquainted with two hulking thugs who tried to run me down, would you now?"

"There are more effective means of elimination. All the same, I'll have someone look into your complaint."

"Not nearly a complaint. Not worth the bother," says Mick.

Vací folds his hands in his lap. "Down to business, then. I'm investigating the death of a Hungarian citizen, Joszef Kovacs."

"The secret police involved in a local citizen's death?" asks Harry. "Why not the Budapest Police?"

Vací looks away, perhaps considering the impertinence of the question. "You are correct. The local authorities would normally investigate such an event. We are led to believe Kovacs had international associations."

Harry nods.

"You," Vací directs his gaze at Harry, "had dinner with Joszef Kovacs the night he died."

"He was good enough to invite me to the baths after which we stopped for a drink."

"Ah yes, Margaret Island." Vací reaches for a cigarette, not bothering to offer any. "How is it you were acquainted with Kovacs?"

"I met him at a tavern, Zsolt Csárda, owned by—"

"Yes, yes. I'm familiar with Zoltán's tavern," interrupts Vací, impatience showing. "It is a long way from Margaret Island."

"True enough," says Harry. He is damned sure he is not going to make this easy.

"And you, MacLeod, did you know Kovacs?"

"We were introduced once," says Mick.

"You know his wife," says Vací.

Mick narrows his eyes. Where the bloody hell is this going? "I met Julianna Kovacs last night."

"Last night and, in fact, before," says Vací. He searches through a sheaf of papers on his desk, stops, points a finger on a page.

Mick does not respond immediately. Calm down, he tells himself, outbursts do nothing but incite. He and Harry must get out of this meeting with their freedom; dignity be damned. He will not be forced to be defensive. "What are you after? Out with it. We won't waste your time with snappish answers if you'll not waste ours with petty questions and innuendo." And your obvious secret service tactics, he wants to add.

Vací's expression tells them he is unsure how much to tell them. Mick watches him loosen the knot of his tie, tighten it again. Finally, he slides the piece of paper toward them. "My command is responsible for Hungary's internal protection. We believe there will be a major breach of security, possibly involving the Regent's son. I am convinced the death of Joszef Kovacs relates to this event."

Now we're getting somewhere.

"Before my men arrived," says Vací, "you searched Kovacs' office. What did you find?"

Mick looks at Harry, raises an eyebrow. Harry nods. Mick leans forward, folds his forearms on Vací's desk. "In mid-July, kidnappers are set to grab Horthy's son on a day he visits his father's residence. From our investigation, it appears he will be held until Horthy appoints a majority of extreme nationalists to his cabinet and Jewish race laws are passed. Within the year, Horthy will be overthrown, power transferred to Arrow Cross party leaders."

To their surprise—they had not expected the truth—Vací slumps back in his chair, puffs out his cheeks, exhales slowly. "For a couple of weeks, we have been aware of this information and have taken precautions. Regent Horthy has been briefed on the situations. There are rumors of something else. I was sure Kovacs had knowledge of this."

"How would Kovacs know?" asks Harry.

"On the surface, Joszef Kovacs and his wife are wealthy merchants, importing goods from Africa and the East, pretty little rugs and statuettes, exporting colored glass and Hungarian lace. In reality, Kovacs made his living buying and selling information. He had no allegiances, no worries about the politics of buyer or seller. He was vigilant, of course. But his only concern was whether payment was made."

Harry considers Vací's disclosure. It could be true. "I was led to believe Kovacs was a Horthy supporter."

A shadow crosses Vací's face. "And an Arrow Cross enthusiast. And a past member of the National Socialist Party. On rare occasion, when it suited his purpose, a subject of the monarchy. I could go on." Vací takes a long puff on his cigarette, blows smoke toward the ceiling. He snickers. "He was never observed to do business with communists. I suspect this lapse had little to do with ideology. More likely, they were unwilling to pay."

Vací rises from his chair, comes around the desk and leans his backside against it. "As you see, there are those who depended on Kovacs and those who wished him dead. We may never know who put him in the river."

Though Vací's candor leaves Harry wondering if they have misjudged him, Vací is not a man worthy of trust. Sharing one bit of information is a small price that may later show profit. When Vací walks toward the window, Mick looks at Harry, a subtle change in his expression. A slight shrug of Harry's left shoulder.

Mick begins anew, "On the night of his death, around midnight, Tennyson Neale brought Kovacs a package. Kovacs paid him. Contents consisted of film canisters, photos apparently taken the night Neale was killed."

"You found this in his office?" asks Vací.

"Affirmative," says Mick.

"More than one?" presses Vací.

"Two packages," says Harry. "Though his wife reported only one was handed over the night Neale was killed."

Vací nods, seemingly unaware when the ash of his cigarette has dropped to the carpet.

Mick stands, takes a few steps toward the opposite end of the room. "From what you say, Kovacs made his money as an intermediary. He paid Neale for the package. In that business, the man must have had sharp instincts. Why not sell it immediately, earn a quick return on his money? Why keep it? Kovacs was killed more than a week later."

Vací lights another cigarette, this time offering the box to each of his guests. "You assume he had a ready buyer. It is possible there was none. Or the buyer urged caution in the wake of Neale's murder."

"Who's likely to buy?" asks Harry, aware that Vací will consider this a naive question from a green agent. Nevertheless, Harry wants to hear his answer.

Vací walks around his desk, clearly composing his thoughts. He straightens a picture on the wall. "The better question 'Who is not?' depends on how Kovacs represents the information." Vací pauses, makes a pronounced bob of his head, his hand in the air. His eyes narrow. "Now it is clear to me. The package. The money exchange. I know why he does not sell the package."

Mick and Harry wait.

"He does not know what he has to sell. If the wife is present, Neale cannot speak frankly. The hour is late. Kovacs pays Neale, expects to meet the next day. Neale is dead. Here is film, but with no explanation. What does the film show? Kovacs cannot risk trying to decipher it. It will look suspicious. Someone will talk. The price goes down if the package has been opened. A fear of tampering, you see. People are particular about their purchases."

Harry assumes the secret police employ film experts. He does not want Vací to question them further on the whereabouts of the film canisters. Hoping to change the direction of the conversation and escape the meeting sooner than later, he says, "Last night, I overheard a conversation between two men. I cannot tell you their names." Partly correct, he tells himself. "These men spoke German. They discussed a plot to assassinate the German ambassador." He lets this sink in, then adds. "As early as next Tuesday."

≣≣≣

Harry and Mick cross Grand Boulevard, a wide thoroughfare filled with honking passenger cars and buzzing electric trolleys, and walk the length of Andrássy Avenue until they reach the quieter Erzébet Square. Harry guides them to a bench, a stately chestnut towering above, its summer blossoms blown about by a promising breeze.

"Vací is desperate," Harry says.

"Wouldn't you be? Allowing the murder of the Führer's ambassador would keep me up at night," says Mick. "You gave him a gift. Both to him and Veesenmayer. What are the chances he'll be grateful?"

"Odds against," says Harry. "At least we avoided the infamous cellar."

"For the present," says Mick. "If I'm going to get it in the neck, I'd be pleased to know the deed was worth it."

"No worries. I think we made a fine impression. We're on his good side." Harry grins. "What are the consequences, long-term that is, of a German ambassador's assassination?"

Mick produces a handkerchief, dabs the sweat from his forehead. "If, as you overheard, the Czechs are blamed, Hitler—ever the opportunist—will invade. Apparently, our intelligence expert," Mick points a finger at Harry, "says Hitler's army is in place, ready to advance in a matter of weeks. No doubt the Czechs will resist. Bloodshed on both sides. Who knows who the winner will be? The Czechs are well armed."

Harry interrupts, "If the Czechs prevail, Hungary's boundaries and leadership remain as they are now. Horthy and Vací maintain power. A weakened Germany, at least temporarily, fails to control more territory on Hungary's borders. The Führer slinks off to lick his wounds. And rearm."

Mick delivers the counterview. "If the Germans overcome the Czechs and keep their word, Hungary regains lost territory. Germany takes most of Czechoslovakia for its own, and gains a path to Poland. At the same time, Hungary is at greater risk, surrounded by German control, Horthy at their mercy, Vací likely out of a job."

"Out of a job. Out of time. They'll not keep him around or alive. He knows too much," says Harry. "They might allow Horthy, the popular war hero, to escape into exile. Not Vací."

"So how does Neale fit into this intrigue?" asks Mick.

"I'm beginning to think Neale was used," says Harry. "Set up or unwittingly caught in the middle of this struggle for power. Mind you, he was selling information to line his own pockets. We won't excuse him for that. But someone cleverer than he made him a pawn."

"Sometimes I think we're nearing the end of a long tunnel, a few steps more and we'll see the light. Other times, we're lost in a hopeless maze, one dim dead-end path after another." Mick makes a series of spiral motions, sending his fingers off in all directions.

"We know a good bit more than we did ten days ago. By a long chalk." Harry stands and brushes down his trousers. "I'm off to uncover another piece of the puzzle."

"What sort of uncovering?" asks Mick.

"The best kind." Harry tips his hat and strolls away.

Chapter Twenty-Seven

10 **June**. After Balas leaves her apartment, Laura paces the sitting room, unable to sleep. When the sun rises, she will go in search of Erik Drucek. She needs to confirm what he suspects, but she knows better than to walk the streets of Budapest at night in a hard summer rain. The Budapest Police, sure to stop and question a lone figure in a hooded cloak, will insist she accompany them to the station. Better to wait and avoid the inevitable complications.

She cannot lie in her bed, the smell of him too repulsive. In a foolish frenzy, sure to rouse the nosy Vilma Gombos next door, she grabs up the sheets and pillows, flings them into the bathtub and runs scalding water to the rim. For an hour, she soaks them until the water cools and she wrings away his foul scent. Afterwards, she paces the apartment once more, stopping at corners, staring at the place where wall meets wall, unable to rid Balas' remarks from her mind. Poets described the hours before dawn as the hours of despair, when soul and spirit wither. For weeks after Marek died, she lay stretched across their bed, awake, deciding how best to join him. It will come soon. Once she keeps her promise.

In first light, she washes and dresses and creeps quietly down the steps to the street. Erik spends early mornings at The Rétes, an out-of-the-way river café on the Buda side. She's taken a message there once, when she could not afford to wait for his call. She assumes no one will know her, especially at this hour. Still, she pins back her hair, wears a brown loose-fitting dress and covers her head with a scarf. On her way across the bridge, she bids good morning to an old street vendor in a worn plaid wool cap, selling sweet breakfast pastries, poppy-seed *pogácsa* and slices of hot cinnamon bread. At half past six, she walks up Halázs Street, not yet crowded with morning workers, and spies the café's small alcove. Outside the door, she pulls up the scarf to hide the lower portion of her face. Four steps into the dimly lit interior, she notes its sparseness and the strong aroma of coffee. It is hot, the air humid after the rain. Two men in separate corners, each sitting alone at a square table, slurp their bowls of coffee. The round-faced man wears workers' overalls, a city insignia on his sleeve. When he looks up briefly, she catches his eye, but he looks away and returns to reading a newspaper that lies flat on the table. The other, a younger man in a plain red shirt and light jacket, faces her. He sits against the wall under a high window, both hands holding the upturned bowl, his hooded eyes following her. She lowers the scarf and says quietly, "I'm looking for Erik."

At first, the young man does not respond, then he lowers the bowl, shakes his head, a slight back and forth motion, and stares past her at a spot on the opposite wall. She finds the young man somewhat familiar-looking, though she cannot place where they might have met. She turns toward the door, as if to leave. There is someone else in the room.

⚏

The sea wave of extended blue umbrellas outside the Kádár café is visible from half a block away. As Harry approaches, he comes upon a milliner's shop, stops to admire the feathered hat and calfskin gloves in the display frame, and imagines the tilt of the hat atop Laura Savic's dark tresses. He has spent the time since Vací's meeting preoccupied with seeing her again. Within the shop, he notices a woman intent over a sewing machine and watches as she drapes a sheer blue cloth, veil-like, along the front of a wide brimmed hat. She weaves several pins through the fabric and looks up at him. He tips his hat. She acknowledges him briefly, a shrug and a brush of her hand, and settles back to her work.

Farther along the street, still at some distance, he recognizes the host standing behind the entryway's brown lectern, pencil in hand, hovering over a folder of pages. The host apparently remembers Harry because he waves and waits for Harry to close the gap between them. "I see you have found her," the host begins.

"Found her?" Harry repeats quizzically.

"Last week," the host reminds him, "when you and your friend inquired about the restaurant bill. You asked about the Englishman and his companion."

"I remember," says Harry.

The host leads him inside, raises his eyebrows followed by a wink. "She is quite beautiful. I trust you have better luck than the last gentleman."

"The last gentleman."

"The Englishman, their lovers' quarrel," whispers the host conspiratorially. "I fear they've separated. We've not seen him since that night."

Nor will you again, Harry laments. Anxiously, he scans the interior, a quick search of the tables. Five stout men around a table in the corner, a burst of conversation, then raucous laughter. Business suits, cocktail glasses and smoldering ashtrays near at hand. There are two aging matrons, freshly coifed in stylish afternoon suits, sipping tea, nibbling delicate sandwiches on delicate plates. Otherwise, nothing. He begins again, at the opposite side, scans once more, careful to observe every table. No one of note.

He stops, focuses his gaze on her. The truth of it dawns, his heart hammering so the nearest patron surely hears his chest expand and his quick intake of breath. His mind resists. A hard lump forms in his throat. The beautiful young woman Neale met the night of his death. The lover with whom he shared a kiss. She sits alone, staring beyond the window, absently tracing the pool of light that reflects off the wine glass at her elbow. Mick was right. Harry knows nothing about Laura Savic.

How could she know that he and Mick made inquiries about the receipt in Neale's pocket? This must be a favorite rendezvous spot. She suggested it, after all. Close to her apartment, she said.

He must recover quickly, conceal his reaction. Act as if he has arrived for lunch, eager to see her. He watches as she searches her purse, pulls out a silver cigarette case, extracts one, and holds it in midair. He reaches inside his jacket.

The flame flickers. "Thank you," she says, a half smile on her lips.

He does not trust himself to speak. An awkward acknowledgement. A clearing of his throat.

"I thought you'd got lost," she says between puffs. "Sit down. We must order before I starve." A small laugh, her head thrown back so he can see the paleness of her neck. She wears a light green dress, the color of spring leaves, a thin matching belt at her waist, her hair combed back from her forehead and brushed up into a twist.

Harry forces himself to look at her, to concentrate on her words. His brain sorts quickly, ticks through the evidence, and revises what he knows. The knot in his stomach hardens. Connections to all three men. What did Mick say? She figures in with Balas. She knew Neale. Chief Gaska was fond of Neale, she said. Neale had no need of a translator, but Laura, installed in perfect position, observed Gaska's habits and appointments. Harry tries not to think of Laura as Neale's murderer, plunging the knife seven times into his body. She is too slight, but she could have been the bait to lure him in, catch him unawares. Doubtless, that would explain Neale's lack of caution. But motive? Passion gone wrong? Her cool demeanor suggests otherwise. Is Laura Savic a buyer or seller of information? For what purpose? He does not want to believe she supports Balas and his extremists.

He pushes aside the inevitable personal questions. How big a fool am I? He realizes that he has prolonged, even damaged, their investigation, endangered Mick's life. Not to mention his own. At some future date, in the wee hours, atop a heavy stool in the sole company of a beefy bartender and several shots of whiskey, he will examine his shortcomings. Admit to himself, at least, what he dares not confess to anyone else. For now, he must make things right.

The waiter arrives, starched white apron tied around his middle, pencil poised. Harry flips open the menu, finds his voice. "I hope

you planned a long lunch. I'm going to have a bit of everything."
To start, he orders hot fish soup, then *paprikás krumpli*—stew with
spiced sausage and potatoes—followed by sweet dumplings with
vanilla custard. "And a bottle of Egri Bikaver."

He reaches across the table, takes her hand, warm to the
touch. In a voice as light as he can manage, "Let's talk about
Tennyson Neale."

She straightens in her chair, her back rigid against it. He
notes the weary lines around her eyes, as if she has not slept.
A pained expression flickers across her face, then disappears.
"I must have mistaken your purpose." She lowers her head
slightly, looks up at him, blinks her long lashes, a small attempt
at flirtation. "I assumed, hoped, this was a romantic invitation."
She wraps a finger around his thumb and squeezes. "I told you
all I know."

Harry waits while the waiter opens the wine, "Just leave it
there," and indicates a spot on the table. When the waiter has
gone, he releases her hand and fills her glass. He has to be clear
without sounding gruff, worse yet, personally injured.

"You neglected to say you were with Neale the night he died,
that you shared a whiskey."

She presses her lips together, touches her neck. He watches
her face.

"Kávé," she says, looking him straight in the eye. "We shared
a cigarette and kávé. Tennyson didn't drink whiskey. Always said
he couldn't stomach the taste of it. Beer, ale as you call it, was
his liking."

"Mmm." He marvels at her calmness, thinks through her
remark. Something doesn't fit about the whiskey. His conscious
mind recognizes it, but he can't lay a finger on what it might be.

"You can't be shocked," she says, a new directness in her gaze. He senses a resignation in her tone.

"Truly, I am."

She tilts her head, twists around to gauge the proximity of the nearest occupied table. "Truth isn't always the best thing."

"There's no one who can hear." He looks around to reassure her.

She gives a small snort, "This is Budapest. There is always someone who hears. Half of the people in this room work for Colonel Vací. Those who don't are relatives of party officials. Most in the kitchen work for Chief Gaska. Usually, they keep their distance. Unless you give them cause."

"I need to know who you work for." He is more than curious as to where she stands, but he does not expect her to reveal it. Is she a paid informant? One thing is certain: She is no one's fool.

She doesn't answer immediately. Her eyes meet his. He senses exhaustion and sadness in her. Before she speaks, she touches his cheek, places two warm fingers on his lips. "If I'm to answer your questions, we must appear as if we are in love." Again, a quick pause. "At least for the moment." She raises her eyebrows in question.

"Not hard to contemplate."

"Laugh now," she says, "and kiss my hand while I tell you a story." Laura lowers her voice, leans forward to speak. In the creation of Czechoslovakia, Komárno was divided, she says. The half north of the Danube went to the new republic, the southern half, south of the Danube, remained with Hungary. Angry Hungarians vowed to take the north back, claiming a majority of the citizenry as Magyars. The hostility began with words, newspaper letters, editorials. Later, there were signs in the streets, rocks through windows. Then stalking and persecuting Czech citizens. Laura learned how vicious the Hungarian extremists could be when the violence claimed her brother, a bullet to his chest in the dead of night as he lay in his bed. Then, her cousin, betrayed by an acquaintance, was kicked to death in an alley.

"You've heard of the Czech resistance." With her napkin, she pretends to wipe a smudge from his chin.

It takes him a moment to realize what she is saying. She is searching his face now.

"This is who you are?" He remembers to smile and touch her arm while his eyes, worried now, stare at hers with interest.

"One of many," she says. "Ours is the most active group. We have lines of communication with the others."

"How long?" he asks. He now understands her reticence, the subtle questions, the distance she maintains. In one sense, he is relieved. In another, he is alarmed.

"I arrived in Budapest with a small group that works to discover what we must overcome, when events will occur. You understand why I cannot divulge more, what it means if the others are caught."

He considers the consequences of her admission. He will not place her in greater danger. "What did Neale have to do with it? That's all I'm after."

"A source. He provided information. We paid for it."

Arriving with two bowls of steaming soup and a cut of brown bread, the waiter fussily arranges the bowls, cautions them to wait for the soup to cool, pours wine. Harry notices that the waiter lingers, as if he requires further instructions. Harry is careful to appear patient, in no hurry, a leisurely lunch with a beautiful woman. He tries the soup. "We'll take our time over the soup," he says. As the waiter is walking away, he turns and looks back at them, an appraising look.

Harry waits a moment longer, unsure of what just happened. "Was Neale further involved? With the organization, I mean?" Perhaps he and Mick have been looking at the wrong motive for Neale's death. There is more to seemingly simple explanations. If Neale was involved with the Czech resistance and others in Budapest were aware, Neale placed himself in a separate realm of espionage.

She looks at him over the rim of her glass. "Tennyson was charming and transparent. He liked his beer and his paydays. Nothing else mattered, as far as I could tell. No higher calling for him. I often wondered if all British operatives were the same."

Harry almost winced. She didn't know Tennyson Neale at all. At least not the Neale he knew. "Who arranged the exchanges?"

"Tennyson and I would meet at various cafés, those that are crowded and popular. Sometimes, we would leave the café, disappear around the corner or down the street, check into a hotel or schedule a massage to throw off suspicion."

"How often?"

"Whenever Tennyson had something for us, he would visit Gaska's office, drop a photo on my desk. He made it appear to the office staff as if he was obsessed with me."

Easy to imagine. "Hence, the preposterous story of the nude photographs."

"Not so preposterous," she says, a widening smile, leaving him to guess at the truth of it.

She breaks off a piece of bread, swirls it in the soup. "On the back of the photo, he would place a number, the price of the documents or photos he was selling. When we could pay, I would contact him."

"You bought something the night he died?" Harry now understands the seemingly random numbers on the back of the photographs.

She gives a little cough and drops a bit of bread into her lap, creating a spot on her dress. She calls over the waiter, sheepishly requests another napkin. She rises, heads for the ladies room, Harry left wondering if she will return or if she needs time to decide what she will tell him.

He waits, sips enough wine to empty the glass. He wishes he could reach into his jacket pocket, retrieve his notebook and record what she has said. She reappears, touches his shoulder, resumes her seat, now very much at ease, ready to talk. Harry plays his role, holding her hand, brushing a wisp of hair from her cheek, the attentive companion.

"The last night I saw Tennyson, he said he had information. Very recent, very significant. Those were his words. A bit after nine o'clock, he called and wanted to meet. This was not like him. Not like him at all. It would be dangerous for both of us. He was to leave soon. A new assignment, he said. But I would remain here in Budapest, exposed. After I spoke to him, I managed to get in contact with my friends. It wasn't easy. I only prayed there was no surveillance on them that night. I told them about the urgency in Tennyson's voice. It had to be important, I assured them. They arranged the exchange spot and time. A lot of money, he wanted. I suspected this was his last opportunity to sell, and he was taking full advantage."

Laura pushes aside the soup, lights a cigarette.

"No reason to kill him." Harry is astounded at the casual nature of her description. His heart hardens, and he feels a growing anger. "You could have stolen the documents and left him alive. Roughed him up a bit."

Her eyes widen. Her throat works for a moment. Eventually, she speaks. "No. No. My God, you think . . ." She grips his sleeve. "No. My friends would not kill Tennyson." She whispers it, surveying the room quickly, anxious that no one overheard.

Relieved at her stunned reaction, Harry breathes—a breath of profound relief—and pats her hand. "Best be careful. Let me handle it. Put your napkin to your lips." He signals the waiter. "The lady isn't feeling well. I'm afraid the soup didn't agree with her. We'll take the bill and be on our way."

Acting as if she is suddenly ill, she rises slowly and leans on him. He tucks her hand into the crook of his elbow, helps her to the door, speaks loudly enough for others to hear, "Fresh air. Take a few deep breaths. A cold drink will help."

卌

"Who then?" asks Harry. "Who else knew where he'd be?"

They sit on a bench in Klauzál Square, deserted except for a kit of pigeons prancing at their feet. She shakes her head.

"There were others in the café that night. Tennyson warned me about them. A group of men watching us from the corner, but I doubt any of them overheard what we were saying. Even so, I never mentioned . . ." He can feel her hesitation. "My God. I wrote the location of the exchange on a napkin." She clamps her hand over her mouth as if to call it back, eyes darting left then right. "We were always careful, I always took everything with me, nothing left behind. But I was angry with him for raising the price. He was being difficult. I walked away, the napkin still on the table. The others might have seen."

"What did you write?"

"The time, the place, all of it. Two o'clock. A path along the river under the Chain Bridge. Under the stairs. Anyone who found it could have arrived before him." Her face is stricken, a nervous tic emerges under one eye. "What have I done? He was concerned that one of them would follow me. After I left, I don't know what he did."

"Not your doing. He was in a rush, forgot to be cautious. He should have picked up the napkin," says Harry.

"He said he would make the exchange the following day. Tomorrow, he said. But I insisted it be that night, told him it was already arranged," she says. "How stupid of me."

That's it, then, thinks Harry. The timeline falls into place. From the café, Neale rushed to Sándor's to develop the images. Then stopped at Kovacs' home to drop one package before showing up at the bridge with the pages he had just developed. Two sales in one night. In a hurry, with a fistful of pounds on his mind, he neglected to be alert. It cost him his life. A lesson for us all.

Laura continues, "You need to know, the exchange never occurred, at least not with my friends. They were run off from the rendezvous point, the money stolen from them. They managed to get away, one of them shot and nearly dead, the other beaten. They never saw Tennyson. Nor did they recognize their attackers. Only that they wore uniforms. We never received the information Tennyson was selling. At first, we assumed he'd arranged it as a swindle to make off with the money, that there actually were no photographs, no papers. He'd made them up. Then, when I went to work that morning, Chief Gaska announced that his body was found. I couldn't believe it. At the end of his life, after the good he had done for us, we doubted him."

"We're surrounded by people who kill for a piece of paper, a sliver of film. Like the rest of us, Tennyson took his chances. More so than most."

He looks across the square. People in twos and threes crowd the sidewalks; vendors crank the striped awnings of their food carts, aromas of cotton candy and grilled sausages fill the air. A boy in a bright blue shirt and knee-high short pants, one arm high in the air, head cocked, eyes glancing backward, races into the open field releasing a ball of string through his fingers until a thin yellow kite rises and holds its place against the sky. The child laughs—a sweet sound of spontaneous joy—and tightens his hold on the string.

She pauses, seeking the right words. "Having our own country, it was a dream of people of my parents' age. It is nothing you would understand. For twenty years now, it is ours. We will not give it up. We will fight. We have armed ourselves. We must do what we can. The French and the British say they will intervene, but we cannot count on them."

A hesitant nod. I would not count on us. No, not by a long shot. He considers the turns of this investigation, the growing number of people and motives. What small actors we are on this unsteady stage.

He breaks the silence. "This is why you're involved with Balas. All business, is it?"

When their eyes meet, he sees sadness and something else, defiance, perhaps. "It's the best way to deal with him."

Harry can't control his next question. "And me?" Harry considers his immediate and unusual attraction to Laura Savic. Then chides himself. What was he thinking? Asking such a question to a woman he's known little more than a week. Perhaps

Tennyson Neale's untimely end has cast a different light on things. Summoning unaccustomed feelings. Feelings he dare not name.

She presses her hand against the bodice of her dress, laughs, a warm laugh, then takes his hand. "Enjoyable as our business has been, it is indeed business. You are an appealing man, Harry Douglas. Not as necessary to us as Kristof Balas, mind you." A deep sigh. "As you've witnessed, his outward charm disappears in an instant. Leaving arrogance, vanity. And remarkable conversation." She pauses, sighs to herself. "He has all manner of secret schemes. He likes to gain power over others, have them in his debt." She reaches to pin up a strand of hair that has escaped her French twist. "At certain times, he is an enthusiastic talker. I am his eager audience. As much as he cares about anyone, I made certain he cares about me, or at least wants to be with me."

"Your gut feeling. Does Balas know anything about Neale's death?" Harry's brain is connecting the pieces. The timeline. The major players. The motive? Which motive? Get the documents for one's own use? Prevent them from getting out? There's the key. Laura's friends need the information and are willing to pay a handsome price for it. She insists they didn't kill Neale, that they never got hands on the documents.

Laura watches the boy with the kite, as if looking to him for her answer. "He may," she says.

"What does that mean? He does or he doesn't." Harry wants to believe she is telling the truth. He marvels once more at her coolness, wishes he could know her in another place and time, break through the facade that is Laura Savic.

"I'm sure he knows something about it, but I don't know what part he played," she says, showing no sign of anger at his disbelief. "Kristof has people who do things for him. Favors, he calls them. He's eager to be Regent, desperate to gain position before the previous leader of Arrow Cross is released from prison."

"He would play the hero if Hungary regains lost parts of your territory, if Czechoslovakia disappears."

She raises a slender finger, a teacher correcting a pupil. "Not necessarily. If the Germans swallow us, take what is ours, it may not be Kristof who ascends to power. Yes, the Germans will send Horthy away, then take Hungary for themselves. Kristof wants to keep things as they are until he becomes the formal leader. He told me he must move quickly. He says he and Arrow Cross will stand up to Hitler, renounce the Jews, strip them of their rights, deport them, and then negotiate a pact. In this way, Hitler will leave Hungary in place—independent and strong. Kristof will be the Regent."

"He believes that, does he?" Harry sits back on the bench, feels the warmth of the sun through his coat, replaces his hat and pushes back the brim. "You think Balas found out Neale was going to sell this information to your friends and had his friends get rid of him?"

"I'm not sure how it went. I think there's another person involved. Someone with something to lose. Perhaps as big a loss as Kristof's." She rises. "Let's walk."

Harry gently pulls her hand so that she again sits down beside him. He tells her about the conversation he overheard between Toth and the unknown accomplice. "Any idea who that might be?" Elbows resting on his knees, Harry looks at her sideways. Balas must have hundreds of contacts in Budapest and elsewhere. Back in Milan, he and Mick would know who they were—the frequency of their meetings, their influence. Balas' networks would have been identified, catalogued, and mapped. Here in

Budapest, he and Mick possess no such information. Harry is seasoned in developing surveillance networks, and knows where to begin. Start with the simplest of notions. Besides Laura, with whom and where has she seen Balas?

She answers quickly. "No names. Kristof never mentioned a name. It is someone he's known for a while. Two nights ago, he rescheduled a dinner date, said he had to meet an old friend." She stopped, as if trying to remember. "No, that's not how he phrased it. An old contact. That's the word. An old contact. Kristof crowed like the rooster he is, said that this person needed his help. One of those quid pro quos, he called it. I asked what he meant. He said, 'Favor for favor. I give him what he wants, he uses his influence.' Later in the conversation, he said, 'not that I will need them, but the old man has the perfect contacts.'"

Old man. Contacts. Just out of reach. The facts out in front, but nowhere near his grasp. "That's all of it?" asks Harry.

"Yes, he said he was off to Zoltán's."

The image springs forth. He smiles. Clear as day. "You say Neale never drank whiskey?"

She looks at him quizzically. "Not in my presence. Never."

"I think I know who has those documents, what they contain, and maybe even why they were taken," says Harry. "I just don't know where they are." He tells her about the title page of the Case Green plan. "It's going to happen soon. Plans are in place. There's to be an assassination. On Tuesday. The German ambassador. The Czech resistance will be blamed. Your people need to leave Budapest immediately. Otherwise, they'll be arrested."

"Erik," she whispers the name. "Then what?"

"Then Case Green becomes Operation Green. Your government, your fortifications, your army must be ready."

"We have to alert them," she says.

"First, you need the plan. To know where the assaults will occur. Sad to say, your friends will not be credible unless they present the details. That's why Neale's price was so high. He knew what he had."

"How do we get it, this plan?" she asks.

"Balas has it hidden somewhere. I'm sure of it." He and Mick don't have time to figure it out. A long shot, at best. It could be anywhere.

"From what you've told me, Balas thinks he has time, a few months, to solidify his leadership. Keeping the invasion plan out of Czech hands will give Balas leverage with the Germans." Harry is not entirely convinced of the argument he is making. He and Mick have to get hands on that plan. More than anything, he knows Balas and his Arrow Cross party are committed to Hungary's independence, establishing a pure, nationalist, anti-Semitic state, at whatever cost. Balas and others of his ilk hate the Czechs. Among other purposes, there is malice in Balas' actions. Politics is one thing; hate another. Mixing the two creates a deadly combination.

"We will not give away our country," she says. "We have the right and the means to defend it."

"He doesn't know you're Czech? Nothing about your background?"

The question makes her snicker. She is, he senses, troubled by the subject. "Only that I'm a pretty girl from the country. That's all he wants to know."

"You're certain?" Harry will not place her in further danger. Harry is sure Balas has killed once. Likely there are others. Such ambition does not hesitate to clear obstacles in its path.

"There's no way he could know. I've told no one," she confirms. "I have an idea where he's hidden it. A place he has mentioned." She pauses. "More than once."

"Will he show you the plan?" Harry asks. "At least tell you where it's kept?"

"He may," she says, tentatively, "if I word my request well. What reason can I give?"

"Appeal to his vanity. Men long to show off their prizes," says Harry. "In Balas' case, he'll likely trade, or pretend to trade, for something that puts him a move ahead. Tell him the matter is urgent. You have information he can use. Information that will affect his faster ascent to the Regency."

"First, I must communicate with my friends. Tell them they must go."

"I can get word to them," Harry says.

"No. I will not compromise them."

"Not to me?"

"Not to anyone."

Chapter Twenty-Eight

11 **June**. Kristof Balas replaces the receiver, frowns, and inhales one last puff. A quick flick of his wrist sends the glowing stub in a long arc through the open window. He watches it land on the street below, and mumbles to himself. How can she know what he does not? Absurd. He will show her she is wrong.

"A problem?" Brinkley arrives, makes himself comfortable in the chair opposite Balas's desk, crosses one leg, displaying his expensive silk socks.

Balas almost growls. "She claims to know something of utmost importance, critical information. She was insistent."

"Who is she?"

"Gaska's interpreter," says Balas.

"Ah. The beautiful Jewess," says Brinkley. "Laura."

"She's no Jew." Balas sneers at the notion.

"Of course she is. Like it or not, there are a few beautiful Jews in Budapest."

"You have the wrong woman." Balas' eyes narrow. "How do you know this?"

"Gaska told me."

"How does Gaska know a Jew from a Christian?" says Balas. One more comment, he'll throw the uninvited Brinkley out.

"Laura told him Madeleine Klapper, the writer, is her grand-mother. As Klapper's writings suggest, she is indeed a Jew."

"Hmmm." Before his meeting with Laura tonight, he will pay Gaska a visit. Right now, he has to get rid of Brinkley. "You informed me. I'll remember it."

Brinkley shrugs, uncrosses his legs, yawns. He is in no hurry. "You'd best remember a lot of things. Keep in mind what we've done. What did you do with Neale's papers?"

"Not now." Balas checks his watch. He has no intention of telling Brinkley anything further. The idea is to know as little as possible. What was done was done. "We have five minutes. What else?"

"I received their report before I came, changed a paragraph or two, a name here and there. Deleted the photos. Nothing of the slightest interest now. Stamped it for the file room. Tennyson Neale, deceased minor operative, fraudulent in his duties, paid the price. End of situation. The bureaucrats will bury it." Brinkley regards his fingernails, an ugly smile on his lips. "I told Douglas and MacLeod to turn in their notes before they depart. At first, they balked, but finally agreed. They'll be on a plane tomorrow morning."

"Their bags will be searched." Balas' voice is sharp. "Nothing gets out. We can't afford for your British colleagues to learn how predatory the Führer has become. It will influence their recommendations."

Brinkley nods.

"You are certain they will be eliminated?" Balas asks.

"Douglas and MacLeod are expendable. The arrangements are secure. Plane crashes in the Tátra mountains. The Bureau has no time for more than a hasty investigation. Two Commonwealth analysts with questionable reputations. End of story. Regrettably, the pilot will be an additional casualty."

"A phone call, nothing more, when they're gone. For good." Balas stands, walks to the door, his tread heavy on the marble. He opens the door wide. "When will I see a favorable article?"

Brinkley recognizes the threat. "Extolling the virtues of the Arrow Cross philosophy?"

"And its leader," says Balas.

"Within the week," Brinkley concedes, his mouth puckering. He tilts his chin, straightens his public school tie and walks out the door.

Balas scratches at his jaw. He trusts her. As much as he trusts any woman. She can't be a damn Jew. He's slept with her, told her things he would tell no one else. My God. His mind races. Where did they meet? Gaska's office. The police do not employ Jews. Employment in any government office is forbidden to Jews. Gaska does not disobey the law. Not now, with Vací watching every move. Her last name? Savic. Not a Jew name. She is alluring, her skin soft, eyes deep and dark. Available. What did she say about her background? Born in the country, that's what she said. Jews don't live in the country. She can't be a Jew. Jews are born in the city. She's not built like a Jew. He pictures her slender body in his bed, in the steaming tub they inhabited the night before. Jews are squarely built with sharp noses and heavy brows. A kink in their hair. The women unattractive. Only a Jew looks at them. Laura is beautiful with straight black hair, smooth olive skin. More like a gypsy.

He picks up the phone. Where is Gaska? He has to sound calm, conversational, work it in with other concerns, questions. No anxiety. He can't just come out with it. Gaska, the celebrated gossip, will spread rumors everywhere. What is a grandmother, after all? One-eighth. One-eighth Jew. In any amount, impure. Like a blanket, within hours the news will cover the city. The others will not forgive him, his standing in the party will collapse. He will be ruined.

He stands at the window, staring at the seven tribes of his ancestors. The Magyars. The pure confederacy. He has spent his life working to restore Hungary's purity. No woman—no Jewess, by God—will stain it. If Brinkley is right, she will pay for this.

Chapter Twenty-Nine

11 June. The night is warm, the air heavy. Harry sits at an outside table at the small café on Fishermen's Bastion, turning pages of the *Magyarság* evening edition, nursing a cup of tepid coffee, a pretense at normality. He keeps one eye on his watch. Thirty meters away, on the west wall of Matthias Church, Mick leans, one foot propped behind him, pretending to enjoy an after-dinner cigarette. For nearly twenty minutes, they have been stationed here.

Buda Castle, its location chosen in the thirteenth century for the high ground above the river, offers the best views of Buda and Pest. At this hour, the castle and surrounding buildings are bathed in light, an eerie glow emanating from the iron lamps that line the streets. The music of Bartók plays in the background.

Five minutes past nine. Two familiar figures emerge on the street, her arm looped through his, her shoulder pressed against him. They walk at a rapid pace along the tree-lined avenue. Laura has been persuasive. Balas has taken the bait.

Soundlessly, Harry slides his chair into the shadow of the café awning. He holds the newspaper high enough to shield his face, low enough to gauge their progress. Out of the corner of his eye, he sees Mick drop his cigarette, stub the remains with his heel and move farther along the wall, head down, hands in his pockets.

Earlier, they had agreed that Harry will follow Laura and Balas into the caves while Mick remains at the entrance. Once Laura and Balas come into sight, there will be no means for Harry to communicate, no signals that might alert others who may be watching.

Laura's afternoon call to Balas was simple enough. She told him she was concerned for his safety. She had come across a vital document called Case Green that provided key information related to Balas' rise to power and the German interest in invading Czechoslovakia and returning Hungary's territories. In the document, Balas' name, she told him, was mentioned more than once. Balas boasted that he knew about Case Green, that it contained no mention of him, nothing as she described. She suggested that the document Balas had might be a decoy, a ploy to deceive him and the Arrow Cross. The Germans were known for such things. He asked how and where she came to possess the document she spoke of. She ignored his questions and insisted, for the security of his own ambitions, that he compare the two versions. She would meet him, she said, at nine o'clock near the entrance to the underground labyrinth at Buda Castle.

Laura glances back as she and Balas enter the caves. She whispers in Balas' ear. The next instant, she turns and looks at Harry, and he feels a nameless apprehension, hears a small voice of admonition. Before they disappear into the dark cavern, Balas takes her by the elbow and Harry reimagines the ugly scene at

Zoltán's, Balas grabbing her wrist and holding on, squeezing until she winced. Harry heads to the entrance and follows them inside, his back to the wall, listening for their footfall. Certain he is undetected, he steps through a low archway and descends a broad staircase, scarcely missing an orange tabby, asleep on the second stair. The cat does not stir from her position, just raises her head and blinks once, languidly, in his direction. Harry has heard rumors of the famed stray cats of Buda Castle.

Down he walks, one long flight, then another until he reaches a vast open space. Around him stands the castle labyrinth—at this hour, empty of tourists. It is an underworld city of towering pillars and walkways lit every few meters by overhead gas lamps, the walls above them blackened over time.

The air is suffocatingly thin. Underground spaces have always chilled him. Visions of blinding darkness and trembling quakes. Overwhelmed by a dizzying vertigo, he sucks in one breath, then another, cursing the black veil that threatens his consciousness. He takes a step back, conceals himself behind a pillar, and drops to his knees. Head down, he fights the nausea, swallows the bile in his throat, and wills his heart to pump harder. Propped against the pillar, he wipes the sweat from his brow. He sees movement ahead. Unsteadily, he heaves himself up. Two figures at some distance walk together, arm-in-arm, the larger figure—Balas—on the left. The white stripes of Laura's dress recede. Harry steps carefully, making no sound, knowing his footsteps will echo throughout the cavern. A draft of wind sifts through the passageway, and he assures himself there is, after all, a continuous source of air within the cave. His targets still in sight, he confirms the gun in his waistband and the knife holster at his ankle.

In the space of two minutes, they walk through a line of sculpted arches. Overhead lights bathe the massive pillars in an orange hue and cast elongated shadows. He follows a trail of steady chatter—Laura's way of telling him her location. He stays well behind them. When he hears the close murmur of conversation, he stops and waits until he is sure they have continued.

Eventually, the broad corridor descends a few steps into a narrower passage. Harry smells the dampness. The temperature drops, and the overhead light grows dimmer. He touches the walls, rife with mottled spots of water. In her light dress, Laura will be chilled. Balas wears a topcoat, its shoulder epaulets bobbing as he walks. The man has been this way before.

Voices drift once again, then stillness. Harry recognizes a tinkling sound—an entry bell—and the creak of a gate opening. A flash of light, a torch of some sort, glows from the ceiling. Crouched low, Harry creeps forward to a wrought iron gate—floor to ceiling, vertical bars evenly spaced—that stands ajar. He notes a heavy lock on the outside. He senses that Laura and Balas are not far from the gate. Harry backtracks a step into deep shadow. Their footsteps recede, and Harry moves forward. He silences the small entry bell and edges through the gate.

Smoke—the heavy presence of oil from the gas lamps—fills the hallway. Harry blinks away the irritation and swallows the cough in his throat. Through the haze, he sees that it is a short passage, one that dead-ends into a blank wall some thirty meters beyond. His heart thumps. The hallway is empty.

On either side, there begins a series of doors, heavily framed with knobs of old bronze and silver, all dark wood, weathered, some splintered, some decayed at the bottom where the moisture has been. On the right, one door is open, light flickering from within, faint sounds of scraping. He edges nearer until he is a mere ten meters away. Laura's voice is indecipherable—its soft timbre echoing off the ceiling and the walls. He dares to move closer, strains to listen.

"So this is where you hide your treasures," she says. "How clever. Here is a slim chance of discovery."

"No chance at all," says Balas.

"You did not say how you came to possess this document," she says.

Harry hears a low grunt, what sounds like a drawer as it slides open and closes again. "There is no harm in telling you now," says Balas. "My people stole it."

"Stole from whom?"

"A British agent, I'm told. No one you would know."

"A British agent," she repeats. "A spy, you mean? Surely he didn't give it up voluntarily."

"He expected to be paid for it," says Balas. "What he got was something different."

"How can you be sure these papers are authentic?"

"A reliable source," says Balas.

"One of your Arrow Cross colleagues?"

"Nothing like that. One of the agent's own countrymen."

"There's a turnabout. You trust such a person?"

"There is no trust involved. He has his special interests. I have mine. I use him. He uses me. We both know who we are. He made it a point to be on the scene when the documents were taken."

Brinkley. Who else could it be? Harry wants to hear more, to confirm his conclusion, but Laura changes topic. "It's cold. Hurry, get your package and let us get out of here. We will compare the two in a warmer place."

"Not yet." He hears Balas clearly, a louder, clearer voice now. "Why did you decide on the labyrinth?"

"How could you forget? Several times, you told me of the royal residence and this enormous place. The underground city, you called it. As a child, you said you explored the caves and found places where no one would find you. I wanted to see what you spoke of. I was disappointed when your meeting cancelled our dinner at the Halaszbasta. I hoped to see it then."

"There is no better view of Budapest." There is a new tone in Balas's voice.

Laura asks. "Is this all of it? Anything else?"

"Anything else?" Balas repeats, his voice loud and harsh. "Now that we're sharing secrets, I have learned that your grandmother is a famous writer."

"Yes. She's quite accomplished."

"A Jew writer," he says. "Is this true?"

"Why do you ask?"

"I have been with a Jewess."

Harry hears a grunt, then sounds of a scuffle. He reaches for his gun and faces the door, his finger on the trigger. He tries to imagine the scene inside.

"You've ruined me," Balas shouts. "You'll pay for this. You Jews will pay."

A sound Harry recognizes as a slap. A short scream from Laura.

Harry plunges forward and plants his feet at the threshold, gun moving left to right. The room is larger and darker than he imagined. Shadows dance on the walls. He cannot make out which shadow is Laura, which is Balas. He sees Balas shove Laura, one large hand to her shoulder. Laura's knees buckle, and her arms go out to stop her fall.

A pistol in Balas' right hand is aimed at Harry. Two sharp cracks fill the chamber and echo into the hallway, sending echoes deep into the labyrinth.

Another loud crack.

Harry pulls the trigger twice. Balas starts forward, stops, starts again. Harry stands firm in the doorway, blocking Balas' path.

Balas tries to shove past Harry. He grabs a fistful of Harry's coat and roars. Harry catches Balas' arm and shoves him back into the room.

Balas charges again. The weight of him knocks the wind from Harry's chest. He manages to stay upright, but Balas is through the door and into the hallway.

Balas reaches the gate and races through, Harry a second behind.

The gate slams shut.

Locked inside, Harry watches Balas flee. Harry fires, but cannot get a clear shot through the bars. Judging from the manner in which Balas moves, the way he holds his left side, Harry is sure he has been wounded. At the entry, Mick will recognize it. Provided Balas exits the way they entered. Is there another way out?

Laura lays crumpled against the wall, legs folded beneath her. Her chest rises and falls. A sharp odor alerts him she is bleeding. She struggles to sit up. A stain darkens on the left side of her dress. He shrugs off his coat, his only thought to stop the blood oozing from her side.

His hand touches hers. Colder than ice. Her fingers tighten around his hand, her voice weak and rough. "Go. Take it to Erik. At The Rétes." She motions to the envelope lying on the floor. In his haste, Balas has left it behind.

Pressing his coat against her side, Harry shushes her, touches her forehead. "First things first," he says. "We'll stop this bleeding. Then, we'll find Erik."

"Now," she whispers. "Take it. Leave me."

Harry calculates the time it will take to reach a hospital. There is a chance. If Mick can open the goddamned gate. Where is Mick? He must have seen Balas, must have heard the echo of shots. What the hell is taking him so long?

Laura closes her eyes and Harry notes the sharpness of her cheekbones, the line of her neck. Her breath evens and slows, raising his hopes. She is strong. He curses the dampness, the cold floor, but there is nowhere else. He dares not move her. Instead, he kneels beside her, one hand a firm pressure on her side, the other holding her hand. He speaks softly, a steady stream of story, whatever comes to mind. He describes the thrilling last furlong at San Siro, a winning flush in Baden-Baden, his work in Milan, early training in London. All the while, he wonders, had she given a thought whether she had walked into a trap? Had he pressured her to do it? She might have refused, might have told him it was dangerous. He might have found another way. He curses himself for not anticipating the extent of Balas' rage.

In the next moments, there exists a mysterious sense of quiet. There is no struggle. His hand holds hers. He hears a rasp of breath. Her eyes open wide, and she smiles at him. "Marek," she says. The air—and with it, that resolute spirit—leaves her, and he is very much alone.

Chapter Thirty

12 **June.** Laura was right. The envelope contains detailed plans for the coming invasion of Czechoslovakia, including maps for Hungary's redrawn boundaries. A deadly plan to further the Reich's reach, prompted by the staged deaths of German citizens and a German ambassador.

Though other men thrust the knife, it is clear Balas and Brinkley murdered Tennyson Neale. Harry remains unsure whether Tennyson died to extend each man's self-interest or as part of a larger plot. Balas wants to secure the Regency before the Germans take control of Czechoslovakia. Likely, Arrow Cross members ambushed Neale that night. Is Brinkley a German sympathizer? Was he instructed to keep the predatory Case Green plan from the British foreign minister? Britain and France are obliged to intervene if Czechoslovakia is attacked. Britain's reluctance is widely known.

After Mick contacted Marton Gaska to report Laura's death and made arrangements to remove her body, Harry and Mick set about examining the packet of photographs. They spend the rest of the night inside a briefing room near Gaska's office piecing together the chain of events that has kept the Case Green plan from seeing the light of day.

They know better than to return to the Gellért. No telling what lays in wait. Still, they must find a way to get the Case Green documents, as well as their full report, to London. They neither trust Brinkley nor the diplomatic pouch.

"You've got hands on our original?"

"No fears," says Mick. "The package is locked in Zoltán's safe."

"Does he know?"

"I told him we needed a favor. I'd pick it up in a day or two. He didn't ask questions."

"Simple enough." Harry and Mick need to put distance between themselves and Balas' followers. "Nagy's a safe contact. We may be able to solve one of our problems." Harry looks at his watch. Almost six o'clock. "Zoltán's bound to be awake. He once told me he sleeps three hours a night. No more."

"Best get to Nagy immediately," says Mick. "According to Brinkley's instructions, our plane flies out in three hours."

"I have a bad feeling about those flight arrangements. From the start, that first day in Neale's flat. That whiskey glass bothered me. Brinkley, this fussy peacock, picks up a stranger's whiskey and tosses it back. It stayed with me."

"I figured he couldn't pass up a drink," says Mick. "No matter the circumstances."

Harry continues, "Turns out Neale never drank whiskey. According to Laura, he never touched it. So whose glass was it, tucked under the bed? The fastidious man who finished it off."

"So, Brinkley had been there already. Searched the place before we arrived," Mick says. "He made sure, or so he thought, there was nothing left to find."

"That bastard set up Neale and had him killed," says Harry. "Brinkley's got his own game. I don't know what it is, but we're definitely not in it to the end. Who's to say Balas' brutes aren't waiting on the tarmac?"

"By now, Gaska may have arrested Balas for Laura's murder."

"Not likely. With sufficient proof, Vací may. Problem is, Laura's dead and I'm hardly a credible witness."

"There are other means," says Mick. "Balas has a bullet in his side."

"Might make for a strong reason for interrogation in Vací's cellar," says Harry. "All the same, we've got priorities. Revenge not among them. Not today, at any rate."

"What about this Erik? He has to be the man I met in the restaurant. Erik Drucek, he told me his name. By his own admission, he's a Czech national doing business in Budapest. No shrinking violet. He can't be too far underground."

"I'll get to him. After we do our job," Harry says. "Doubtless he's waiting for her to contact him, most likely at this Rétes place."

"You don't have to do this alone," says Mick.

"I'll handle it."

卌

Zoltán is not pleased to see them. He opens the door, as if he's been expecting them, and hurries them inside. He secures the shades on either side of the door.

"These two, I am telling myself, they will turn up. I am asking myself, what have they done? I am dreaming in my bed. An intense dream. A raven-haired country woman. Voluptuous, she is. Skillful, larger than life. A happy woman, laughing, singing in my ear. Likely to make me happy. Ach. A loud banging on the tavern door. Five o'clock. The sun not yet shining. I am asking, who can it be? A lost patron who cannot find his way. No, he will go elsewhere. A real woman, in the flesh, who desires Zoltán. There are such women. With hope in my blood, I am finding my slippers. I am wrapping my robe. Who is it? Who is banging on my door? No one but your stiff friend. British Brinkley."

"Brinkley." They say it together. "What did he want?"

"He is asking for you. Excited, he is. Concerned, he says. Do I know the police will close my tavern if I am abetting a crime. What crime? I am asking him. Is this a threat? Is he now working for Gaska?"

"It wouldn't be Gaska who sent him. We've just come from there."

"Who then?" asks Zoltán.

"Balas," says Mick.

Zoltán frowns, pulls cups from the bar, pours dark liquid from the brewed pot, thrusts them at Harry and Mick. "I am telling him nothing. I am telling him to go. He is interrupting my dreams."

"You think he's still around?" asks Harry.

"I see him getting into taxi."

"This was an hour ago?"

Zoltán shrugs, nods.

Mick stands to one side of the window, lifts the shade with one finger and checks the street. He walks the length of the room, cracks the back door and steps into the alleyway. "A stray cat. Nothing more," he reports. "I came for the package I left in your safe."

"And a phone," says Harry. "If I may, I need to make a call."

Zoltán grunts, heads down the hallway to his office, points, without looking, to a black phone at the end of the bar. "Careful what you will say."

On the first ring, Nagy answers. It is early, he explains, his secretary not yet in. Magda leaves for London this evening, the two of them and a dozen packers are adding final touches to a glass order bound for Vienna's Imperial Hotel. The shipment is to be loaded on a Bulgarian barge and sent upriver tomorrow morning.

"That's precisely why I'm calling," says Harry. "I've a gift to get to London by tomorrow. I'm wondering if Magda would mind adding it to her luggage."

"A gift?" Nagy repeats.

"For a friend, a lady. It's her birthday. She gets upset if the gift is even the slightest bit late," says Harry.

"Ah, an expectant lover. A dire situation," says Nagy.

"I wouldn't ask if it weren't," says Harry.

A moment of silence, as if Nagy is considering it or looking to Magda for a response. Finally, he says, "We're working in the warehouse. 42 Kopaszi gát. There are three warehouses under the Rákóczi Bridge on the Buda side. Come to the first one. My office is on the second level overlooking the factory floor."

"I'll get a taxi," Harry begins.

Zoltán interrupts, his hand covering the mouthpiece. He whispers, "It is buried among the wharves along the river. We will use the delivery truck."

Mick pulls Zoltán's arm, shakes his head. "Too risky. Balas's people are watching. They won't like it."

"Hah," Zoltán says. "Always they are watching." He puts his arm around Mick's shoulders, a smile fading as quickly as it surfaces. "You know nothing of Budapest."

‖‖‖

The truck slows and stops. Two warning thumps on the partition that divides the driver's cab from the cargo bed send Harry and Mick to the floor. A single beam of brightness shines through the top of the partition and falls on the rear entry door, providing just enough light for them to avoid the barrels and boxes scattered about. As Zoltán instructed them, they jam themselves behind a tool bin and the cab partition, a sliver of space wide enough for two men if they lay sideways and do not move. They cover themselves with a tattered tarpaulin, stinking of motor oil. Harry wonders how many others have hidden themselves here and for what purpose—bootlegging? cigarettes? Zoltán is involved in countless schemes. Lying still, they listen to the exchange between Zoltán and another man. The language is Hungarian. In the last two weeks, their command of the language has improved, and they pick up enough of the conversation to understand.

A courteous tone from Zoltán, "Good morning, friend." Several words Harry cannot decode, then, "Work on a hot June morning."

A murmur from the outside, the pitch of a question.

"Nothing in the truck now, a pick up," they hear Zoltán say. "From the wharf."

Another question.

"Of course. Around the back. Have a look. My boss can wait." Zoltán's laugh vibrates the cab, carries through the partition.

Mick nudges Harry's foot. What now?

They feel the weight shift as Zoltán jumps from the seat of the cab to the ground, hear footsteps walking along the side. The hinge of the rear door creaks as it opens.

A new voice. "The barrels. What's in them?"

"Empty," Zoltán says. "Allow me to open them so you will be satisfied."

"We will not waste your boss' time," the man says.

"My boss, your boss. These bastards and their wasted time." Zoltán laughs. "To me, one hour is like another." Another hearty laugh.

The door slams shut. Harry and Mick exhale.

IIIII

They find Jan and Magda in the second floor office, packing a box of gold trimmed stemware. Jan explains, "The restaurant manager is in a panic. The Führer arrives next week. Apparently, he has appalling manners, but insists on a finely set table for lunch and dinner. The china and stemware must be different for each meal."

"One more reason to deny the man's sanity," says Zoltán.

"But good for business," winks Jan.

Harry relates the events of the last twenty-four hours, not all of them, but enough.

"The documents provide information about Germany's plans for both Czechoslovakia and Hungary. Poland in the long term. To prevent their release, a man was killed. The British and French governments must be informed," adds Mick. "This knowledge will affect their decisions."

"It is your job to get the documents to these people?" asks Nagy. Harry nods.

"And you are running from the Arrow Cross," says Magda.

"More than likely," says Harry.

"I recognized the man who stopped me," says Zoltán. "He is Arrow Cross."

"The first thing is to get these invasion plans to London," says Mick.

"What are you asking?" Nagy turns his attention to Harry.

"They are asking me to transport them," says Magda.

Harry nods.

"No. I must decline," says Nagy, no warmth in his voice. "It is too dangerous."

Magda walks to the row of windows overlooking the factory floor, stares down at the assistants packing and labeling the boxes of glassware. She looks at Mick, then at Harry. "My husband worries for me, but we must help. Our country's future lies in cold hands."

"Magda, you are crossing the Austrian and German borders. At the checkpoints, they will search your bags, and take extra pleasure in doing so. You said so yourself. If you are caught . . ." Nagy turns toward his wife.

"They will not suspect. There must be a way," she says.

"Our sons," Nagy reminds her.

"Yes, our sons. We must save them from this madman's dream," she says, staring down again at the workers below.

Harry wonders what he can offer in return for Nagy's support. Refuge? Asylum? "When your play is finished, there are places in London," he pauses, "for your sons and family members," he adds, remembering their conversation on the train.

Nagy's face tells Harry he is not persuaded, but he is thinking. No one speaks.

"A serious offer," Harry says.

Unsmiling, Nagy looks at his wife.

"How many pages?" she asks.

Mick produces their report and the Case Green invasion plan. "Nine, total."

"It will not do to put them in your luggage," Nagy advises. "They will tear it apart looking."

"You forget, my love," she picks up the hem of her long skirt and twirls in a broad circle, one arm extended, eyes to the ceiling, a theatrical pose. "I am merely an empty-headed actress studying lines for a new play. The Countess Maritza can be most convincing."

"I have an idea," says Harry.

Chapter Thirty-One

12 **June**. The evening is cool for mid-June, a fine drizzle has wet the pavement. Magda Nagy, slim and elegant, steps from the taxi. She is dressed in a powder-blue travelling suit, her blonde curls tucked under a gray-and-blue stiff linen hat. Delicate white feathers decorate its crown, and a finely tatted veil covers her forehead. She wears matching suede gloves and shoes, and carries a shoulder bag of brown Catalonian leather, the initials MN set in gold and pressed into its cover.

As Magda and Jan emerge, one porter covers them with an umbrella while another goes round to the boot and discharges two large trunks, a single round hat box, and two makeup cases. As is her custom when she travels, Magda requests, upon her arrival, that a railway porter deliver her cases to the baggage car. This evening, in particular, she is careful not to deviate from her usual practice. Jan carries a square cardboard box, double-taped at the corners and tied with a green ribbon.

On their way to the departure platform she smiles and waves to a scattering of admirers. Jan hangs back several steps and keeps one eye on the luggage as it is loaded, one eye on his glamorous wife. He takes note of the baggage car's location. At the entry door to her carriage, she holds his face, kisses him on both cheeks, then whispers in his ear, "Take care, my love."

He holds her hand, his voice low, "I'll be waiting for your call."

"From Hoek Van Holland," she says. "Ten hours." She calculates the time of her arrival. "Six o'clock. Too early for the sleepy ones in our house." She laughs, determined to wipe the frown from his face.

"No matter the hour. You will call the moment you are safe." He holds tight to her hand.

"I'll be fine. You must trust in that. Do not appear sad." A faint smile, a reassuring nod.

Smoothly, she detaches his hand, takes the box from the crook of his elbow, and touches his cheek. He steadies her while she climbs the two steps to the darkened railway carriage.

The porter directs her to the compartment. She stops in the aisle, looks in. There is one other passenger—a small gray-haired man in a vested linen suit, comfortably established on the forward chair next to the window. One hand rests on a cane that stands upright beside his right leg. The porter turns the latch and slides open the door. The occupant lifts his head, politely doffs his hat, and acknowledges her with a tap of his cane. He is humming a familiar tune. She nods a greeting and sits down in the opposite chair.

The compartment is finely decorated in dull-red brocade, gleaming brass hardware finishing the door and windows. Four upholstered chairs add to its warmth. Magda notes the silk-shaded lanterns above each seat.

The steamy windows provide no clear view of the platform. Removing a glove, she wipes a wide circle on the glass. Only then does she notice the dozens of uniformed police officers patrolling the platforms, walking to and fro, peering in the carriage windows, batons swinging at their sides. Gaska's men. Why so many?

She finds Jan in the crowd, blows him a kiss. A uniformed officer approaches him and begins to talk. She watches the man's lips and tries to decode what he is saying. Jan frowns, takes a step back. She presses her face closer to the glass. There is something amiss in the tilt of Jan's head, his expression. Another officer arrives. What now? The man reaches inside his jacket, brings forth a piece of paper. A photograph. Jan shakes his head several times, looks up and stares directly at her. "No" she sees him say. The officers move away, turn back to glance at him, and say something else. Jan nods. Again, he stares at her—a look of concern, a new tension about his shoulders. He holds her gaze, his eyes fierce—trying to send a message—and does not look away until the train lurches from the platform.

"Is everything all right?" her travelling companion asks.

"Oh." She realizes how her expression must appear. "Is it apparent? My husband and I are not often apart. I will miss him so. He is not happy." She removes a second glove, places it on the chair next to her, on top of the leather bag. "But it must be done," she says.

"No man will find happiness when separated from a beautiful woman." He taps his cane. "I am János Teller."

"Magda Nagy," she extends her hand.

When she arrived in the compartment, she had meant to place the green-ribboned box on the railing above her seat, out of the way, out of sight. She gets as far as lifting it over her head when János Teller stands and takes it from her. She tenses.

"Here?" He moves a smaller bag out of the way, his own, she surmises.

"A little to the left, perhaps, behind your bag, if you please." She adds quickly, "I wouldn't want it to fall upon our heads."

"Not much harm. It's very light." A question on his face.

"A gift for a friend," she says.

ﬀﬀ

She awakens with a jolt. The train has slowed to a stop, the rain heavy, slanting down from the roof of a station. Through the window, she watches a line of Austrian border guards in oilskin capes—raindrops bouncing off the brims of their hats, wetting their faces—make their way along the platform and disappear two by two into the railway cars. Heavy footsteps and loud voices fill the corridor.

The door slides open. Two men enter without speaking. Once inside, their presence fills the compartment, the smell of dampness and authority.

"We wish to inspect the passengers on this train," one of them says, the cape's upturned collar shadows his face. "Your papers, if you please."

Teller offers his passport first. A quick examination. A grunt of acceptance from the guard. Magda reaches into her leather bag, holds out her passport and letter of transit. The second guard, the one who has not spoken, takes them. A cursory glance. A longer look, closer, at her face. A hint of recognition. He looks at his colleague, raises his chin, tilts his head in her direction, a faint smile. When they both doff their hats, she sees they are mere boys, barely older than her own. No doubt, ordered out on a stormy night while their superiors lounge in the station, enjoying their after-dinner Schnapps.

"Thank you, madame," they say and back out the door.

Magda and Teller exchange a look. Afterward, he studies the knob of his cane and replaces the passport in his coat pocket.

"Odd," he remarks. "They're usually more thorough."

"They are anxious to complete their task and find a place out of the rain."

Ten minutes elapse, then twenty. She stands and stretches at the window. The rain has abated, so much that she can see the stationmaster emerge from the ticket office and look at his watch. He signals to the engineer.

"This is taking an undue amount of time," she says.

"Highly unusual," agrees Teller.

She lowers herself to the edge of the chair. Now the rain has stopped altogether. Another group of officers appears on the platform. In single file, at attention, they face their commander. After a few words of instruction, they break ranks and head toward the railway cars.

Within two minutes, an officer peers into the compartment. Once again, she hands him her passport.

"No need." He turns to János Teller, looks him up and down. "Stand up, remove your hat and coat," his voice hard, precise.

Teller looks surprised but does as he is told. The officer shines a light in Teller's face, makes him turn around.

The time has come, she thinks. How stupid we have been. In her mind, she sees an alarming image, a newspaper photo of a bayonetted blonde actress and an older man—János Teller—dead in a gutter. She pushes the image away and concentrates on the officer's commands.

"You're looking for someone," she says, taking a chance at conversation.

"Yes, madame. Have you seen either of these men?" The officer holds out a photograph. Two men in Budapest. On the riverside of the Gellért Hotel.

She leans forward, makes a show of studying the photograph. "I recognize the hotel," she says, a slight chuckle to cover her shock. "But not the men. They look quite harmless," she ventures, trying to keep the emotion from her voice. "What have they done?"

The officer pauses, lowers the photo. "Far from harmless, madame. They are wanted for murder. We were informed they are aboard this train."

"Murder," she repeats, her tone now solemn, contrite. "May I see the photograph once more?"

She stares at the faces of Harry Douglas and Mick MacLeod. "If they are aboard, I trust you will find them quickly."

She realizes, then, what had so alarmed her husband on the departure platform in Budapest.

█████

An hour later, the train crosses into Germany. At the border station, passengers are ordered off the train. A harsh glare illuminates a row of flags—black swastikas on a red background—draped in precise formation along the length of the station. The "Horst Wessel March," the Nazi Party anthem, blares from speakers that hang from every corner of the station. Magda counts four sentries at the entry and exit doors, rigidly erect, eyes forward, faces impassive. Another officer hovers inside the entry door, permitting one passenger at a time to enter.

As the passengers climb down, it begins to rain. First-class passengers are lined single file against the wall, under an overhanging canopy. The others stand alongside their assigned carriage, holding newspapers over their heads and hunching their shoulders against the downpour. An officer leads a sharp-nosed German shepherd, straining on a black leash, along the platform. Occasionally, the dog stops to sniff the passengers and their belongings. The sight infuriates her. She wants to approach the officer inside to demand that all passengers enter the station, at least permitted to stand out of the rain. She controls the impulse, knowing it will call attention to her.

Farther along the platform at the third railway carriage, a small commotion is occurring. The dog stops to sit beside a suitcase tied with a yellow ribbon. What looks to be a grandmother—an older woman with a black scarf tied under her chin—and a child are ordered to come forward. Two powerful torches shine upon them. The woman shields her eyes, but keeps hold of the child's hand. Magda hears loud talking, nothing polite.

"You better come along." An officer with gleaming high black boots leads them away to an outbuilding, separated from the station by a wall. The suitcase is left behind. Where is he taking them? There are words, graffiti on the side of the building. She peers at a sign attached to the building. *Jews not welcome. Don't buy from Jews. God's wrath on Jews.* She watches the woman and the child grow dim as they are marched, hand in hand, down the dark path. Before they disappear from view, the woman pulls the girl close, wraps her in her shawl, kisses her head. A heavy door opens and closes.

Magda's heart aches. Hours earlier, she had been so confident. Why had she thought she could slip through untouched, undetected? A little humility would have stopped her fantasies. She has not sufficiently understood this German machine. Jan tried to warn her. What can she do if they question her papers? Search her belongings? She is, above all, an accomplished actress, but she has no script for this role. Only a seething anger and a growing dread.

Inside, the passport control table is set beneath another huge red and black flag. Two dozen eyes stare at her as she enters. She had not expected so many. It is quiet inside, no blaring music. Indeed, the room is silent, save for the panting of another German shepherd sitting beside the table, eyes scanning and alert, ready to leap at the slightest command.

Magda is the only passenger in the room. Whatever happens here is invisible, she realizes. A rush of anxiety. Her lips are dry. Beads of sweat rise on her neck.

A photographer steps forward, motions to a spot on the floor. Using a big black apparatus with flash, he takes two photos, light flashing with each click of the shutter, blinding her so that she has to close her eyes and turn away. He points to a door, tells her to step into a smaller room, its only furnishings a steel table and two wooden chairs. The room smells of cleaning fluid. She wets her lips and tries to swallow. Finally, three men in dark suits enter. One of them, the taller and paler-skinned of the three, seems to be the leader. He talks, the others listen. In his right hand, he holds the passenger manifest, a listing of each passenger by name and seat or compartment number.

He makes a head-to-toe inspection, pausing too long at her hat. A smirk of disapproval. Or suspicion? When she suggested it to Harry, he told her stories about women smuggling secrets in the crowns of their hats and slits in their gloves. 'It's been done. They're wise to it.'

"Passport. Papers." A statement, not a request. A lifeless voice.

She wills her hand not to tremble as she opens the flap and reaches into the leather bag. Indeed, she looks at him directly and smiles as she places the items in his hand.

In the tense stillness, he makes more than one inspection of her documents, thumbing through the passport, turning the pages slowly. She studies his manicured fingers. He holds her papers up to the light, hands them to his colleagues, waits for them to look, takes them back.

"Father?"

"My father is dead," she replies.

"Mother?"

She thinks, what has my mother to do with this? "My mother is Hungarian."

He scowls, says something under his breath to the man standing beside him.

"Profession?"

"Actress. I am Magda Nagy," she says. "Perhaps you've seen my work." Her heart pounds, but she smiles and bows, makes a wide gesture with her arms as if sweeping onto the stage, gathering accolades of the audience.

Out of the corner of her eye, almost out of the angle of her vision, she notes one of the men say something to his colleague. They share a joke.

"We will look at your luggage," he says. He snaps his fingers. A cart wheels into the small room, taking up much of the space. He walks around the cart and uses a smooth elongated baton to thump, one by one, all sides of her trunks.

"Your trunks have been searched. Everything is in order," he says. "Now your hat."

"My hat," she repeats.

"Yes, madame. Remove your hat."

He waits for her to unpin and place it on the table. Their eyes briefly meet. With the tip of his baton, he holds the hat aloft, studies it, drops it to the floor. The heel of one polished black shoe crushes the fragile white feathers. She feels a red blush creep from her neck to her cheeks, but says nothing.

When the hatbox is opened, he pushes the baton down into the box, exerting pressure on the bottom. The man next to him unzips the makeup cases and pokes through the contents. The cardboard box with the green ribbon sits alone on the table.

"What is this?" He shakes the box.

"A gift. Glass flutes." She has prepared herself for this part of the inspection. "For champagne," she adds.

"The French and their champagne," he muses, a tight-lipped smile.

She reminds herself how many times she has acted the courageous heroine. Convincingly so, even in the midst of darkness.

"We'll see how much French champagne these glasses hold," he says, narrowing his eyes. Again, he stares at the picture on her passport, cocks his head to one side, purses his lips.

She moves to touch his sleeve, desperate to distract him.

Without raising his eyes, he takes a small step back, putting a greater distance between them. The move is calm, deliberate, no urgency in his manner.

The box is dismantled, four glass flutes removed and set one by one on the table, the paper packing falling to the floor. She blinks several times, bites her lower lip, and brings her eyes back to him.

He kicks at the wads of packing paper. "Search them," he commands.

His colleague, the one with flat pale eyes, picks the papers from the floor, flattens them on the table, and examines each sheet, front and back. "Nothing," he says. He replaces the glass flutes in the box and hands the box to the third man who walks with it from the room.

Still, this examination does not seem to satisfy the leader. His eyes search her gloves, then fix on the leather bag in her hand.

"And this?"

"This satchel contains my papers," she says mildly, her face calm.

"Open it." A challenge.

She shrugs. "Most of it is the script to my new play." She works to unclasp the lock, opens the flap. "The long train ride is perfect for studying my lines." She stops, careful not to overstate.

"It is possible we will keep it." He eyes the gold clasp.

"If you must," she concedes, then, "It is a sentimental gift from my husband."

He seems unmoved.

She reaches into the satchel and hands him the script. He reads the title aloud, "The Countess Maritza." He flips through the pages, watching her face as he does so.

She has little time to think. "At least let me retain my papers and the script. You've already impounded my favorite hat." Demurely, she lowers her eyes, looks up at him coquettishly, and winks, "What's left of it."

"You're in no position, madame, to make requests." He taps the baton on the script's front page, creating a small dent.

Undeterred, she tries again. "You are right, of course," she concedes. "It is just that I am to play the lead." She claps her hands together, gives a brief toss of her head, and smiles at him, a dazzling smile, eyes full of mischief. "And I must know what the heroine is to say, mustn't I?" Then, she laughs.

She catches a slight movement of his lips, the beginning of a cold smile.

"A Hungarian playwright?" he asks.

She moves closer and points to a name beneath the title. "Emmerich Kálmán."

"Kálmán. I have no familiarity with him." He drops the script onto the table, eyes it a moment longer.

A uniformed officer appears, whispers in his ear.

His next move strikes her as odd. "You will excuse me." He gives a signal to the rest, bows in her direction, clicks his heels, pivots and is gone, the door closing swiftly behind them.

Her heart almost stops.

⊞⊞

At the ticket station in Cologne, a box awaited her, the seamstress making good on her promise. "One of my costumes," she explains to Teller when the porter appears at the compartment door.

"Hmmm," he eyes the box. She notices he has been more watchful since her experience at the border crossing.

"Would you like to see it?" she asks. She rises to receive it.

To her surprise, Teller rises too. He retrieves his bag and bids a hurried goodbye. She watches him step down from the train. It is the last stop in Nazi-occupied territory.

The train picks up speed as it pulls away from the station. Within minutes, the engine races across the border and slips into the low country of the western Netherlands on its way to the ferry terminal at Hoek van Holland. Alone now, Magda opens the compartment window and watches the darkened village houses stream past. One more leg of the trip and she will be in London. Exhausted. The air is fresh and cool, and she inhales it, feeling as if she has held her breath the better part of the night. Her eyes fall on a dark object that lay beside Teller's chair. Oh dear. He's left his cane behind. How will he manage? With sudden clarity she whispers, "*Sunyi gazember.* Sneaky bastard." Her body begins a violent shiver, an uncontrollable shuddering of fear and relief. Her hands grip the window sash, the wind whistling as the train speeds through the darkness. She grabs the ugly prop and hurls it out the window, angry at her own naiveté. At Teller's word, that Nazi thug stole four exquisite champagne glasses and ruined her favorite hat. Lovely white dove feathers that she shall never find again. In the face of such danger, it is a silly thought. A strangely comforting silly thought. She dare not tell Jan. No need to burden him with further worry with what might have been.

The train slows as it passes through a small village. She is thankful beyond words for the sight of the Dutch signs on the posts. Long, loud shouts to the sky. Triumphant, she settles back, shedding tears of relief, dabbing at her nose, pressing her eyes with the lace handkerchief.

Beside her in the chair, she feels for the leather bag, withdraws the play's script, and unfastens three brass brads that bind it together. She leafs through each page, turning it front to back, laying one sheet aside, then another. At the final page, she eyes two stacks, one substantially thinner than the other. She aligns the corners of the larger stack, and using the brads, rebinds the manuscript. The shorter stack, exactly nine pages in length, contains not the first mention of the beautiful Hungarian Countess Maritza.

Chapter Thirty-Two

12 **June.** The daylight is gone, the street almost dark. They sit in a back corner pretending to read the evening news at a table scarred with cigarette burns. The tables around them bustle with students and factory workers.

"How long?" asks Mick.

"Until he shows," says Harry, appearing to concentrate on the photograph on page three.

"It's been two hours. I've had my bloody fill of sweet kávé. My teeth are beginning to rot."

"Drink something else."

"Why don't I go?"

"Go where? We can't get into the factory before eleven when the last shift leaves. This place is as safe as any. Besides, you'll know him when he arrives. I won't."

"Talk of the devil and he will appear," says Mick, raising an eyebrow toward the door.

"Is that how the saying goes?"

Erik Drucek makes his way to the bar, orders a drink, and takes a swift look around.

"Looking for a chair," Harry says under his breath.

"Looking for Laura. When he comes this way, I'll catch his eye."

Drucek stands with one hand on the bar; the other holds a mug of ale. The bartender nods his head once, lowers his eyes, and slides his hand across the bar to Drucek.

"Message received," whispers Mick.

Drucek turns, in no hurry, and walks in their direction. For a moment, he and Mick stare at each other. He finds a vacant stool by the window and looks out, his back to the room. He gulps his beer and seems not to notice when three men dressed in dark green work uniforms—soiled at the end of the workday—come from the other side of the bar and sit at a long table near the back door. They make a show of laughing and slapping the table. Harry realizes the display is subterfuge for Drucek, who retraces his steps, hands the bartender what appears to be payment for his drink, and leaves.

Harry waits.

"Stay here," Harry approaches the bar. The bartender slides a mug toward him, nothing he's ordered, a small slip of paper visible beneath it. Harry drops a few forints on the bar.

‖‖‖

One hundred meters ahead on the right, Drucek emerges from a doorway. He stops, waits for a line of traffic, then crosses the road and walks to the corner. As the note instructed, Harry and Mick proceed to the next street and look for an address. Before they can knock, a generously endowed woman in a crisp red apron throws wide the door. She shouts into the street and stands back from the entry.

"Come, come in. Your rooms are waiting. First, you must have something to eat."

The entryway closes around them, overly warm, smelling of boiled cabbage and fresh onions. A wave of a heavy cooking spoon directs them to a downward staircase. In a bare basement, Erik Drucek sits alone at a table, a blue-checkered tablecloth its sole decoration. He indicates chairs and cigarettes. Overhead, floorboards squeak. They hear people talking, feet scuffling. Mick looks up.

"A small hotel. You met the proprietress." Drucek lights a cigarette and looks to Mick. "We've met before."

"King Leopold," Mick says.

"I remember." Drucek gives a brief smile, then turns to Harry, wasting no time. "You have word from Laura."

Harry hands him the envelope.

Drucek opens it, withdraws four pages, reads the first. He looks up, eyes wide, "How did you get it?"

"Kristof Balas. Laura managed to get it from him."

"Where is she? I waited for her signal."

"She died last night acquiring this. She insisted I bring it to you."

Drucek covers his eyes, whispers to himself. "I was afraid. She did too much. I warned her."

"When did she join your group?"

"Her husband was our leader."

"Her husband?"

"Marek. He fought for Czechoslovakia. Politically and in the press. Then, guns and bombs. Last year, he was killed in the fighting. After it, she was not the same."

"Meaning what?"

"She became obsessed. She left her family, came to Budapest. She refused to talk of defeat. She was determined to get information for our cause. Nothing else mattered. She took great risks." Drucek sits motionless.

Mick breaks the silence. "Even if it meant her life?"

"They were in love. She promised him." Drucek's eyes glisten, tears staining his cheeks. He wipes them with the back of his hand and looks at Harry. "You're Douglas."

Harry nods.

"She trusted you."

"What now?"

"Now we know they are coming." Drucek's face is drawn with fatigue.

"Soon," Harry says.

"Some will deny it," says Drucek. "Now there is proof."

"What will you do?"

"We will fight," says Drucek. "The British and French have promised to help us."

Chapter Thirty-Three

12 **June**. Two blasts of the whistle signal the end of shift. A crowd of men, some walking, more on bicycles, moves quickly through the gate, and spills out onto the street. A dark silhouette paces the loading dock until Harry and Mick arrive.

"You must leave immediately." Nagy tells them of his encounter at the railway station, the broad circulation of photographs. "Come this way."

They climb an iron staircase to the second floor. The sign on the door, in Hungarian and German, reads "Plant Manager." Inside, Nagy lights the desk lamp, turns up the volume on the radio, and signals them to stand back from the window. From the bottom drawer he extracts a small black book, picks up the telephone, and waits for the connection. He speaks quietly in Hungarian, tears off a strip of paper, writes a few words, hands it to them, and replaces the receiver.

Ava Vicktor, Bulgarian, Pier 15, 02:00

He takes back the paper, lights a match, burns the paper, and lowers the radio volume. One hand in the air—a stop sign of sorts—he speaks clearly, as if giving a command to his plant manager, "Assign two men to pick up and deliver a shipment to Bratislava. Four crates of chipped glass on the *Lauro*, Pier 5. Departing at two." For half a minute, Nagy says nothing. "Yes, I regret the late notice, but the crates must go. An immediate need. Inform me when the shipment arrives."

Harry furrows his brow, looks at Mick.

Nagy snaps off the lamp, leaves the radio on, ushers them out the door. In the hallway, in a whisper, he explains. "You are to go to the *Ava Vicktor*. Pier 15. The captain will know. The other is a diversion. Meant for the customs agents who will be dispatched to the *Lauro* on Pier 5 to inspect crates filled with glass. In truth, the *Lauro* captain can say he knows nothing. Four crates that never arrived. Who knows where they are? It happens every day. Two workers on Pier 15 will draw no attention."

Mick says, "The authorities won't wonder what happened to the glass shipment?"

Nagy shrugs. "They will ask questions. By then, you will be gone."

Nagy herds them into a small utility room that smells of sweat and dirty linens.

"A rich fragrance," Mick remarks.

"You must smell like a bargeman," says Nagy.

In the dark, they change into the clothes of a dockworker, rough serge trousers, long-sleeved shirt, knit cap, thick socks, and rubber boots.

Nagy lifts two jackets from a peg by the door. "It is cold on the river, even in June."

Outside in the street, there are sounds of footfalls, running, whistles blowing.

Nagy lifts the window an inch, listens. "Street patrol. Odd at this hour. You may have been followed. How did you get here?"

"A friend let us off downriver half a kilometer. We worked our way back."

"Someone has seen you."

They ride an elevator to the third floor, hurry across a catwalk and, on the other side, take stairs down to the second floor of the factory. Nagy keeps his voice low, "Disembark at Bratislava. The captain will direct you to a car. It will take you to Krakow. From there, I cannot help you."

Nagy leads them to the opposite side of the building, away from the river. They walk up a steep incline, through a maze of overhead conveyor belts and packing bins. Nagy stops at the fourth bin, collapses one side of it, and focuses a torch beam on a square hatch cut into the floor. "This leads to a storm drain that empties, after a few hundred meters, into a tributary of the Danube. Near the end of the pipe, keep right toward the wharves. Farther along, the piers are numbered."

"Your escape hatch," Harry notes.

"It's a matter of time before Arrow Cross takes control. Every Jew will need to get out of the country." Nagy shakes his head.

On hands and knees, Nagy pries open the hatch. He presses the torch into Mick's hand and indicates the top of a ladder. "The captain sails at two. Wait within the pipe until just before. When you emerge, you'll see Pier 15 in the distance. Go near. The captain will see you. Follow his lead." He grips Mick's arm one last time. "Now go."

Mick nods his thanks and descends first, the top of his head disappearing into the black hole, the torch's small circle of light guiding him down the steps.

Harry reaches for Nagy's hand.

Nagy takes hold, "See you in London, friend."

Harry stops on the ladder's fourth rung, half in, half out of the hole. He touches his cap, "Drinks on me."

〰〰〰

At the bottom of the ladder, they find a long wide pipe that slopes downward toward the river. The stench of rotting trash and the sickly odor of dead animals almost gag them. The pipe was built for shorter men, and they duck their heads against its ceiling. Reminded of his claustrophobia, Harry shivers, decides now is not the time for self-indulgence. They slosh through a shallow stand of water, the cold of it seeping into their boots, wetting their socks and the edge of their trousers. Farther on, the water deepens until it covers their knees. The larger pipe divides into two narrower drains, one bearing sharply left, the other at a slight right angle.

"Is this it?" Harry asks.

Mick shines the torch into each pipe. "On the left side, the water is diverted into a narrow canal. From Nagy's instructions, we're to keep straight on, then right near the exit."

"Douse the light." Harry moves quickly to stand in front of Mick as if to block his view.

Ahead, they hear the sound of footsteps on gravel, a grunt of exertion, the heavy clunk of a gate.

"Did you see it?" they hear someone say. "A light inside."

They dare not move, fearful the slightest slosh of water will betray them.

"I don't see anything," says another.

The voices are close. Harry and Mick stand in pitch-black, ticking off minutes in their head, knowing it is nigh on two o'clock.

A voice calls through the gate, "Who's in there? Come out now. We won't shoot you."

The other laughs. "Just a reflection. Where's my torch?"

Harry finds Mick's arm, pulls downward, a signal to drop into the filthy water should the torchlight come near.

A circle of light moves back and forth across the water. "The eyes of rats. A river of trash. That's all."

Finally, they hear the footsteps recede.

Harry and Mick inch forward. On the right, they see the end of the drain and hear the sound of rushing water. The floor drops abruptly, and they stumble down and see the gate they heard closing. A half circle of iron cordons off the bottom of the pipe. A lock holds fast the gate.

"Time to practice our alpine skills," Harry whispers.

"Or we could push it open, like so," says Mick. The rusted lock gives way.

They check their watches and fight a rising sense of panic. Ten minutes past two. They may be too late. Where is Pier 15?

⧜

From a concealed corner on the wharf, Harry and Mick peer at the Bulgarian barge, *Ava Vicktor*, tied at the end of the pier and illuminated by a decrepit streetlamp. Three men load and secure a stack of crates, their loud directives carrying into the night. Harry and Mick creep along the outer walls of the warehouses that line the river, stopping in shadowed doorways, looking for a signal from the bridge of the *Ava Vicktor*.

They hear the clop of horse's hooves. An approaching port officer comes close, parallel with the barge, not twenty meters from where they are hidden. The officer halts the horse, blocking the way forward.

Harry scans the area. There is no question of getting past the port officer without being seen. Likewise, they cannot move left or right. Behind them is a narrow alley. It means fading back among the warehouses, retracing their steps, working back another way. If they cut across a section closer to the barge, they risk exposure and a request for papers they do not have.

They make out the captain, supervising the loading. See him hold up his hand. Hear a string of words, a strong voice in German. "Ho! Jákó! It is you. What about my money? A man pays his debts. My money. Where is it?"

The port officer, Jákó they assume, waves his hand dismissively, spurs his horse and rides off in the other direction, toward the farthest pier on the quay. The captain stares after him, and hollers once more. Knowing the man will not turn to face him, he jerks his head at Harry and Mick, who race up the pier and scramble aboard the *Ava Vicktor*.

The captain motions them behind the wheelhouse out of the light and comes around, hands on hips. He is a slight man with hooded eyes and thick hair. A day's growth of beard darkens his weathered face. He wears a flannel shirt beneath his open seaman's jacket and a loose muffler tied on his neck.

He fishes a cigarette from the pocket of his trousers, raises his chin. "Captain Petar Todorov. One minute more, I will be gone." He tosses Mick a small container. Shoe polish. "You must look like a Bulgarian. After, see the mate. Bargemen don't stand around when there's work to be done."

One nightmare to another, thinks Harry. Mick finds a piece of cloth on the deck and begins to rub his rosy Scottish cheeks, willing to do whatever it takes to leave Budapest behind.

†††††

Four hours north to Bratislava, the barge pushes hard against the black water. When they reach the port, the sun has begun to rise, a light fog lies across the city. Church bells toll six. The barge slows; engines quiet. The air smells of petrol. The mate jumps ashore; a crewman throws him a mooring rope. Falling in line with the others, Harry and Mick move to unload the cargo. A barge sounds its horn.

"No time," snaps Todorov, pulling them inside the wheelhouse. "It will be too late. The car is waiting."

"How will we find it?"

Todorov points out the window. "Five minutes. Stay on the north side of the bank. Run fast until the wharf buildings disappear. The way becomes a towpath, then houses. Turn left on Belluš Street. Walk then, no running. You will see a small gray house with rough shutters. The car is there—an Opel, blue or black. Depends on the driver. Get in the back seat. Lie flat. He will take you to Krakow."

Todorov hands them each an envelope, "Your papers."

They do not know what to say, how to thank the man. Mick extends his hand, surprised by the warmth of Todorov's grip, "We're damn grateful. Thank you."

A quick affirmation, the supposed smile of hardened Bulgarian river captains.

Todorov follows them off the gangway, pulls down the brim of his battered hat. "You know nothing of my boat."

Chapter Thirty-Four

30 **September, London.** The weather outside is typically London, cool and breezy with plenty of clouds, the occasional drizzle. Savoy's American Bar is warm and quiet, the hour too late for the Fleet Street press trade, too early for the after-theatre crowd.

"Friday night usually this dead?" Harry settles himself at the end of the bar on an electric-blue stool. He looks around, appreciating the creamy Art Deco decor, the photographs on the wall—Savoy's famous guests.

"A monotonous night on the Strand," laments the Head Barman, Phil Craddock. He wears a black vest over a crisp white shirt, buttoned at the cuff. "You'll have the piano man for company." A slow, sensual interpretation of Sammy Fain's "I'll Be Seeing You" drifts through. Four individuals stand around the grand piano, all dressed in evening clothes. Guests of the hotel, Harry assumes. Two silver-haired men have shed their tuxedo jackets and loosened their black ties, the formal event they attended obviously come and gone. A dark-haired woman in rich burgundy sways to the music, eyes closed, while a statuesque blonde in green satin leans against the curve of the piano and sips from an almost-empty martini glass.

Mick takes the stool next to Harry. "It speaks to me."

"To the whole bloody world, apparently," says Craddock. "We admired it, too, the first thousand times ole Davey banged it out." The pianist grins, raises his chin in acknowledgement. "Every night, we suffer that song. God knows why it made its way across the big pond. Long about midnight, our ears yearn for a bit of variety. What'll it be, chaps?"

"An English Porter," says Mick.

"This is the American Bar, pal. It's all about the whiskey." Craddock feigns an American gangster pose and accent.

Mick laughs. "A fine Highland single malt, then. Remind me of home, will you?"

Harry says, "Canadian or American. Whatever you've a mind. Make it neat."

From the mirrored shelves, Craddock selects two bottles and dispenses two glasses, years of practice evident in the precise quantity of pour. He sets them down. "A nip of the peat bog for the Scotsman, and a taste of Kentucky for you, sir."

Harry continues to study the photographs on the opposite wall. "Who's the handsome bloke on the right?"

"That's our Robin Hood. Australian actor, name of Errol Flynn. Big opening at the Odeon in May. Every damn bit as striking in the flesh. Spent a few nights on that very stool. You haven't seen the film?"

Mick lifts his glass, waits—a wry smile on his face—for Harry's response.

"Been travelling," Harry says.

"Back for a spell, then?" asks Craddock. His pencil-thin mustache—a reflection of Errol Flynn—twitches.

"Looks that way." Harry is reminded of their dinner two nights ago with Magda, her sons, and her mother. A tasty Algerian place in Soho. Thankfully, the Nagy household located a suitable flat in Holborn, a short walk from Magda's work at the Palace Theatre.

Mick savors his Dalwhinnie and nibbles from a bowl of salted crisps.

At the opposite end of the bar, a young bartender in a belted apron wipes a row of glasses. The green satin requests another martini, but the others in her party are ready to go, and so she smiles apologetically, withdraws her request, and follows the others through the archway that leads to the lobby. The piano man plays the last chords of "Smoke Gets in Your Eyes," then gently closes the keys' cover.

"Mind if I smoke?" Harry asks. He fishes his pipe and a tin of tobacco out of his coat pocket.

"Whatever suits," says Craddock.

Behind the bar, on the far counter, stands a finely crafted box of polished inlaid wood, four round knobs aligned at the bottom. Harry recognizes the expensive Marconi. Craddock turns to the younger bartender, his demeanor serious now. "Find the station, lad. Turn the speaker this way."

"Yes sir, Mr. Craddock," says the young man. He regards Harry and Mick, "We'll have the BBC coming in."

Static, a turn of one knob, then another until a strong voice comes clear. "This is the BBC broadcasting this night from London. Here is the news. Prime Minister Neville Chamberlain arrived back in the UK today, holding an agreement signed by Adolf Hitler, which stated the German leader's desire never to go to war with Britain again. The two men met at the Munich conference between Britain, Germany, Italy, and France yesterday, convened to decide the future of Czechoslovakia's Sudetenland. Mr. Chamberlain declared that the accord with the Germans signals 'peace for our time' after he had read it to a jubilant crowd gathered at Heston airport in west London. The German leader stated in the agreement: 'We are determined to continue our efforts to remove possible sources of difference and thus to contribute to assure the peace of Europe.' Many MPs are bound to criticize the agreement as part of the Prime Minister's appeasement of German aggression in Europe. Mr. Chamberlain's personal pact will be little comfort to the Czechoslovakian government which has been forced to hand over the region of Sudetenland to Germany, despite not being present at the conference."

Harry's tobacco tin slips from his hand. He and Mick stare into the mirror. The face of Eric Drucek flashes through Harry's mind. *The British and French have promised to help us.*

The radio report continues. "After greeting members of the public at the airport, Mr. Chamberlain appeared in front of another rejoicing throng on the balcony of Buckingham Palace with the King and Queen, and again later outside 10 Downing Street. The British Prime Minister mobilized the Royal Navy four days ago when Germany announced it was building massive fortifications in Rhineland. But the conservative leader has always expressed his desire to find a peaceful solution to the Führer's wish to create a new—and enlarged—German homeland in Europe."

"That's it, then," says Craddock. He walks to the radio and turns the knob.

Davey, the piano man, stands at the end of the bar, a cigarette dangling from his fingers. "Tragedy that. Rotten shame. Just a delay. War is bound to come. Enough is not enough for those brutes."

Craddock says, "We've got no taste for it. Nineteen eighteen is still fresh. Not twenty years ago we lost our best boys."

Davey counters, "Even so, we had an agreement with the Czechs. A treaty. We and the French betrayed them and didn't have the decency to tell them."

Unwavering, Craddock replies, "Not the first time one nation made promises and neglected to make good."

Davey crushes his cigarette. "Is Chamberlain ignorant? The PM can't be daft enough to believe that Nazi peasant."

Craddock shrugs, "No clear answers there. I'm glad for peace. Praise be." He wipes the bar again. "What about you chaps?"

Mick is shaking his head, eyes on the floor, fists balled at his side. His coat already on. It's clear he's working hard not to punch something.

Harry catches him by the arm, raises his glass. "Worth a second go?"

Mick turns, a grim face.

Harry follows him to the door. "See you tomorrow, then."

Mick's voice is tight, heat in his words. "I'm done in." He jams one fist into his coat pocket. "I like to believe we're of some small use. When we risk our lives for swine like Balas and Brinkley to triumph, that's something else again."

"You know how this works. These battles are bigger than we are." Harry blocks his exit, looks him in the eye. "We can't clean up the troubles that politicians start."

They face off for a long beat until Mick pushes past him. He gives Harry a glance before turning the knob. A flare of anger. "I have to get out. Before I stop caring. I won't let them have that."

Harry stands in the doorway watching Mick walk away, listening to his footsteps on the pavement. He had seen more than temporary frustration in Mick's eyes. From the start, he has known Mick is a rare species. Sure of purpose. Pure of heart. Unthinkable as it is, Harry would sooner see Mick out of the Service than transformed into a beaten skeptic within it.

Harry no longer wonders what altered Tennyson Neale's loyalties. Decisions hard to stomach. Powerful men with misguided assumptions and personal ambitions. Unprincipled compromises. No doubt Neale woke one day to find he was wounded in a way he had not foreseen. His badge of honor had vanished into a gray hole.

No matter Harry's opinion of Chamberlain's betrayal, the shadowy world of espionage is Harry's work. The job runs deep. He is not about to give it up. He has found his place in the world and the best in himself. He has no delusions, no need for moral comfort. Only hunger for the next assignment. He knows he must deal with contradiction, deception, evil. He must walk in darkness. He must run with bastards like Balas and Brinkley and nurse the coldness in his heart. As long as the Service will have him, he will do its bidding. It is the only life he wants to live.

He resumes his place at the end of the bar, loosens his tie, and raises the empty glass. "The same. A double."

When Craddock shows him the door, Harry wanders, giving little care where his feet take him. The air smells of lilacs. Unmercifully, Laura's memory has not faded, her face clear in his mind. Her hand warm in his. She is with him now, walking in step, leaning into his shoulder, stopping to straighten his tie. Her lips brush his ear. She takes his arm, her body against his.

No matter what he must do, whatever small deed or large, however long it will take, Balas and his like will pay for what they have done to Laura Savic and Tennyson Neale.

Historical Notes
and Further Reading

In March 1939, six months after Britain signed the Munich Agreement, German troops poured into Czechoslovakia and dismantled the Czechoslovak government, Hitler calling the Munich Agreement "just a scrap of paper." Poland seemed the next likely victim of Nazi aggression. Because Britain and France failed to protect Czechoslovakia, Hitler was confident the two countries would not go to war. Thus, on 1 September 1939, German soldiers, tanks and planes crossed the border into Poland. Two days later, on 3 September 1939, Britain and France declared war on Germany. This action marked the beginning of World War II in Europe.

In Hungary, the Arrow Cross Party fully subscribed to the Nazi ideology of master races and supported a political order based on the authority of the strongest and "purest." When the Germans finally deposed Miklós Horthy in 1944, leaders of the Arrow Cross Party held power from October 1944 to March 1945. During these five months, up to 15,000 civilians were murdered and 80,000 Jews and Romani were deported from Hungary to concentration camps in Austria. After the war, more than 6,000 Arrow Cross leaders were tried by Hungarian courts as war criminals.

In researching background for this novel, I reviewed books and articles on the topics of Hungarian politics, the Arrow Cross Party, and the German invasion of Czechoslovakia. Useful sources included:

Braham, R. *The Politics of Genocide: The Holocaust in Hungary.* New York: Columbia University Press, 1994.

Bryant, Chad. *Prague in Black Nazi Rule and Czech Nationalism.* Cambridge: Harvard University Press, 2009.

Crowhurst, Patrick. *Hitler and Czechoslovakia in World War II: Domination and Retaliation.* London: Bloomsbury Publishing, 2013.

Lackó, M. *Arrow-Cross Men: National Socialists 1935–1944.* Budapest: Akadémiai Kiadó, 1969.

Murray, Williamson. *The Change in the European Balance of Power, 1938–1940.* Princeton: Princeton University Press, 1984.

Rothwell, Victor. *The Origins of the Second World War.* Manchester: Manchester University Press, 2001.

Sakmyster, Thomas. *Hungary's Admiral on Horseback: Miklós Horthy, 1918–1944.* California: Helena History Press LLC, 2022.

Acknowledgments

The real Harry (born Henry) Douglas was my mother's father. He was born on 1 May 1887 in the lowland district of Ayr, Scotland, to Edith McKinnell Douglas and Henry Douglas, a slater by trade. As a young teenager, Harry immigrated to the northeastern United States and learned the skills of masonry, bricklaying and plastering. In 1917 at age thirty, Harry joined the Canadian Expeditionary Force where he served as Lance Corporal in the 6th Battalion 2nd Canadian Engineers in France, Belgium, and Germany. Discharged on 27 May 1919, he returned home to Quincy, Massachusetts, where he met and married Agnes Mylott. Together, they moved to New Jersey and New York and raised two daughters, Edith Douglas Corley and Nancy Douglas Teets. Though not formally educated, Harry was well informed and well read. He was known to read the encyclopedia from cover to cover. He never missed his daily newspaper and always had a book or puzzle in his lap. He enjoyed editing others' work, creating word puzzles, and savoring his daily glass of Ballantine Ale. Harry was never without his pipe and can of sweet-smelling tobacco. Harry died on 24 May 1965 in Miami, Florida. No doubt he would have thoroughly enjoyed his rebirth as a tall (the real Harry stood 5'4"), handsome, reckless foreign agent.

I am grateful for early readers of this manuscript. Thanks to Justus Doenecke for his thoughtful editing and detailed notes regarding persons and events of the period; to Carol Doenecke and Marilyn Wittner for their attentive reading and recommendations; to Marshall Craig for his focused deliberations on time, space, and dialogue. Special recognition goes to Sterling Watson and Laura Lippman for their critical commentary and suggested changes, both of which greatly improved this project.

Deepest gratitude and love belong to my husband John, first listener and editor, who brought a gifted mind, a willing ear, and the perfect turn of phrase to our nightly cocktail revision sessions.

Finally, I cannot discount the well-timed contributions of the charming and chubby Duffy, who occasionally took a leisurely stroll across my keyboard and offered a warm paw when inspiration waned.

About the Author

Writer and illustrator Susan C. Turner's recent work concentrates in the crime/mystery arena. She prefers to set her narratives in the pre- and postwar periods of the 1930s and 1940s. *Mission Budapest* is second in a series featuring characters Harry Douglas and Mick MacLeod. The first book in this collection, *The Truth About Otis Battersby*, was published in 2022. The third novel, coming in winter 2023, is entitled *Assignment in Oran*.

Born in New York, she has lived in Miami and London, and now resides in Tampa with husband John, and articulate and loveable cat, Duffy.

www.ingramcontent.com/pod-product-compliance
Lightning Source LLC
Chambersburg PA
CBHW030617120726
47904CB00006B/1931

* 9 7 8 0 9 8 4 7 2 3 2 7 0 *